THE COAL MINER'S WIFE

LYNETTE REES

Boldwood

First published in Great Britain in 2026 by Boldwood Books Ltd.

Cover Design by Colin Thomas

Cover Images: Colin Thomas

A CIP catalogue record for this book is available from the British Library.

Paperback ISBN 978-1-83633-813-0

Large Print ISBN 978-1-83633-812-3

Hardback ISBN 978-1-83633-811-6

Trade Paperback ISBN 978-1-80656-379-1

Ebook ISBN 978-1-83633-814-7

Kindle ISBN 978-1-83633-815-4

Audio CD ISBN 978-1-83633-806-2

MP3 CD ISBN 978-1-83633-807-9

Digital audio download ISBN 978-1-83633-810-9

This book is printed on certified sustainable paper. Boldwood Books is dedicated to putting sustainability at the heart of our business. For more information please visit https://www.boldwoodbooks.com/about-us/sustainability/

Boldwood Books Ltd, 23 Bowerdean Street, London, SW6 3TN

www.boldwoodbooks.com

For all those women who had the courage and opportunity to leave an abusive relationship, thereby forging better lives for themselves.

1

MERTHYR TYDFIL, FEBRUARY 1889

Elin Edwards lifted the poker and began rattling the fire in the hearth, sending a flurry of furious sparks up the chimney. At least it hadn't gone out, but unusually there'd been no one here at her parents-in-laws' house when she arrived home from work. She'd lived here with her husband, Wyndham, for just a few weeks, but Elin sincerely had her doubts about the union.

It was most unusual for Elin to have found the house all in darkness at this time of the day, as Olwen would usually be here fussing over something on the stove for Frank. But tonight, she had an eerie feeling as she unlocked the door. In normal circumstances, there'd be no need to use her key as the door wasn't usually locked, with someone being home, but she'd been given a key by the woman for emergency purposes and maybe this was one such time.

Once she'd added coal to the fire from the scuttle and banked it up, she placed the metal blower across it, finally, covering it with a sheet of yesterday's newspaper, to draw it up. As she did so, she glanced at the main headline – something to do with the levels of crime in the town – but then her attention was drawn to a smaller article, just below it. *Has Jack the Ripper Left London?* It went on to explain that following the murders of five prostitutes in the Whitechapel area, the police suspected the perpetrator might have moved on elsewhere, as the killings had ceased, at least for the time being. The last, and most gruesome murder of all, had been of Mary Jane Kelly in early November 1888, three months ago.

Elin shuddered at the thought of it. For weeks people had spoken about those murders. There'd been all sorts of rumours and theories as to the killer's identity. From the description issued, some thought he might be in the medical profession, while others presumed he might even be a member of the royal family. But whoever he was, he hadn't been caught as yet.

Tonight, though, she realised it was time to have a word with her husband as she wasn't happy with how things were going between them. It wasn't that it was marry in haste, repent at leisure, as the saying went, oh no. Because there'd been ample time to get to know one another before wedlock, she thought she knew her husband very well indeed. The courtship had gone on for two whole years. She recalled now how she'd first encountered Wyndham while out walking one Sunday afternoon.

It was while she was out strolling on a beautiful spring day, deep in reflection, when she almost bumped headfirst into a handsome young man on the canal bank. He steadied her and told her not to apologise, as what a lovely thing it was for her to bump into him. His lively chatter had excited her, as her heart leapt in his company. Before she realised it, they were courting. And now newlyweds of some weeks.

So why was she feeling disconcerted and disappointed now? She shouldn't be, should she? Her husband had employment as a collier at the nearby Gethin Coal Pit, while she worked for the

Langton family, who owned a confectionery business, as a nursemaid for the widowed mother of the family, Muriel Langton.

She and Wyn had a roof over their heads, even if they didn't own the property, so she should be supremely grateful.

Wyn's parents had kindly given them their front room to use in combination as both a bedroom and a living room – the agreement being that they'd also have the run of the house as in the scullery – but the main living room was to be kept private to Wyn's parents when they needed it. That arrangement suited them very well as Elin hated the idea of having to spend every waking hour when at home with the pair. Oh, they were nice enough, but she valued her privacy and theirs too; she'd for a long time dreamt of spending cosy evenings curled up by the fireside with her husband in that little room, but somehow that never happened. Since the wedding, all she saw of him was when she dished up meals in the scullery or when he turned his back on her in bed after performing his husbandly duties. That's when he had the energy to do so, as what was becoming a pattern now was for him on returning from a day shift at the coal pit, to wash and change, eat the meal she'd prepared, and then take off to the pub, or often it happened the other way about.

It was understandable that many a miner acquired a raging thirst after working at the pit, and it was the reason for Wyn visiting the pub, but was it too much to ask that he spend just one evening at home with her? Where they might chat about the day's events, wrapped up in one another's arms with her head resting on his shoulder? She longed for that sort of intimacy. It wasn't just that her husband was constantly absent from the home, he was spending money out of the family coffers too, money that should be shared between the two of them. None of this boded well for her future thoughts about starting a family together.

That's what she'd do, she decided; she'd tell him tonight when he arrived home from work that it just wasn't on.

* * *

Elin filled the old battered kettle with water from the pump in the yard, trying to focus on the task in hand rather than the uneasy sensation threatening to consume her. She placed it on the hob to boil just as there was a persistent-sounding knock at the front door, startling her. Feeling puzzled, she went to answer it, knowing it couldn't be a member of the family as they'd have walked right in.

She was surprised to see the anxious-looking face of their next-door neighbour, Mrs Evans. Dilys Evans was about the same age as Olwen and a very good neighbour and friend to the woman.

'Hello, dear,' she said as she gripped the fringes of her shawl around her head and shoulders. It was a bitter evening, and the woman's fingers appeared blue, so Elin ushered the woman inside out of the cold.

'Please come in and sit down, Mrs Evans,' Elin said, smiling, thinking the woman had popped around to borrow something from Olwen, which she often did, despite there being a perfectly good shop at the end of the row. But then again, Elin thought, maybe the woman had trouble making ends meet as she was widowed, and Olwen never seemed to mind sparing a cup of milk or a few spoonfuls of sugar to put in the woman's tea – she was kind-hearted that way.

Dilys smiled gratefully as she stepped over the threshold,

lowering the shawl from her head as she did so, but leaving it in place around her shoulders.

'I won't stop long,' she said as she followed Elin to the scullery, easing herself into a chair at the wooden table. She sucked in a sharp breath between her teeth. 'It's your mother-in-law, dear...'

Elin's hand went to her chest as though wounded in some way. 'Olwen? What's happened to her?' She took a seat at the table opposite the woman as her heart began to thud anxiously.

Dilys shook her head. 'It was just this afternoon; she was at my house when she got taken sick with pains in her chest. Awful it was. There was no one else around as you were all out at work, but I managed to arrange for my son to take her on the horse and cart to the doctor's surgery. She's still there right now. They've not returned yet. I thought I'd better let you know as no doubt Frank and Wyndham are still working at the pit.'

Elin nodded at her. 'Aye, they both are. They'll be home in about twenty minutes. But how long has it been since your son and Olwen left here?'

'A good couple of hours. I'm getting right worried about her now; that's why I came to see you as soon as I noticed you were home from work.' She frowned and shook her head.

'You stay and rest for a while, Mrs Evans. I was about to brew up. You can wait here with me if you like?'

'Yes, thank you,' said Dilys. 'I'm on pins with worry about Olwen.'

The woman shot her a smile of gratitude as Elin stood to check on the fire, which had now drawn up nicely. She particularly wanted to keep the heat in the house, for when her mother-in-law arrived home. She removed the metal blower, screwed up the sheet of newspaper covering it and threw it into the flames of the fire, watching it burn for a short while. It was all yesterday's news anyhow.

While she and Dilys took a cup of tea together, the women sat in silence, not sure what to say to the other, the only noise being the ticking of the mantel clock.

The silence was then broken by a sharp hammering on the front door. Startled, Elin rose from her chair to answer the urgent-sounding summons.

2

Elin drew the door open wide to find herself staring down at the face of a young lad of around twelve years of age. There was something familiar about him as he stood there in his coal-dusted clothing, a large flat cap shading his face.

Wasn't that Dai Phillips's boy from across the street? She remembered something about him recently starting work at the pit, which accounted for his dirty, dishevelled clothing, but he'd grown so much of late, she hardly recognised him. 'Hello?' she said hesitantly, wondering what he wanted.

'Hello, miss.' He startled as though suddenly remembering it was polite to remove his cap, so he did so and, clutching it in his hands, carried on. 'I've been sent to tell you that Doctor Penry-Jones has examined Mrs Edwards and he's keeping her at his surgery for the present time.'

'Who sent you?' she asked, gazing intently at the lad. 'Was it the doctor himself?'

He shook his head. 'No, it was Joshua.'

Now Elin understood. So it was Mrs Evans's son who had sent the message.

Elin heard a scraping sound behind her as Dilys drew out her chair to stand, dragging it across the flagstone floor. She turned towards her and said, 'Did you hear that?'

'Aye,' said Dilys as she approached, peering at the lad over Elin's shoulder. 'Any more information other than that for us, Thomas? Did my son say when he might be returning home?'

The lad shook his head. 'No, sorry, Mrs Evans. I just happened to be visiting the surgery myself as I injured my arm underground. The foreman sent me there, see.' He drew up his jacket sleeve to display a bandaged arm. Elin winced at the thought of it. A lad so young as that, working in those conditions, didn't seem right to her. He readjusted his sleeve as he carried on. 'That's when your son recognised me and gave me a penny to bring you the message. Sounds like he won't be back any time soon to me, missus.'

'Oh dear,' said the woman, frowning. 'I wish I'd gone with them both now, but there wasn't any room for me on the cart as well.'

Elin turned to touch the woman's arm in reassurance, then, turning back, fixed her gaze on the lad. 'Thank you, Thomas. You go home now, as your mam will be looking for you,' she said. If his mother had heard he'd been injured at the pit, she might be frantic with worry by now.

Smiling as though pleased with himself, Thomas turned his back and made his way across the road, his hands tucked deep in his trouser pockets. Elin had considered giving him another penny for his trouble, but money was in short supply, especially the way Wyn was sinking all that ale of late.

Should she find him and tell him what had gone on? And where on earth was his father? He should have returned from work by now too.

She turned towards Mrs Evans. 'Can you wait here, please,

while I try to find my husband? He's probably at the p—' she cut herself off short before uttering the word '—pub.' And then as though trying to make light of it, added, 'He goes there following his shift sometimes. Says he has a raging thirst after a day's graft.'

The woman spoke softly. 'I quite understand, *cariad*. There's no need to explain to me. I was a miner's wife myself many moons ago. They're hard-working men but some have their demons to slay – particularly after what they witness working in that dark hellhole all day long.'

With some alarm, Elin grabbed her cloak from the peg near the front door and wrapped it around her shoulders. She wondered which pub Wyn might have gone to, as there were several in Abercanaid. She made eye contact with Mrs Evans.

'Try the one on the canal bank, first,' the woman advised. 'It's the one most popular with the miners.'

Elin forced a smile. Of course, it all made sense, as it was one of the nearest to the pit.

'Go now, dear. I'll stop here in case there's any news about Olwen.'

As Elin scurried along the gaslit street, her heartbeat seemed to quicken with each step. Darkness had fallen fast and she hated being out here on her own, where she feared every shadow or footstep behind her. She'd never set foot in a pub in all her born days. Her own father wasn't a drinking man at all, and even her uncle was a temperate sort of drinker, only having the odd drink at home for special family occasions such as Christmas and birthdays. This was all new territory for her.

She made her way towards the canal bank, needing to ascend a small path to reach it. Realising it might be a little slippery with ice as the temperature had dropped lately, she clung on to an iron railing on the approach. What would she tell Wyn when she found him? Not intending to unduly alarm him, she decided to keep what she said brief, having no real idea what had happened to his mother. After all, Thomas hadn't imparted all that much information to her.

From a distance away, she could hear the raucous sounds of men's voices emanating from the *Llwyn yr Eos* public house. The Welsh name meant 'grove of the nightingale'. Well, she'd never seen nor heard any nightingales in these parts, but they must have been here once upon a time to name the pub as such, she surmised.

Beneath the hazy glow of a gas lamp, she noticed a man with a tankard in hand having a conversation with a woman, who was leaning in to him. Was that his wife? But the way the man now had his hand wrapped around the woman's waist and was almost kissing her cheek as he listened to her, she guessed not. Since when did she know any married couples who carried on in that sort of fashion? Her parents certainly didn't and neither did Wyn's. Being intimate was for the bedroom, wasn't it?

As she approached the pub's entrance, she caught the man's attention.

'Who are you looking for, lovely girl?' He broke free from his companion, seeming interested in Elin now. A sickening thought grabbed her by the throat. Surely, he didn't think she'd come here seeking a man? As though she was so hard up and desperate that any gentleman who had plenty of money to flash around would do for an evening?

'I... I'm looking for Wyndham Edwards...' Her voice trembled as she spoke and she drew her cloak tightly around her shoulders as though it would somehow ward off any menacing presence from the man.

'Wyndham, you say?' He had her full attention now as he stepped towards her. 'You're not his girlfriend, are you?'

'No, I'm ruddy well not! I'm his wife!' she said, raising her voice at his suggestion. What was going on here? Was her husband canoodling of an evening with a common tart like she'd witnessed that fellow just do? It would make sense though, all those absences and not wanting her company of an evening.

The man stiffened his posture, caught off guard. 'Oh, I see,' he said, narrowing his gaze. 'Well, you'll not find him in that pub I just came out of there. Try one of the others in the village. I dare say you'll find him in one of those, though...' He hesitated for a moment, before adding, 'I'd send some man in ahead of you just in case you see something you shouldn't like!' Then he threw back his head and laughed uproariously, pleased with himself that he'd managed to knock her off balance. And to add insult to injury, the woman joined him in his laughter too.

Elin could still hear their malicious peals of laughter resounding in her ears as she walked away, feeling thoroughly defeated. Was this what most married men did of an evening after a hard day's shift underground? Filled their bellies and then left their wives at home all alone while they sought some sort of sport elsewhere? She gritted her teeth, chin jutting out in defiance as she marched back towards the village, totally forgetting the path that was iced over and, in her reverie, she found herself slipping downwards until she landed in a crumpled heap, feeling grazed and sore. And then at that final humiliation, the tears flowed freely.

Elin took a composing breath as she scrambled to her feet, all the while chastising herself for not having taken more care. Now where to? She brushed down her skirts and headed off to the nearest pub, which was a couple of streets away. Thank goodness no one had seen her tumble – that would have been hard to bear on top of everything else.

Finally, when she rounded the corner, she noticed the pub door was ajar. There was no one standing outside this one, and for that she was grateful.

The first thing she noticed as she entered the establishment was the strong smell of alcohol and tobacco. The odour reminded her of that on her husband when he returned home of a night: stale sweat, swigged beer and the stench of pipe smoke. It made her want to expel the contents of her stomach onto the pavement, and thankfully, she'd not had time to eat as yet, or she was sure that she would have done.

Blinking, she noticed two young men at the bar with their backs to her, deep in conversation with one another. Across the way, in the corner, was an elderly man with a sour expression on his face, nursing a pint of what looked like ale. This pub appeared a far cry from the other, which had seemed teeming with life.

The stocky barman glanced up as she approached, looking surprised to see her. 'Can I help you, miss?' he asked. He had slicked-down hair, sported a clean shirt and navy waistcoat, and a bar towel was casually draped over his shoulder. He was a large-built fellow, appearing as though he could handle himself and any rough customers if necessary.

Looking into his warm brown eyes, she said, 'It's, er, Mrs, not Miss. My name is Mrs Edwards, and I'm married to Wyndham. Do you know him?'

The man had just drawn a pint from the pump for one of the young men, which he lifted and placed on the bar in front of him. Then taking the payment from the man, he looked at her and said, 'Aye, I know him. No, sorry, Mrs Edwards. Your husband has not been here this evening.'

'Please,' she persisted. 'I've just called to the Llwyn and he wasn't there. It's important that I find him as his mother has been taken ill.'

Hearing the distress in her voice, the barman said, 'If I were you, I'd try the White Hart Inn in Upper Abercanaid, Chapel Square. There's a man who runs a card school there.'

'Pardon?' Elin blinked several times. 'You mean he's teaching men like my husband how to play cards?'

The man chuckled. 'Er, no, not exactly.' He looked both left and right in case someone was listening. 'It's a card game all right the men are playing, but it's not for me to explain exactly what is going on, but let's just say someone comes away with a pocketful of coins afterwards!'

Elin gulped. 'Gambling!' she yelled.

'Shush!' He waved his arm in an attempt to silence her. 'Yes. But please keep your voice down as the wrong folk might get to hear of it and the police will try to shut it down.'

'And so they jolly well should!' she said, feeling quite affronted that Wyn would do such a thing behind her back. Not only was he abandoning her of late, but he was probably also spending more money on his nights out than she initially realised. Suddenly, she felt quite weary.

'Are you all right, love? You've gone quite pale there,' the barman said, coming around the counter and guiding her over to a table and chair, encouraging her to sit. At that point she couldn't have cared less who saw her in a pub, never mind seated at a table. 'I'll just fetch you a glass of water.'

'I... I think I could do with something stronger than that,' she heard herself saying.

'I'll fetch you a nip of brandy instead then, shall I?' He raised a pair of quizzical eyebrows.

The only time she'd ever tried brandy was when Mrs

Langton had presented all the staff with a celebratory drink on her birthday once, telling them to choose between a small glass of sherry or brandy. She'd chosen the latter, recalling how it had warmed her to the core, and how much she'd liked the sensation.

'Yes, please.'

The barman left her side to fetch the glass of brandy, which he presented to her along with a jug of water, but instead of diluting it, she knocked it back, all in one go, neat. Watching in astonishment, his eyes widened, he said, 'You really needed that, Mrs Edwards, didn't you?'

She smiled gratefully and nodded, wiping her mouth with the back of her hand. There was no doubt in her mind that she had needed it and if she had more money, she'd have ordered another, but she wasn't like her husband, oh no. She had more sense than to spend the family coffers on such frivolities. If it hadn't been for her own wage coming in, they might well have starved this week, and to think not only was he swigging the ale every evening, he was playing card games for money too!

Leaving a couple of coins on the table to cover the cost of the brandy, she stood to leave, heading for the door, which caused the barman to come rushing over. 'No,' he said, quietly displaying his open palm.

'But I must pay what's owed,' she protested.

'No, have it on me. I'll pay for it this time. You be on your way now, Mrs Edwards. And I hope you find that husband of yours.' He picked up the coins and deposited them into her hand.

Feeling it was useless to argue, she gratefully accepted them, dropping them into her skirt pocket. The way the man was talking, she got the impression that maybe he knew Wyn very well and what he got up to. Did he feel sorry for her? Did he know something she didn't?

Overcome by his kindness, she thanked him and left the pub, covering her head with the hood of her cloak. A thick grey fog had descended so she could only see a few feet in the distance ahead. The fog was commonplace enough in Merthyr Tydfil, what with all the heavy industry in the town and all those smoking chimneys, but she could have done without it tonight of all nights, as it cast an eerie smoky shroud over the village.

By the time she arrived at the White Hart, which was on the periphery of a cobbled street at Chapel Square, she sighed deeply. Now what? Should she enter, wailing like a banshee, demanding her husband abandon his card game and come home immediately, or should she try a gentler approach? Deciding on the latter, she pushed open the pub door.

Heart thudding beneath her blouse, her eyes scanned the low-ceilinged, dark room. A layer of smoke filled the place as all heads turned in her direction. There was no sign of Wyn, so she surmised maybe that barman was wrong, but then out of the throng, she saw someone she recognised headed towards her. It was Billy Joseph, a man who worked with Wyn at the pit.

'What on earth brings you here, Elin?' He blinked in astonishment.

Swallowing hard, she held her head erect; defeat was not in her sights right now. 'I'm looking for my husband,' she said firmly, and she glanced both right and left to see who was watching her, which turned out to be most of the establishment, all of whom, to her relief, appeared to be male.

Billy narrowed his gaze. 'What do you want him for?'

Elin felt her hackles rise, and raising her voice, even though she'd initially thought to go for the soft approach, she said, 'It is a matter of extreme importance and not because he hasn't shown up for his supper!' she snarled, thinking that's what most of those men were inwardly laughing about. The fact that Wyndham Edwards's missus had his dinner on the table and was so incensed she'd throw it at him, or even worse, in the bin. But nothing that evening could be further from the truth. She hadn't even had time to prepare anything.

Billy softened his stance and smiled at her. 'All right, love, just checking, that's all.'

'And I know full well why you're checking an' all, because he's been playing a card game for money,' she whispered behind her gloved hand. Then she watched Billy's eyes enlarge so much so that the whites were on show. He'd be wondering now how she knew that! Thought they had one up on their wives did these men!

Billy cleared his throat before saying, 'As you know, then yes, he's in the middle of an important card game in the back. He's not to be disturbed...'

'Look, it's his mother; she's been taken ill, and it sounds quite serious...'

Billy's mouth opened as though he was about to say something, then he closed it. 'Aw, not Olwen?'

She nodded. 'So, please tell Wyn he must return home at once. I'll wait for him outside.'

'B... but I can't do that. It's a very important game; there's a lot of money at stake here. There'll be one or two sorts who won't put up with any interruption from me nor anyone else for that matter – especially that fella from the China area of the town who owns a pub. There's a lot riding on this particular game, I've been told.'

'I've no interest in some fella from China!' she spat. 'Who I am interested in, though, is my ruddy husband! If you won't go and fetch him because you're too scared to, then I will!' Elin held her chin with determination as she brushed past Billy and headed through the bar room until she found a door. It seemed as though everyone in the pub was watching her as, gingerly, she tried to turn the brass knob. It wouldn't budge.

'You won't get it to open, love. It's locked,' said a gentleman with a bushy moustache, standing behind her. He appeared friendly enough and was probably of middle age, about the same age as her parents-in-law.

Appealing to his better nature, she said, 'Look, I've heard my husband is in the middle of a card game, but his mother has taken ill. He needs to come home *immediately*!'

This time, this man showed no cowardice as Billy had. 'I'll tell you what I can do; I'll pass a message inside the room. There's two men stood behind that locked door, you see, on guard should the police arrive. If I knock and tell them who I am, they'll open it and I'll ask them to give your husband a message from you, though I can't guarantee he'll leave the game. There's too much money at stake...'

Elin nodded appreciatively. 'I'd be grateful if you do pass that message on and tell him I'll wait outside for just ten minutes.'

The man smiled at her. 'I'll see what I can do for you. Who is your husband?'

'Wyndham Edwards.' On the mention of her husband's name, the man paled, and she wondered why. 'What's wrong? Can't you pass the message on for me?'

'It's not that. It's just...' he said, hesitating for a moment, an uncertain look in his eyes.

'Go on, tell me, please.' She was frustrated now, realising she'd come this far and there was obviously something wrong – which the man before her knew but she didn't.

Shaking his head, he said, 'Your husband owes one or two in that room a lot of money. And I mean *a lot*. He was hoping to play that game tonight to try to win some of it back with a view to clearing his debts.'

'Debts? I didn't know he had any.'

'Oh, aye. He does. He's been borrowing money from folk, right, left and centre.'

Elin felt a rush of fear engulf her. She knew Wyn had been frittering their finances away lately, but not to such an extent. And where was he getting the money to participate in this important card game? It sounded to her like he was up against some fairly wealthy sorts if they owned pubs!

'Please pass that message on anyhow and my job here will be done!' she yelled, not caring who could hear her. 'And it's up to him how he responds to his mother being taken ill. She was still at the doctor's surgery the last I heard, but it sounds serious to me.'

The man nodded sympathetically as he placed a hand on her forearm. 'Yes, I will, dear. I think it's best you leave anyhow. Don't wait for your husband, in case you are needed.'

Forcing a smile at the man, she turned and left the pub. It felt as though she were walking through the Red Sea as the crowd parted to allow her through.

* * *

Elin entered the house with trepidation. She could sense that something had changed since she'd left, knew it inside herself. Mrs Evans was standing over Frank, who was seated with a bowl of cawl in front of him, his meal untouched. He looked up at her with large, hooded eyes, which were dripping with tears.

Mrs Evans left his side to approach her. 'Sit down, dear. We've just received some sad news...' she explained. 'Joshua just returned home without Olwen.' Gently, she guided Elin so she might sit by the table too. 'I'm sorry to have to tell you this: your mother-in-law passed away at the doctor's surgery earlier.' Dilys sniffed and, pausing for a moment to find her voice, continued, 'My son waited for a while to speak to the doctor out of respect and to discover what might have happened. The doctor explained that he thought it was heart-related. She was on borrowed time anyway, as he put it.'

Elin glanced at her father-in-law who was staring at the bowl of cawl before him. It was as if he wasn't present somehow, as if he was someplace else in his mind, and maybe he was, as that was the only way he could cope with such devastating news. Only moments ago, he must have been about to eat his supper as usual, but then had been given the news that would change his life forever.

'Wyn,' she said now, looking up at Dilys's face and realising she must be feeling it too – she'd just lost a friend and a good neighbour she'd known for years.

'Did you manage to find him?' Mrs Evans's face was full of concern.

Elin nodded slowly. 'Yes, eventually.'

'Then why is he not with you? Here back at home where he's needed?' Mrs Evans pursed her lips with disapproval.

What could she say to the woman that would not land her husband in it nor disappoint his father? So instead, she didn't quite lie, but told a partial truth to save feelings. 'He's on his way here now...'

'But what can possibly be causing the delay?' Mrs Evans frowned.

Realising that if it was some time before Wyn returned home, it was going to look very bad for him in the woman's eyes, Elin rose to her feet. Facing her, softly, she said, 'You go home now, Mrs Evans. You've been very kind to stay here all this time, but Joshua needs you as he's going to be most upset, I'm sure. I'll see to the men here.'

In some ways she realised she was telling the woman, *You mind your own business, and I'll mind mine!* But she'd said what needed to be said in such a kind and tactful way that the woman hadn't realised the barbs behind her words.

Mrs Evans forced a smile, reached for her shawl on the back of a chair and wrapped it around her shoulders. 'Well, if you're quite sure, dear.' Then glancing at Frank, who exhibited a catatonic stare in the direction of the wall behind her, added, 'But please don't hesitate to knock on my door if you need anything.' She lowered her voice. 'That lamb cawl will be stone cold by now. My son called here with the news just before Frank was about to eat it. Right hungry he was an' all... Maybe you can warm it up for him later?'

Elin nodded. 'Yes, he probably doesn't have the stomach for it right now. I'll make him a cup of tea and warm the cawl later.'

The woman then left them to it, returning to her house next door. Elin turned her attention to her father-in-law as she reseated herself at the table. 'Frank, you do understand what has happened, don't you?'

He nodded as a tear slid down his cheek and into his bowl.

* * *

After she'd sent Frank to bed, Elin waited up for her husband to return home. Rest was what he needed right now. He'd be in no fit state to return to the pit tomorrow, and neither would she be to work at the big house. But for the time being, her role was to comfort her husband when he returned; there was no time for her to be upset. There would be time for that later, in privacy, when she knew she wouldn't be disturbed. What was important now was to ensure her husband knew of his mother's death.

She lay on the couch with her cloak draped over her, eventually falling into a fitful sleep where she dreamt she was searching everywhere for her husband, but she couldn't find him anywhere. Then she heard it, his key in the door as he stumbled into the room, startling her awake. He sounded unsteady on his feet and seemed to be breathing heavily. A strong smell of alcohol permeated the air.

A flickering candle emitted a low light, casting shadows on the wall, and there was an eerie reflection in the mirror as Elin glanced at the mantel clock. It was fifteen minutes past three in the morning and Wyn needed to be in work by six. A sudden rage consumed her as she jumped to her feet. He'd gone to that pub knowing he'd have to rise for work first thing, and even though she'd passed a message on about his mother being taken ill, he'd not heeded it, instead putting his thirst for beer and his lust for gambling above all else.

'Why didn't you come home earlier when I summoned you!' she snapped.

'Shurrup, woman,' he slurred and then to her disgust, he hiccupped and belched loudly. 'I hope you've kept me something to eat. I'm famished!'

For some reason she couldn't fathom, he seemed very pleased with himself and then she figured it out.

'You stayed behind at the White Hart because you were on a winning streak?' she said in disbelief.

'Precisely! I managed to pay off a debt or two and I've got some money left to enjoy!' His voice was gleeful as he jingled the coins in his trouser pocket.

'You disgust me!' she shouted, forgetting about her father-in-law in bed upstairs. But, before she had time to think on it further, she felt it – her husband's fist in her face.

She rebounded backwards against the wall. There was an almighty pain in her cheek as her neck snapped backwards, and then she felt her body slide down the wallpapered wall, slumping onto the cold tiled floor.

And then all went black. There'd been no time to prepare and even if she'd known it was coming, it would have been difficult to defend herself.

3

As Elin came to, she emitted a low groan. What had happened to her? Her eyes slowly adjusted as the room came into focus. She managed to pull herself onto her feet, glancing at the mantel clock as she did so, which now read twenty minutes past four. A surge of reality washed over her. She'd been out cold for well over an hour. Had she tripped over something? But then, suddenly, the horrors of the past few hours came rushing towards her like an out-of-control steam train. A memory of searching for her husband to give him the news that his mother was very sick and now, sadly, she'd since passed away.

Wyn should have followed her back home. But he hadn't returned until gone three o'clock. A vision of his sneering face danced before her eyes. He'd been violent when she'd stood up to him and now her cheek felt sore, and the pounding in her head felt akin to a series of rhythmic hammer blows. The sickening realisation that he'd struck her full force in the face. That's what happened, she recalled. She must have fallen when he'd punched her in the face, striking her head against the wall. It must have eventually knocked her out. She vaguely remembered how he hadn't even checked she was all right afterwards, nor shown any remorse by the look of it; that's how drunk he'd been at the time but following that, she remembered no more until waking up.

A sudden bout of nausea caught her unaware and had her retching violently. She just managed to make it to the yard outside where she vomited into an old metal bucket. Wiping her mouth with a handkerchief she'd found in her pocket, she made her way to the pump. Cleaning the bucket out could wait until she'd had something to drink.

The nausea had now subsided and a powerful thirst consumed her. She filled a large tin cup that was attached on a chain beside the pump, and began to drink thirstily, until realising it might cause her to vomit again. She slowed down and began to sip from it instead. Once sated, she realised she must try to speak to her husband again. She guessed he'd gone to bed.

And that's where she found him, spark out, still in the previous day's clothing, lying face down on the bed. She was sorely tempted to grab the bucket of vomit to tip over his head – he deserved it – but that might only cause further anger from him. And in that moment, an overwhelming feeling of sadness swept over her.

Oh, Wyn, why did you hurt me so? It's not just that you've hit me for the first time ever, it's the fact you've been hurting me every day since our marriage began, in one form or another.

Gently, she leaned over the bed as he snored loudly, and she shook his arm. He stirred momentarily, grunted, opened one eye, then closed it and promptly fell back to sleep, snoring again. It was of no use, she realised, disgusted. He couldn't even rouse himself enough for her to inform him that his mother had passed away. Regretfully, she resigned herself to the fact he was going to have to sleep it all off.

A thought occurred then – Frank! What about him? He ought to be getting ready for work this morning. She'd wait a while and then rouse him to see what he wanted to do. Thankfully, he hadn't drunk too much last night. He'd just seemed vacant, out of things, as though what had occurred hadn't been real. It was a way of coping, she supposed.

Things would be busy soon enough, regarding her mother-in-law's death. She ought to savour this time she had alone. There'd be callers arriving at the house and Olwen's body brought home. There'd be so much to arrange; the undertaker and chapel minister would need contacting, but before that she'd need to get a message to her employer to say she couldn't go to work today. A sickening feeling of letting Mrs Langton down today of all days, when she was desperately needed, engulfed her. Mrs Langton had asked her yesterday if she might help as her son, Lawrence, was due home from London in a couple of days' time. He worked as a lawyer there, and his mother was set on throwing a dinner party. She wanted Elin to accompany her to Merthyr town where a new grocery shop had opened that sold all manner of things that Cook could prepare for the party.

Nothing was too good for the son of the house. Elin had begun to picture the young man as a right mam's boy, the golden-haired child. According to Cook, there was another son, Benjamin, whose name was never spoken and no one at the house had any idea why, except that a previous member of staff, who had now retired from service, had once said he'd been sent away in disgrace for some misdemeanour. This was while his father was still alive.

Despite having worked at the big house for a few months,

Elin had yet to meet the woman's elder son. When he'd last arrived home for a few days at Christmas, Elin had been unwell with that horrible influenza that had been doing the rounds in the village, so she'd been bed-bound for a number of days and, consequently, had not been able to meet the man. By the time she'd returned to her position in January, he'd already left, headed for his London office. Not that she particularly wanted or needed to meet him; as far as she could see he was far too busy in the big city with his own affairs to be much help to his ailing mother. Why couldn't he start his own practice in Merthyr Tydfil to help support her? she often wondered. Surely it would be better for him to be close at hand rather than away from home in a bustling city?

Yes, she had to put her own family first. She was just going to have to send word to the house that she couldn't make it today.

Sighing deeply, she made her way to the scullery to prepare some tea and toast – she'd be no use to anyone with an empty stomach – then she'd swill out that old bucket and fetch coal with it to light the fire. Later, she'd check on Frank to see what he wanted to do. There was no way on God's green earth he'd go to work today. Surely not?

Following some sustenance, she began to feel more herself, if not a little tired as she'd only had a few hours of disturbed sleep – lying on the couch and sometimes the floor overnight.

She left the scullery to make her way upstairs. Swallowing hard, she tapped softly on the door to her parent-in-law's bedroom. When no reply was forthcoming, she tapped again, then slowly turned the knob. Throwing the door open wide, she gasped. Frank was nowhere to be seen! And from how neat and tidy the bed appeared, it evidently hadn't been slept in overnight.

This just didn't make any sense whatsoever. Last night when

she'd gone in search of Wyn, Mrs Evans had been here to keep an eye on Frank when he eventually came home. She'd seen him with her own eyes. Though of course she'd assumed he'd gone to bed but maybe he hadn't; he might have slipped out the front door while she was in the scullery.

Fearful now, she made her way back downstairs and almost wept with relief to see her husband still asleep in their bed. How on earth could she explain when he awoke that his mother was dead and his father missing?

She approached the front door and with relief opened it to see Thomas across the road sitting on his doorstep. She beckoned him over. Maybe he had a day off from the pit due to yesterday's injury.

'Hello again, you,' she said kindly. 'Do you think you could take a message to someone for me? I'll give you something for your time?' It was money she'd have been concerned about spending yesterday, but nevertheless, she thought, maybe her husband's turn of fortune since would ease things for them both.

Digging his hands into his trouser pockets, the lad nodded eagerly. 'I should say I can!' His eyes were shining bright. A puzzled expression swept over his face and she realised maybe she looked a right sight. Smoothing down her hair, she said, 'Just hang on here and I'll write one out for you to take.' She stepped back inside the house, and rummaging around in the bureau drawer in the room she shared with Wyn, she located what she was after: a sheet of paper and a pencil. Quickly she scribbled out the note:

Dear Mrs Langton,

I'm sorry I can't come into work today as there has been a close family bereavement. My mother-in-law passed away suddenly yesterday evening, which has left us all in a state of shock. I hope you understand. I plan to return to work within a few days.

Yours sincerely,
Mrs Elin Edwards

There was no envelope for her to slip the letter into, so she neatly folded the sheet of paper and handed it to Thomas, as she explained to him which house the letter needed delivering to. The large residence, though, would be hard to miss with its three storeys, standing loud and proud below the canal bank, its vast garden sporting colourful flower beds and ornamental fountains with neatly trimmed shrubbery. All in all, it was quite an impressive property, a far cry from the smaller houses packed closely together in the village, where the working-class folk lived cheek to jowl. There were one or two other large houses in Abercanaid, but none quite as grand as the Langton one.

'When you've delivered it, and waited for a reply, bring it to me and I'll pay you,' she instructed. If she hadn't been so upset, she'd have had a good old chuckle at the lad's desire to please. It was obvious he could see copper coins dancing before his very eyes as no doubt Mrs Langton would also pay him to send a reply in kind back to her.

Thomas, though, appeared a little wary before leaving.

'What's the matter?' Her forehead creased into a soft frown.

'I... I've never been to a big house like that before, miss. What do I do? Bow or curtsy or something like that?'

She shook her head and smiled at him. 'No, nothing like that. There really is nothing for you to fear. I actually work there for Mrs Langton. All you need to know is you don't knock at the main front door; go around to the rear of the property instead – it's the back door that the servants use. Knock there and one of the staff will answer you. Just tell them you've brought a message from Mrs Edwards for Mrs Langton and it awaits a reply. Oh, and of course, remove your cap before speaking to anyone and say "please" or "thank you" as necessary. It's common sense really.'

He nodded now as though he were happier at the prospect of approaching the house.

Elin handed the letter to him and watched him head off down the street. At least now she wouldn't be leaving them entirely in the lurch without knowing the reason for her absence. Mrs Langton would have to take one of the other maids shopping to Merthyr town with her instead, maybe young Molly or even the ageing Beatrice.

Lawrence Langton was the least of her worries when she had an errant husband asleep in the back room to deal with.

* * *

It wasn't until midday that Wyn roused himself, and Elin took that as an opportunity to approach him.

She drew near to where he perched on the side of the bed, head inclined, hair tousled, clothing a crumpled mess and still reeking strongly of alcohol. He looked up at her and, rubbing his eyes, gasped.

'My word, Elin – what on earth has happened to you?'

'How do you mean?' She frowned. 'Shouldn't it be me asking you that same thing: what on earth has happened to *you*?'

'It's your face, my sweet. It looks a bit swollen; you're going to have a right shiner by there.' He pointed to her cheek.

A large lump had formed in her throat, which was now threatening to choke her. 'I beg your pardon! Don't you remember who caused it, Wyn?' She blinked in disbelief. How could he not remember last night?

'I'm sorry, I don't,' he said, shaking his head, his palms splayed in an open gesture. It was as if he was denying he could ever do such a thing. In his mind he was innocent of all wrong-doing towards her.

'It was you, Wyn! You did this to me with that fist of yours!' She pointed to her face.

'Me? I've never put a hand to a woman in my ruddy life!'

Her husband seemed quite affronted now when it was she, herself, who ought to be rightly affronted!

Noting the expression on her face, realisation dawned for him. She wasn't one for lying, oh no, she wasn't.

Wyn's hand flew to his mouth. 'I'm sorry, Elin. Did I really do that to you?'

Slowly, she nodded, and, in that moment, she could sense his shock, could tell how mortified he was by such a suggestion.

Then he was on his feet and cradling her in his arms. 'Let me tell you, this will never, ever happen again,' he promised. 'It was the ruddy drink; it turned me into a demon!'

'Those are only meaningless words though, Wyn. You hurt me more than you'll ever know last night, and not only physically, but emotionally too. I was looking for you to tell you that your mother had taken ill.'

'Oh, I had no idea. I'm sorry. Where is she now?'

'That's just it though, Wyn... She's dead!' There was no other way to say it. No other way to spell it out to him, only to say the words folk hated to hear.

It was as though a bucket of ice-cold water had been sloshed all over him and he was standing there, dripping – sodden wet and as cold as his dead mother.

'B... but I don't understand, Elin. How can that possibly be?'

As best she could, she explained what had happened.

'So, where is she now? Where is my mother?'

'Still at the doctor's house. We're going to need to contact the undertaker to transport her body back home.'

He nodded.

'But first, I'm going to brew up and make you something to eat. We need our wits about us today, as on top of all of this your father has gone missing.'

Wyn remained sitting on the edge of the bed and slowly shook his head in disbelief.

* * *

Her husband was in a state of shock as he ate the breakfast of bacon, fried egg and crusty bread she'd prepared. He was going through the motions, shovelling forkfuls into his mouth. His eyes seemed without light. But then she reminded herself that's how his father had been. And now he was missing.

Gently, she reached out to him across the table, touching his free hand. 'Wyn,' she said softly, 'what are you going to do next?'

He shuddered and then fixed his gaze on her, looking as though he'd just woken from a bad dream. 'I... I don't really know.'

'Shall I tell you what I think you ought to do?' He was in no fit state to make any decisions right now, what with the shock of his mother's death, his father's disappearance and the realisation of how he'd physically hurt her the previous night.

'Yes, please go on,' he said. 'Although I don't deserve any help whatsoever from you after what I did to you last night.' There were tears in his eyes now.

Elin took a breath of composure and let it out. 'I think you should go to see the undertaker as soon as possible and explain what's occurred and where your mother's body now rests at the doctor's surgery. Request that either her body is brought back here before the burial, or...' She glanced at the ceiling as she tried to think things through.

'Or what?'

'Or maybe it would be a good idea if her body was taken to the chapel to rest there instead before a service is booked for the funeral. This is only a small house, of course, and there wouldn't be much room here. I know that ordinarily, people bring their loved ones home before a funeral – in the parlour or some other room – but we...' she sucked in a breath, feeling a little guilty '... but we are now residing in that room, so it wouldn't be practical.'

He lifted his head. 'Yes, you are right. I shall do that. I'll go to see Mr Pritchard straight after breakfast.'

Over the years, Vaughan Pritchard had seen to the funeral offices of many from Abercanaid and the surrounding areas, and before him his father, Zacheriah, had done the very same. These days the old man was still involved but not to such a great extent. It was Vaughan and his eldest son and daughter who saw to most things now.

Elin huffed out a breath of relief. No matter how her husband had behaved towards her last night, she realised she had to put it all to one side out of respect for her mother-in-law. 'What about your father, Wyn? Shall I go in search of him for you?'

'Oh no.' He shook his head vigorously. 'You'd better stay here in case we have any callers. I'll look for him after I've paid a visit to the undertaker's house.'

She wondered for a moment why he was so insistent she remain at home. There wouldn't be any callers yet, as hardly anyone knew his mother had passed away.

When she stood to clear the breakfast dishes away, she touched her throbbing cheek and winced – it was still sore to touch. She dreaded to think how she appeared to others. Leaving the dirty dishes soaking in the sink, she made her way to the living room. There, above the fireplace, was the mirror. Steeling herself, she took a peep, gasping in horror when she saw the bruising coming out on her face. The swelling had increased and a purple and blue patch had begun to radiate from her cheek to just beneath her lower eyelid. That would end up being a right shiner for sure. Now it made sense why young Thomas had been looking at her curiously earlier. She would bathe it with a cold wet flannel when Wyn left the house.

No wonder Wyn wasn't keen for her to go out right now. People would see the bruise and put two and two together. She realised he must be cringing inside. All of this would only add to the misery, but it couldn't be helped. No one had forced him to raise a hand to her. He had only himself to blame.

Before leaving the house, with tears in his eyes, Wyn took her hand and said, 'I'll make it up to you I swear, Elin. Please don't think too badly of me. This is a turning point, my love.'

Elin swallowed hard. Could she believe this man? This man stood before her looking like a shadow of his former self? After all, before today he'd not laid a finger on her. His constant drinking and absence from the home did not bode well. But everyone deserved a second chance, didn't they?

* * *

After washing and tidying herself up, changing out of yesterday's dress into a dark one to indicate a period of mourning, and then brushing her long hair and pinning it up neatly,

Elin dropped into the armchair, holding a cold, wet flannel to her sore cheek.

She didn't know how long she'd been sleeping when a gentle tapping sounded on the front door. Startled, she glanced at the mantel clock, relieved to see she'd only been asleep for about twenty minutes and the flannel had now fallen to the floor, but those minutes had been enough to rejuvenate and restore her. She retrieved the flannel and placed it on a low table beside the armchair.

Drawing back the front door, she saw Dilys there, with tears in her eyes. 'Good morning, *cariad*. I don't expect you've had much sleep, have you?'

Elin didn't have the heart to tell her neighbour she'd disturbed her, so she just shook her head and forced a smile. 'Not a lot, no. But I feel a bit better now after a wash and brush-up. Come in,' she offered, as she watched the diminutive figure step over the threshold. 'Have a seat,' she said after the woman had followed her into the living room.

Dilys did as told and looked at her now, studying her face, then she narrowed her gaze. '*Duw, duw*.' She tutted, shaking her head. 'What's happened to you then, since I saw you last night?'

Oh dear, this was going to be difficult for Elin to explain. She struggled to think of something to satisfy the woman's curiosity, but her delay in doing so must have told the woman it wasn't something everyday that had caused her to look this way.

'I... er...' She was about to say she'd tripped over the rug and carelessly bumped into the edge of the mantelpiece when Dilys cut in.

'You don't have to explain, dear. It's happened to me over the years. My Walter was handy with his fists, but only when he'd been in drink. I'm guessing that's what happened to you.'

Dilys didn't appear to be expecting a reply nor an explanation, but Elin replied anyhow. 'Yes, something like that, Mrs Evans.'

'I'll tell you what, I'll nip back next door and bring you some soothing balm. I swear by it. My sister gets it from somewhere. It's so handy as it contains some sort of herb that heals bruises.' She rose to her feet.

'I'd appreciate that. Thank you. While you're gone, I'll put the kettle on.'

'Thank you, dear. I'm parched.' The woman smiled, rising to her feet.

Now Dilys knew about her little secret Elin realised she had a confidante. She wasn't one for spilling her guts to all and sundry, oh no, but Dilys had explained how she'd been through the exact same thing. In the village there were some who thrived on gossip – it was that sort of area. The houses were packed closely together here like sardines in a tin can, so if someone in the house across the road as much as sneezed then someone somewhere would know about it. Some folk could be too familiar at times – wanting to know all your business. Elin quickly realised that Dilys Evans was not one of those people. The woman preferred to keep herself to herself and was a good ally to have by her side.

Dilys returned within minutes, in which time the kettle had almost boiled. She handed Elin a small brown glass jar.

Removing the lid, Elin closed her eyes and took a sniff. It wasn't unpleasant at all. 'It smells like fresh grass or hay,' she said, looking at the woman.

'Yes,' said Mrs Evans, seeming quite pleased with herself. 'It's a soothing salve that contains something called comfrey. I think it's some sort of plant. There are other good things in there too that promote healing. Put some on your bruising while I sort the tea out,' she said helpfully. 'You won't need too much of it, just a little to smooth over the affected area.' Then she left the room for the scullery to brew up for them both.

Elin nodded gratefully. Then, dipping a couple of fingers into the cold balm, she applied it to her swollen cheek, wincing as she caught sight of herself in the mantel mirror. If only she had something to conceal the bruise.

When the woman returned with two cups in matching saucers, she laid them down on a low table between both armchairs. Elin didn't usually use this room, but what did it matter now? Olwen was dead and would never sit in here ever again.

'Now how does that feel?' Dilys smiled at her.

'It feels very soothing. Thank you so much, Mrs Evans. Please sit yourself down. You have been so helpful to me.'

'Dilys, please,' said the woman as she seated herself. She stretched over towards the table and took her cup of tea as Elin sat opposite and followed suit.

This felt like the calm before the storm. Soon her husband would return and then she'd find out what the next step would be.

'You look anxious, my dear,' Dilys observed as she set her cup back down on its saucer.

'I am more than usual. Frank's bed wasn't slept in last night and we've no idea where he is.'

'That's not good, is it?' said Dilys with a frown. 'I wouldn't worry too much about him though, as I saw him passing my window this morning. My guess is he's gone to the pit.'

'Oh, why didn't I think of that?!' Elin put the heel of her hand to her forehead. 'I don't think he ought to be working today of all days, mind you.'

'Maybe he's not gone down in the pit cage. Perhaps he's just gone to explain to the foreman why he and Wyn won't be in work today.'

'Aye, maybe. I had to do the same thing myself. I sent young Thomas with a letter to let Mrs Langton know I can't go to work for her this morning. And she particularly needed me today too.'

'Oh, why is that?' Dilys quirked a curious eyebrow.

'That lawyer son of hers will be returning from London for a few days and she wanted to get some special provisions in for him.'

Dilys nodded knowingly. 'That's only to be expected, I suppose. I'd do the same for my Joshua if I were in her position. And to be honest, it's perfectly understandable when the black sheep is no longer around...' She pursed her lips and shook her head.

'I had heard a whisper about that, though I've not encountered him at all.' She took a sip of her tea, which had now cooled so it was comfortable on the tongue.

'Well, you wouldn't have, would you? He was supposedly shipped off to some relative in Scotland in disgrace when it all happened.'

Elin laid down her teacup on the table and sat forward in her chair. 'What happened though, Dilys? That's what I don't know.'

Dilys lowered her voice in a surreptitious manner as though she were about to reveal the most awful thing – the secret of all secrets. 'Supposedly, and I have this on good authority from someone who worked at the house at the time, he was embezzling funds from the sweet factory to fund his gambling addiction...'

Elin gasped. Mrs Evans's words struck a chord with her.

The woman carried on. 'Apparently, he'd been put in charge

of the company finances. I was informed he has a good head on him and is clever with figures. Though a little too clever for his own good, if you ask me. Then one day, the accountant his father employed noticed a discrepancy in the books and all the key staff were called in to explain the missing money. What hurt his parents so much though wasn't just that their own son had stolen from them, but he'd tried to blame his brother for it!'

'Oh, my goodness!' said Elin, her hand flying to her mouth. 'No wonder Mrs Langton likes to fuss over Lawrence, then.'

Dilys nodded. 'Aye, there's no doubt about it, she's trying to make amends to him. In the first instance, both she and her husband, William, believed him, giving Lawrence a hard time of it. That was until the police were summoned and a very clever constable caught Benjamin out with some untruth or another. It was then he confessed all and was sent away in disgrace.'

Elin felt as though she'd been punched in the stomach and all the wind had been taken out of her. How could she possibly face the woman and her son now, knowing all of this? She was sure the other staff wouldn't know quite how serious it had all been. In some ways, she'd rather have not known at all.

She was about to ask a question when she heard the front door opening and closing. Surely Wyn couldn't be back so soon? The doctor's surgery was in the nearby village of Troedyrhiw. Exchanging a curious glance with Dilys, she held her breath.

But it wasn't Wyn who entered the living room but Frank, with his flat cap in his hand. There were dark rings beneath his glassy eyes. He appeared to have aged overnight.

'I'm so sorry if I've worried you...' he said solemnly.

Elin released the breath she'd been holding. 'Here, take my seat by the fire,' she said kindly, rising from the armchair. 'Now don't you go worrying. You must be absolutely perished. I'll fetch you a hot cup of sweet tea.' She patted his gnarled hand.

He nodded gratefully. 'I need something,' he said.

'How about a bite to eat too?' Dilys offered.

He raised his palm. 'No, I can't. I couldn't eat a morsel. Thank you, though. I don't have the stomach for it.'

'But where were you?' Elin blinked. 'Your bed doesn't look slept in.'

'I was here until about two o'clock this morning, then I just found myself walking around the streets. I didn't know what to do with myself, to be honest with you. I did pop back home when you were sleeping, Elin. I didn't want to disturb you and knew I'd not sleep a wink no matter how I tried, so instead, I called to the pit to have a chat with the foreman.'

'That's when I saw you,' said Dilys. 'Passing my window.'

'Oh, I see.' He glanced up at Elin and for a second, she thought he was going to enquire about her bruised cheek but instead, he asked, 'How come you were sleeping on the couch anyway?'

'Oh, Wyn was snoring too loudly last night.' She forced a smile, feeling guilty for lying to her father-in-law, but surely it would hurt him more if she were to tell him the truth. 'Then, as I was stumbling in the dark as I got confused where I was, I hit my cheek on the mantelpiece...'

He nodded at her. 'You'll have to take more care in future,' he warned.

'Aye. I'll just fetch you that tea.' Then turning towards Dilys she added, 'You'll stop for another cup?'

'No, thank you. I'd better return home. I've things to do,' Dilys said, rising from her chair. 'Now if either of you need me, you only have to ask, and I'll be here in a trice.'

'That's so kind of you,' Elin said, and then she left the pair of them to fetch a pot of tea. When she returned, the woman had gone.

4

Wyn returned home waving a brown envelope in his hand. 'I've been to the undertaker's and sorted things out,' he said. 'I never thought this time yesterday, I'd be saying this to you...'

'I feel the same way too,' Elin sympathised. 'One good thing, your father's back home.'

'I'd totally forgotten about the old man. My head is so full of stuff, it's swimming. I can't think straight. Is he all right?'

She nodded. 'Yes. He's numb with shock though. He'd been wandering around during the night, came home about two o'clock in the morning, noticed me sleeping on the couch and left again. Went to the pit by all accounts to explain to the foreman why you both wouldn't be in work today.'

'He's a bloody old fool wandering around in the cold like that.' Wyn shook his head. 'Might have caught his death and then we'd be burying the pair of them!'

'He's all right, honestly. I made him a hot cup of sweet tea, which he drank, and then he took to his bed. We need to let him sleep. Wouldn't touch any food though. So, what did Mr Pritchard say?'

'I didn't get to speak to him; he was out on a call somewhere. I dealt with his son, who took all the details. I need to pay a deposit later. He's gone to fetch my mother's body from the doctor's surgery to perform last offices on her and then, by tonight, she'll be lying at rest at the chapel.' He looked at her and she could see the sadness in his eyes. 'It's funny to think that very same chapel is the one where she went to Sunday school as a child, and the same one where she married my father. Most people's lives in this village revolve around the chapel or—'

'The pub in some cases.' It had slipped out without her thinking about it, and now she wished she'd bit her tongue, as the hurt in his eyes was clear.

'You have a point there,' he said finally, blinking away tears. 'But believe me, I'll be a changed man. You'll have nothing to worry about any more. You won't have to fear my fists, as I'll not be drinking from now on, and as for the gambling, after that win last night, I can clear most of my debts. But then again, I'll need some of the money right now to help with the funeral, as Dad hasn't got much.'

She nodded, but all the while she wondered: once the funeral was paid for, how would he get the money to pay off those debts?

Wyn left the house again soon after, saying he had some people to see, and Elin wondered who those people were.

* * *

Realising there'd be callers arriving soon, Elin tidied up the house. Her mother-in-law came from a large family, being the eldest of seven children. One brother and sister were now deceased, but the other four siblings and their families lived in neighbouring villages. Elin knew they'd at some point wish to pay their respects. But who were the people Wyn had gone to see? Were they a couple of his creditors? Which, if that was the case, meant that he was a debtor. It would have been most unwise to bring the matter up following last night's volatile behaviour. She couldn't be certain he would not strike her again, whether in drink or when sober. The whole episode had left her feeling slightly on edge. Before marriage, she'd been a confident woman, but these past few weeks had made her feel like a shadow of her former self.

To keep her mind off things she sought to keep herself busy. So, it was with some irritation that there was a knock on the door. Hoping it would be Dilys and not someone turning up earlier than expected to pay their respects, she made her way to the front of the house.

She smoothed down her hair and opened the front door, to be met with a pair of the most overpowering cerulean-blue eyes she'd ever seen in her life, glistening like the shimmering sun on the sea at Swansea Bay. The eyes belonged to a tall, handsome man who wore a long, very expensive-looking tailored jacket, white shirt and silver-grey cravat. He removed his top hat to address her.

'Elin? Mrs Elin Edwards?'

Her cheeks grew hot as she realised a blush must be spreading across her face. It was most unusual for someone of his standing to be knocking on her door. She had no idea who he was, and she noted a small crowd had gathered behind him in amusement. It was then she noticed his coach and driver parked down the road, and she could see that Thomas and his friend seemed most interested in the black horse that was attached to the coach, both sleek and shiny in their own way.

Desperate not to invite a further audience, she said, 'You'd better come inside, sir.'

It was then that her heart began to beat profoundly. Was this man something to do with her husband's gambling? Was he someone he owed money to? A moneylender, perhaps?

'Thank you, Mrs Edwards.'

She smiled tentatively, stepping aside to allow him access into the small passageway. He followed her into the living room.

'Please take a seat.' She gestured with her hand, pleased that she had cleaned and tidied the room recently and there was still a small fire kindling in the grate. The room now smelled of beeswax and lavender from having polished all the wooden surfaces. It might not have been the smartest room ever, but it had a nice and cosy feel about it.

The man did as bid, placing his top hat upside down on the small table beside him. He looked uncertain for a moment as though not quite knowing what to say, and there was an awkward silence until Elin asked, 'Can I get you anything? A cup of tea or a glass of water, perhaps?'

He shook his head and held up his palm. 'No, thank you. I've just had one with my mother.'

His mother? It was then something occurred to her. 'Are you Lawrence Langton?'

His smile reached his eyes, making them appear warm and friendly. 'I am the one and the very same. Now won't you please sit, as you're making me feel most uncomfortable, me being seated while you're standing.'

She smiled again, though not tentatively this time. Now she knew who he was, she felt more at ease. She let out a little breath, brushed down the skirts of her dress and sat in the armchair opposite him.

The man clasped his leather-gloved hands together and then made direct eye contact. 'To tell you the truth, I would have left well alone, but it's my mother; she wanted to check on your welfare after receiving that letter from you earlier this morning...'

'Oh, I see. Please tell Mrs Langton not to worry about anything. I just need a few days off until my mother-in-law is laid to rest.'

'Yes, it's most understandable you require some compassionate leave. And we both offer our condolences to you and your family. I suppose really it wasn't just that though; she's wondering if there's anything we can do for you. According to her, you're a very valuable member of staff. I know she holds you in high regard, Mrs Edwards.'

Elin beamed on hearing him say those words. She knew of course that the woman thought well of her but for someone else to say it, she felt appreciated and respected. 'It's very kind of your mother to offer help, but it's all in hand. Please thank her for me though.' She hesitated a moment, studying his handsome-looking face. He had a strong sculptured jaw and those thick-lashed eyes of his seemed to be boring a hole into her soul, and she realised he was someone whose appearance made an impression on those he encountered. 'I thought though...'

'You're looking puzzled? For some reason, you were obviously not expecting to see me here today of all days?' He raised his eyebrows as he awaited her answer.

'Yes, I thought you weren't due back from London for another day or two? I was supposed to accompany your mother to Merthyr town today to purchase some provisions before your arrival.'

He raised his eyebrows in bemusement. 'Ha, that. Yes.

Mother does tend to make a bit of a fuss of the prodigal son whenever he arrives home!' He chuckled.

Shouldn't it be the other way around? Elin thought. Wouldn't Benjamin be the prodigal one? But she said nothing about it, as it wasn't her place to do so. 'So, you arrived earlier than expected?'

'Yes. I had the opportunity to slip away as an important court case was cancelled, so there was no need for me to remain in London after all. I thought I'd surprise the old girl by coming home early.'

Elin could well imagine that would have surprised her all right, and she could picture the delight on her employer's face to see her handsome son walking through the front door. She thought he couldn't be all that much younger than Wyn, but Wyn had a more weather-beaten, less polished appearance of late, especially since he'd taken to the drink.

A beam of sunlight was shining in through the window and settled on her face, dazzling her. She made to rise out of her seat to draw the curtains a little. The sun's rays could be strong at this time of the day, even in winter, on the window. Though they didn't get to see too much of it.

'I hope you don't mind me asking...' he said when she'd reseated herself. 'But what happened to your face?'

Taken aback by his forthright remark, her breath hitched in her throat. She couldn't believe he'd asked her such an impertinent question. She was about to give him the tale about tripping over the fireside rug and falling and catching her cheek on the mantelpiece when he spoke softly. 'I am sorry. Please forgive me for asking you, but you have such a beautiful complexion, that bruising looks out of place. I mean I couldn't help but noticing a little swelling when I first spoke to you at the door, but when the sun streamed in through the window it settled on that side of your face, and it became evident that somehow you'd injured yourself.'

She nodded. 'I did, yes.'

'Is it sore?' A look of concern furrowed his brow.

'Yes, it is but I've been bathing it in cold water and applied a little balm.'

He gazed at her for the longest time as though captivated by her. 'Look, you don't have to answer this question, but did someone do that to you?'

She nodded and gulped and then to her horror, tears began to fill her eyes. She didn't want to break down in front of this stranger but the past day or so had been such a shocking experience that she was unable to hold back, and in a way, it was a release for her.

'I'm sorry, I'm afraid I've managed to open the floodgates for you. Here, take this.' He handed her a silver silk handkerchief from his top pocket, which she gratefully accepted, dabbing at her eyes and, when she had finished, she made to hand it back to him.

'No, you keep it, please. I have plenty of them,' he enthused. 'My dear, you've been through a lot, and this probably isn't the best time to discuss your domestic arrangements but never forget if you're ever in trouble, we have spare bedrooms at our house. Mother would rather see you stay with us than physically hurt in any way at all. Do you understand me?' She nodded and watched him stand. He drew close to her and patted her hand. 'Now you stay where you are. There's no need to see me out. Have a good cry if you need to. In my profession, I've seen many women, many of whom are from the upper echelons of society, who have been hurt by their menfolk. A lot of them have money to deal with such things and I've sorted out new domestic arrangements for them, whereby their cruel husbands have to part with their filthy lucre so that their wives can find somewhere else to abide.' He glanced around the room before continuing. 'The working classes are not quite as fortunate, I'm afraid...'

In that moment, she realised never was a truer word spoken.

* * *

Once Lawrence had left, Elin sat there in the armchair reflecting on what had just occurred. She couldn't believe how she'd broken down in front of a total stranger like that. Yet, the man hadn't seemed to mind at all. What she didn't want though from anyone was pity. Though it wasn't pity he had shown her but compassion. He'd left, telling her to take as much time as she needed – the house would continue to run without her for a while, he'd said, and to remember that she was a 'deeply valued member of staff'.

There weren't many people in this life that she took to straight away, but Lawrence Langton was one of them. She'd felt comfortable in his presence. Must have done so to have cried like that in front of him. She hadn't named her husband, but both understood that Lawrence knew the truth of who had hurt her like that.

She managed to rest a while longer before she heard a stirring from above. She realised that her father-in-law was getting out of bed. Hopefully the rest would have done him some good. Fussing around him and trying to encourage him to eat would help to take her mind off things.

* * *

Early afternoon, the first caller to arrive at the house was Issac Probert, minister of the local chapel where Olwen's body was to be taken to rest and where her funeral would be held later that week. Mr Probert was an elderly man, but his countenance was that of a much younger person. In his line of work, he hadn't succumbed to immorality or 'good living' in as much as partaking of alcohol. He ate well, took a little exercise, kept his brain sharp, and practised the word of God every day. He liked to keep himself in fine fettle so that he could be there for his flock.

Elin answered the door to him and showed him into the living room where Frank was already seated.

'Ahh, that we meet on such an auspicious occasion, sadly,' he said as he nodded at Frank.

Frank raised an open palm to the man. He knew him well of course as he and his wife had been regular chapel-goers.

Elin offered him a seat and went to fetch refreshments for both men. As she boiled the kettle, from the open scullery door she could hear them chatting: Frank was explaining how unexpected Olwen's death had been and Mr Probert was passing on his condolences. Every so often, her mind drifted away, surprising herself as the image of Lawrence Langton danced before her eyes. She remembered his kindness towards her and began to see something in the man that she did not see in her husband. As the minister was in close proximity, she immediately felt guilty for thinking that way.

Yet she still couldn't get the man out of her mind. Puffs of steam emerged from the kettle's spout as she wondered whether their paths would ever cross again – or if he'd have already left for London by the time she returned to work.

As she brought the tray into the living room, she inhaled the intense odour of coffee. Most valley people drank tea at home and only occasionally drank coffee at the taverns that were springing up in Merthyr town. The idea was to keep men out of the pubs and in coffee shops instead, something approved of by the Temperance Society. And they were proving popular.

They did have some in the house though. Elin's mother-in-law had been partial to a cup of coffee so she occasionally purchased some and tended to drink it on special occasions. It wasn't as cheap as tea though, but it made a nice change.

Elin poured the drinks and was about to add sugar to the minister's cup when he held up his hand. 'No sugar for me, thank you, Mrs Edwards.'

'Oh?' That was most unusual as the coffee had such a strong flavour. She'd never known anyone refuse a little sugar before, as most used it to temper the bitterness.

'Yes, I only allow things into my body that will do it good.' He smiled. 'After all, the Good Book says, "If ye be willing and obedient, ye shall eat the good of the land" – Isaiah chapter one, verse nineteen.'

'Following the teachings of the Bible must be doing you some good, Mr Probert,' Elin enthused, 'as you look fit and healthy for your age.'

'I am that!' the minister said proudly. 'I'm eighty years old! Now tell me then...' He accepted the cup and saucer offered from Elin's outstretched hand. 'What happened to Olwen? Was she ill?'

Elin hesitated, glancing at her father-in-law to see if he'd speak up, but he remained mute. Feeling uncomfortable by his silence and not wishing to be rude to Mr Probert, she said, 'Not that we were aware of.' She turned to her father-in-law. 'Frank?'

Frank looked at the pair of them with enquiring eyes, so similar to his son's though his were hooded with age. 'Not that she'd been diagnosed with anything, but I remember her telling me that as a young child her lips would sometimes turn blue. And once...' He was obviously thinking back now. 'Once I remember her fainting in the snow. But to be honest, I didn't think she had a bad heart like the doctor has indicated. Well, not to that extent anyhow.'

Elin thought of the recent times when Olwen had seemed out of breath, such as when she caught her struggling to carry the coal bucket into the house. She'd ended up taking it herself, relieving her mother-in-law of her heavy load. Or other occasions when she'd found her fast asleep on the couch in the afternoon and it had taken a time to rouse her. Looking back, all the signs were there, but Elin said nothing about it, because she didn't want to upset Frank. But surely, he must have noticed a gradual decline in his wife's health, too?

The minister nodded. 'What it is,' he said sagely as he replaced his cup in its saucer, 'is that we learn to live with the deficit in life. What I mean is, as our bodies age, we get so used to slowing down that it becomes normal for us. It can happen so gradually that we don't really notice it. Many of my congregation have told me the same thing.'

No wonder Mr Probert was keeping an eye on his own health then, Elin thought. The man had no family of his own to speak of, just a housekeeper to take care of him. But then again, he didn't have to partake of the physical toil that many men from Merthyr had to, as his profession was in preaching the word of God. It wasn't lifting a pickaxe in the bowels of the earth. Yet, what he did was every bit as important, maybe even more so than the miners who toiled underground. His job was to keep those same men, women and children of the village on the straight and narrow, and he needed to keep himself fit to enable him to do so. Elin had a lot of time for Mr Probert. He was a godly man and if anyone had troubles, he welcomed them into his office at the chapel to speak with them.

As Frank began to tell the minister of his wife's early years and their married life, Elin guessed that the man would be storing up anecdotes to recite at the woman's funeral. Opening up did seem to be helping Frank too. She could never imagine the man would have ever laid a finger on Olwen. He seemed to have held her in high esteem and obviously had loved her dearly.

5

Following a few days of neighbours and family calling to the house, it was time for the funeral to take place. These days were particularly hard for Elin, as pressure had been put on her to play the hospitable hostess and she just wasn't in the mood for it; her emotions were all over the place. Wyn wasn't much help to her, though he had managed to stay out of the pub at least, but whether he kept away from any gambling dens, she couldn't be sure.

The main thing she decided was to keep on going for her mother-in-law's sake. She had both liked and respected the woman so much.

When they arrived at the chapel, the first thing Elin noticed were the strains of '*Ar Hyd y Nos*' – otherwise known as 'All Through the Night' in English – emanating from the pipe organ, played by Mr Cornelius Plumber, a pious man who often held his nose in the air as though he thought he were better than everyone else. While most of the men from Abercanaid did manual work in the shape of coal mining or ironworking, this man worked as a 'clerk of the works' at some solicitor's office in

Merthyr town. His hands were too lily white and baby soft to have partaken of any hard graft. He was unmarried and she wondered if that was because no woman would have him.

She was pulled up sharp by her mean thoughts. The man was a decent organist; she'd give him that much, she supposed.

A few people stood with their heads lowered as she, her father-in-law and husband walked solemnly down the chapel aisle behind the coffin, which was being carried by four pall-bearers. It was decorated on top with a large bouquet of white lilies. The lily had been Olwen's favourite flower – that was something Elin prided herself on remembering, and she was glad that she had, as neither Wyn nor his father seemed aware of it. Only she and Dilys next door were mindful of that, so it was a nice touch to have them at her funeral.

The organ music ceased abruptly after the coffin was laid to rest on a pedestal in front of the pulpit and they seated themselves in the front pew. Then all went quiet as Mr Probert took his place on the platform with a sombre expression on his face.

'We are gathered here today on this sad occasion…' he began. Not a pin could be heard dropping as he spoke about the woman's life, mentioning how Olwen Jones had been brought up on a mountain farm overlooking the village of Abercanaid and what a happy childhood she'd had with her brothers and sisters. There was mention of how she'd met and married Frank Edwards and how they had one child, who was a devoted son to them both. Of course, a lot of what Mr Probert said had come from his previous visit to the house. Although he'd known Olwen very well, there were little touches to his sermon that Elin guessed the man wouldn't have known otherwise. Like the time her father had carried her as a toddler on his strong shoulders over the mountain to Aberdare as there was a singing competition they wanted to enter. And they'd won it too as 'The Jones Family from Abercanaid'.

Elin noticed some of Olwen's family smiling at the memory. It must have taken them back to many years ago.

Then one of her brothers, David Jones, was summoned to the pulpit to give a reading from the gospel of John – it said something about the Father's house having many rooms and how Jesus prepares a place for us there.

Elin could see how choked up the man was. It couldn't have been easy for him to read that out, knowing his sister was lying there lifeless in that coffin just below him.

Finally, a hymn was sung and the service ended in prayer, then the coffin was transported by the same four pall-bearers to the undertaker's horse-drawn hearse, ready for Olwen's final journey to the cemetery.

It wasn't common in the Welsh Valleys for women to attend a burial, it being more usual to return to the house to help prepare food following the service. Several women attended the house including Olwen's sisters, friends and neighbours.

Elin often thought how unfair it was that womenfolk were expected to remain at home while the men attended the graveside. Often what happened was that many of those same men ended up sloping off to the pub and did not return to the house at all! The ones she knew for certain who would return were close family members and the minister. She was confident Wyn would attend though, despite being recently tempted by drink – he wouldn't want to let his mother down. As for the rest, she doubted very much she'd ever see hide nor hair of those varmints again.

But true to his word, Wyn turned up at the house an hour later, with Frank, Olwen's brothers, the minister and a couple of other men who she'd not seen before, not even at the chapel.

Frank explained to her that Mr Dean and Mr Saunders, who were quite elderly, had worked with Olwen before her marriage to Frank – they obviously thought highly of the woman.

Elin watched as Dilys and Mrs Merriman from down the street handed around piled-up plates of ham and cheese sandwiches, while Olwen's sister doled out cups of tea and slices of fruit cake.

Sighing to herself at the sadness of the day and how they were all now expected to prepare for a life without Olwen in it, she headed off to the scullery to begin washing some used crockery, preferring to clean and tidy up as she went along. She'd learned that from working at the big house for Mrs Langton – a habit she liked to adhere to, avoiding things piling up around her, as that seemed to cause more hard work in the long run.

It was while she gazed out of the window as she washed up that her mind turned to Lawrence Langton. She'd been charmed by his presence and surprised how sympathetic he was to the plight she now found herself in. Not many men she knew would be like that. She imagined he was well used to dealing with people. But despite that, she could tell the man was genuine and she put a lot of that down to his mother's influence – Muriel had a way with people herself.

'Elin!'

As she turned suddenly, a plate slid out of her hand and back into the soapy water, causing a big splash.

Wyn was standing behind her, a frown on his face.

'Yes?' She blinked several times.

'Are you going deaf or something? I said your name a couple of times and you didn't respond to me.'

She chewed her bottom lip, feeling guilty that her mind had been elsewhere – on another man she wasn't even wed to, no less! 'Sorry, it's just that today is such a sad day...' she said, shaking her head.

'I know.' He headed towards her and placed a hand on her shoulder. For a moment, she thought he'd say something reassuring, something to calm her restless spirit and boost her morale – especially after how he'd behaved so abominably towards her of late. But instead, he looked into her eyes and said, 'As soon as you're able, will you pour a few glasses of whisky for the men?'

She nodded.

'Except...' he added, and relief flooded through her. She preempted he'd say, 'except for me', fully intending on sticking to his promise to keep off the booze, but instead he went on, 'for Mr Probert, as you know he doesn't partake in the evils of drink!' Then he threw back his head and laughed, which made her feel quite uncomfortable, given the situation a few nights previously.

Forcing a smile, she watched as he left the scullery, no doubt about to charm all and sundry with his witty repartee and insincerity – why was she the only one who could see through him? But what else could she do? Today was all about her mother-in-law and not about causing a scene by telling her husband he wasn't to touch a drop of the hard stuff. She reassured herself that maybe Wyn needed one or two drinks just to get through today. Her father-in-law was different; he knew when to stop when he'd had enough. If only his son were the same.

She dried her hands on a kitchen towel and then set about pouring the drinks and brewing up a pot of tea. Tentatively, she carried the tray into the living room. Mr Probert was standing near the window, speaking to Mrs Merriman, so she passed him a cup of tea and then made her way over to the men. The women had been at the house a lot earlier and had drunk copious amounts of tea, so she didn't bother offering again, and it would be unseemly to hand them a glass of whisky, so she bypassed those. It made her think of her secret snifter in the pub, recently. She wondered what Wyn would make of that if he knew she'd been drinking neat brandy!

He was standing now with his back to the hearth, in the midst of relating some tale or another from the coal pit. She handed a whisky glass to him and then the remainder of the glasses to the other men. Wyn was the only one not to thank her.

Funny, she thought, he's standing in front of that fireplace there with an audience, charming them all. They probably imagine he's a good man, yet only a few nights ago, he struck me in that exact same place – if only they knew the truth of it. What would they think of him then?

And in that moment, a seed of hatred began to grow in her heart.

But it was he, himself, who had planted it there.

* * *

The following day, Wyn and Frank rose at dawn to return to work at the coal pit. It seemed strange to see them togged up in their dirty, dusty working gear after being smartly dressed for yesterday's funeral, and Elin knew that when they returned home after a twelve-hour shift, their faces would be caked with coal dust.

After quickly tidying up the scullery, Elin donned her cloak and bonnet and made her way to the Langton residence. She hoped Mrs Langton would not be too upset with her for taking a few days' leave of absence from work, but then again, she reassured herself that it had been the woman's own son's idea and not her own.

As Elin reached the main wrought-iron gates, which were open wide, she glanced up at the three-storey house, her stomach unsettled. She was being silly; she hadn't been away all that long, but was it the fear of settling back down into a routine again and having to explain herself that was making her anxious or the thought of seeing Lawrence Langton once again?

She needn't have worried as the first person she encountered was Cook, who seemed supremely pleased to see her.

'Am I glad you've returned!' exclaimed Mrs Brightman, who was a large-boned lady, with chubby, ruddy cheeks and a twinkle in her violet eyes. The hair beneath her mob cap was as white as the driven snow and a pair of round silver-framed spectacles were precariously perched on her small button nose. 'How have things been? I've heard all about it from Mrs Langton.'

Elin let out a little sigh. 'The funeral went very well but everything happened so suddenly, my mind has been in a whirl ever since.'

'I'm not surprised. Here, allow me to take your bonnet and cloak. You can have a cup of coffee with me as I'm due a break.'

'Shouldn't I just crack on?' asked Elin, frowning. 'I better not lounge around as soon as I've just got here.'

Cook's face broke into an almighty grin. 'It's all right. We're all taking a bit of advantage as Mr Langton junior has taken his mother to Pontypridd for the day on some sort of business. That's why the gates are open, as they left in the coach. They won't be back for ages. We're all up to speed with our jobs in any case...' She huffed out a breath. 'I've been up since the crack of dawn with Molly to get the breakfasts ready earlier than usual. Floss and Beatrice have completed their tasks in the laundry room for the time being, so we'll take coffee together. I've even baked a cake for us, coffee and walnut!'

Elin smiled. She'd not been expecting such a reception on her return and it was a nice surprise. It was obvious that everyone had missed her and from what Cook told her around the table when they were all seated, so had Muriel Langton herself.

Cook and Molly were quick to fill Elin in on everything that had gone on since her absence. The dinner party had taken place to welcome Lawrence home, and a young lady named Arabella Armitage was invited, along with some business associates and family friends. According to Molly, it had turned into a riotous evening as, out of the blue, Master Benjamin had shown up, causing quite a stir.

Elin gasped to hear that. Wasn't the man supposedly secluded away from public gaze in Scotland, since falling into disgrace? And if true, how would the wronged brother feel about that?

* * *

The rest of the day passed by without incident, Elin keeping herself busy by sorting out Mrs Langton's wardrobe, colour co-ordinating the woman's outfits and checking for anything requiring repair. Mrs O'Bryant, who lived in the village, was an excellent seamstress. A marvel who was able to turn her hand to all sorts of repairs: anything from shortening a garment to invisible mending. Elin resolved to take the clothes to her house tomorrow.

Then, kneeling, she checked the woman's footwear, which was being stored in the bottom of her walnut double wardrobe.

Hmm, these wouldn't see the light of day again. What a sad thought. They were peach satin dancing shoes, but the heels were too precarious for her employer to wear these days. Mrs

Langton occasionally needed someone to take her by the arm to guide her, as she could be a little unsteady on her feet, particularly if she was having one of her dizzy spells. She imagined the woman some forty years younger than she was now, all dressed up and wearing those shoes, adorning a stunning peach silk ball gown with a rose in her hair.

I bet she made a pretty picture back in the day!

For a moment she imagined herself wearing that gown and shoes while being whisked around a ballroom, maybe the one at Cyfarthfa Castle, in the arms of Lawrence Langton. He was looking at her adoringly, with an expression of longing in his eyes, and she felt the rise and fall of her chest. He had eyes for no one else, except her.

The sounds of Molly giggling with Floss outside on the landing brought her back to reality, and the daydream began to slip away. No doubt the girls were taking full advantage of their employer being away from the house and were now exploring it. She couldn't blame them, she supposed. It wasn't often the staff had free rein at the house. But today, Elin intended to carry on working hard for the woman as she was so grateful for all the time off allotted to her for the funeral and afterwards; many employers wouldn't have allowed that. When Mrs Langton returned from Pontypridd, Elin vowed to ask her if she'd like to sell the shoes or pass them on to someone else she knew.

All the other shoes were still suitable. There was a stout pair of walking shoes, two stylish pairs of shoes for special occasions, a pair of ankle boots and a pair of carpet slippers. Elin figured the walking shoes could do with being resoled and heeled, along with one of the more stylish pairs. She'd take them to the cobbler shop tomorrow after dropping Mrs Langton's clothing off for repair.

Feeling satisfied with her decision, she turned her attention towards the chest of drawers in the corner of the room, where she proceeded to neatly fold all of Mrs Langton's lace-edged handkerchiefs, stockings and petticoats, reminding her of the handkerchief Lawrence had recently given her – she still had it and ought to return it to him; she might have brought it back today if she'd been thinking straight. *Or is it that you want to hang on to it for as long as possible?* a little voice inside chastised her. How silly she was being. She resolved now to return it to the man as soon as possible.

None of the other staff were allowed access to the woman's personal items, only Elin. She kept the drawers neat by tidying them on a daily basis. Since she'd been away from the house they had become a jumbled mess, so she took care of them. Later, if the gardener was still around, she planned on asking him for some fresh flowers for the vase on Mrs Langton's dressing table. She plucked the old blooms from the vase, now sad and wilted, sighing heavily. No one had thought to freshen up the water in the vase since she'd been away. Shaking her head, she tossed the neglected flowers into an old metal waste bin she'd brought with her. All her efforts were her way of saying, 'I'm back! Thank you so much, Mrs Langton, for allowing me compassionate leave!'

Elin walked around the large garden in search of Dewi Price. He was always about somewhere. If he wasn't to be found at work in the garden itself, then he'd be in his shed, sorting out his gardening tools or taking a little break there with a cup of tea. Her eyes were drawn to a wooded area where the man was busy raking the lawn and dropping the collected leaves from overhanging trees into an old wheelbarrow. Dewi had been working for the Langton family since he was a young man. He'd been most loyal to them over the years and it was obvious how much they valued and respected him.

'Hello, Mr Price.' She waved at the elderly man.

He deposited a flurry of dead leaves and smiled at her. 'Well, hello there, Mrs Edwards. It's good to see you back at the house!' he enthused, leaning on his rake.

'Thank you.' She returned the smile. 'I was hoping you could help me with something?'

'Oh, aye? What's that?' He rubbed his forehead with his free hand, which was smudged with dirt, knocking back the peak of his cap as though to get a better view of her.

'I was thinking of surprising Mrs Langton with some fresh blooms for her bedroom.'

He nodded. 'There are some colourful pansies, daffodils and snowdrops in full bloom – you're welcome to take what you want – oh, and there's some pretty purple heather what's managed to survive winter in the rockery area.'

She nodded enthusiastically. 'Thank you, Mr Price. Those'll do nicely. How are you keeping these days?' Her face took on a more sombre expression as she realised the man hadn't been well in recent weeks. He'd lost a lot of weight and had developed a persistent cough that wouldn't seem to leave him.

'I'm all right, thanks,' he said, forcing a smile, obviously putting a brave face on things. 'My wife makes a hot toddy for me when I get home from work of an evening and she said she'll pick up a bottle of tonic from the doctor by the time I return home this evening.'

Somehow, Elin didn't feel a bottle of tonic was what the man needed right now. What he did need was a thorough medical examination, but that cost money. Money the man and his family probably couldn't afford to spend, as it was only enough to put food on the table. He walked to work from the Georgetown area and back home again every day. She didn't know how he managed it in his condition, and there was tending to the garden as well, which could be hard, gruelling work for him. She resolved there and then to have a word with Mrs Langton about the situation. She was extremely fond of Dewi and would hate to see something happen to the man.

After constructing a floral arrangement of yellow and blue pansies and white crocuses interspersed with heather, she placed it on the dressing table and then arranged the daffodils in a crystal vase half filled with water. She'd place these on the windowsill, feeling that daffs were a cheerful sort of a flower; they always reminded her of spring and the hope of bright days ahead.

At the end of the day, she bid Cook goodbye in the kitchen, donned her bonnet and draped her cloak around her shoulders and was about to leave via the back door when Molly burst in.

'The mistress is home!' she yelled at the pair of them. That put paid to Elin quietly leaving; it would be rude of her to slip out when Mrs Langton and her son were arriving. In any case, she needed to thank the pair for their care and concern these past few days.

Cook cast Molly a stern glance. 'Have you offered the mistress any refreshment after her long journey today?'

Molly flushed from the neck up until her face was a vivid shade of pink. 'Er, sorry, Mrs Brightman, I didn't think...'

'That's just the thing though, isn't it, Molly?' Cook continued. 'You never do think! Go and ask her at once what the pair of them would like. Silly girl!' She shook her head, glancing at the ceiling, obviously frustrated at the lack of foresight on Molly's part.

The young maid nodded, shame-faced, and then turned her back to leave the kitchen. Cook could be quite sharp with the girl at times, but then again, Molly didn't exactly show much initiative. She returned a few minutes later with Mrs Langton's order of a pot of coffee for two with some of Cook's special coffee and walnut cake.

'Just as well I kept some of it back then!' Cook sniffed, upset that Molly had mentioned the cake to the mistress when it was intended as a little treat for the staff.

'I can take it through to them, before I leave,' Elin offered.

'Very well.' Cook smiled, then, looking at Molly, said, 'Brew up the coffee and cut a couple of slices of cake, girl! Not too thick, mind you! They don't want doorstep slices like you cut that last time! Make sure you leave some for the staff too. You ought not to have mentioned that cake to them – it was for us. There's a fruit cake in the larder for those pair!'

What on earth has got into Cook today? Elin had never seen her this irritated before. She wasn't usually so abrasive to Molly or derogatory towards their employer.

'Then,' barked Cook, pointing across the room, 'you can wash up those pots in the sink!'

Elin noticed tears forming in the girl's eyes. Molly was such a sensitive soul. Elin smiled at her.

A few minutes later, Elin headed to the sitting room with a full tray in her hands. She'd removed her cape and bonnet out of respect, leaving them on a chair in the kitchen.

Tentatively, she rapped on the door.

'Please enter!'

Elin's heart thudded at the sound of Lawrence's voice.

She was about to push the door when it was opened suddenly for her from the other side. Lawrence beamed broadly when he realised it was Elin who had brought their refreshment.

'We meet again, Mrs Edwards,' he said softly. 'Let me take that tray from you.'

Elin was thankful he did so, as the way she was inwardly all of a tremble was making her fear she'd drop the thing. She nodded her thanks as he placed the tray on a low table in the middle of the room, then she glanced around to locate Mrs Langton. But there was no sign of the woman, whose favourite place to sit was in the floral armchair near the long-latticed window.

'Where's Mrs Langton?' she asked, wondering whether to pour for her.

'She's just gone upstairs to change into something more comfortable,' Lawrence said with a smile. 'The trip has taken a lot out of her today.'

'Perhaps I'd better go upstairs to help her as she's sometimes a little unsteady on her feet?' she suggested, feeling a little alarmed.

'Mother will be absolutely fine!' He waved a hand of dismissal. 'She had no choice but to manage in your absence.'

Elin was surprised to hear that, as she imagined one of the other maids would have assisted the woman – dressing her in the mornings and last thing at night for bed.

'B... but how did your mother manage?'

'She just took her time to do things, but she coped.' He smiled. 'Of course, I offered to step into the breech as it were, but Mother said that was hardly appropriate.'

Elin nodded with understanding. 'Shall I pour your coffee then?' she asked. 'Or wait for your mother to return?'

'You can fill both cups, if you don't mind. Mother won't be long.'

In some ways Elin wished Mrs Langton was already present in the room as she didn't quite know what to say to her son. She poured the steaming hot brown liquid from the silver coffee jug, added a little milk, and then passed a cup over to Lawrence. 'Would you like sugar in that?'

He nodded. 'Yes, please. I'll have two demerara sugar cubes in mine.'

She lifted the silver tongs and plopped two cubes into his awaiting cup, then stirred it. All the while, he seemed to be watching her in a curious fashion, and she wondered what on earth he was thinking.

Before she had a chance to say any more, Mrs Langton appeared in the room with a beaming smile on her face. 'How lovely to see you back here, dear,' she enthused. She clasped her hands together. 'And you've brought us a tray of coffee too. But shouldn't you have finished work by now?' She glanced at the mantel clock and then furrowed her silver eyebrows in puzzlement.

'Good evening, Mrs Langton,' Elin said as she dipped her knee, causing Lawrence to shoot her a bemused grin. What was he finding so funny? It was normal for her to behave this way as a gesture of etiquette towards her employer. Yet, she supposed it did seem strange as he had a way of making her feel that he wasn't above her. Far from it; in his presence it seemed as though they were on the same level – yet how could they be when he was a London lawyer and she a companion and helper to his mother? They were hardly of the same social status or ilk.

Elin continued. 'I was about to leave, ma'am, when I heard of your arrival. I thought it would be rude of me to leave as you were arriving, especially as you...'

Now Lawrence had his head tilted to one side as though eager to hear what she had to say next, but for some reason she felt tongue-tied in his presence. She didn't know what it was, but he was disarming even though he didn't act like her superior.

Finally, she found her voice. 'Especially as you have been so good to me, allowing me compassionate leave.'

Mrs Langton nodded. 'It was the very least I could do, Elin, under the circumstances.'

Elin watched the woman take her usual place in the armchair before taking a cup of coffee and a slice of cake to her, setting them down on the nearby small table.

'Oh, to what do we owe this great honour?' Muriel Langton chuckled.

For a moment, Elin had no idea what she meant by that remark but then she realised she must be referring to Cook's cake. She'd need to be careful about what she said, as obviously the cake hadn't been meant for her employers.

'Mrs Brightman thought it would be a lovely treat on your return home, ma'am,' she said diplomatically.

'Please inform Cook before you leave that was very kind of her and well appreciated.' Mrs Langton paused for a moment. 'And speaking of appreciation, that was a very thoughtful thing you did, Elin.'

'Oh?'

'Tidying up my bedroom and creating that floral arrangement, so kind of you.'

'It's nothing, honestly.' Elin shrugged, feeling slightly embarrassed in front of the woman's son.

'Mrs Edwards,' said Lawrence firmly, 'when someone offers you a compliment you need to know how to respond and not just shrug it off.'

'Sorry.' She blushed, and bit on her lower lip, feeling like a scolded child for a moment, but that feeling changed when he winked at her. Elin wasn't quite sure how to respond so she made her excuses and left the room.

As she closed the double doors behind her and stood in the hallway, she heard Mrs Langton say, 'What a lovely young lady she is...'

She paused for a moment, her heart hammering in her chest as she waited to hear Lawrence reply to his mother. 'Isn't she just! Simply delightful!'

* * *

Elin arrived home from work, exhausted from the events of the past week or so, surprised to see there was no sign of her husband. When her mother-in-law had been alive, if she were late home from work then both father and son would be seated at the table while she dished up something hot for them. And for that, Elin was extremely grateful, but now she was dismayed to see that Frank was seated at the table with only a cup of tea before him. A surge of guilt coursed through her veins.

I should not have stopped on at the Langtons'. I ought to have rushed home here to cook something for him.

'I'm sorry, Frank,' she said, laying down her wicker basket on the pine table. Luckily, Cook had given her some of that delicious coffee and walnut cake to bring home, which she placed on a plate for her father-in-law. 'Here, have some of this with your cup of tea and I'll get the supper going.'

Frank waved his hand. 'It's all right. I don't have the appetite for a meal, but I'll try some of that cake you've brought,' he said weakly.

She laid it beside his cup of tea. 'I'm going to prepare a beef stew with dumplings so you can have as much or as little as you like,' she said, smiling as she watched him nibble on the cake. At least he was eating something. These past few days he'd barely eaten at all. Wyn had returned to the pit, but the foreman thought it best Frank take a few more days' leave.

She removed her cape and bonnet, hanging them on a peg

behind the door. Smoothing down her hair, she said, 'Has there been any sign of Wyn yet?'

Frank shook his head. 'No, not yet. He's probably gone to the pub, I expect. By the time that stew's cooked, he'll show up, starving as usual.' He shot her a smile.

A gnawing feeling played at the pit of her stomach. The last thing she wanted or needed was for Wyn to turn up drunk again after spending money they desperately needed. And what if he carried on gambling, too?

Her mother-in-law's shoes were hard to fill, the woman having been the heart and soul of the house. That fire Elin had once kindled with Wyn had now long since diminished. In her heart, she knew things would never feel the same again; the trust had gone and her love was dwindling like the embers of the fire in the hearth.

* * *

It was gone eight o'clock when Wyn returned home with a self-satisfied grin plastered across his face, and a dead goose beneath his armpit, its neck hanging limply. Flinging it on top of the scullery table, he said, 'Here, you can pluck that! We'll have it for tomorrow's meal.' Then, turning, he sniffed the air. 'By goodness, something smells right tasty! What have you cooking there?'

'Beef stew,' said Elin, feeling relieved he seemed sober. She had feared he'd come home via the pub. Her forehead creased into a soft frown. 'But how did you come by the goose, Wyn?'

'I got it as payment for doing a job for a farmer!'

Elin blinked. 'Farmer? What farmer?'

'Dick Constable who lives in that farm overlooking the village. He needed help to mend some fences as his sheep have been escaping from the field. Lost a few of them lately, he has. Couldn't afford to do so any longer so he came looking for me!' He hitched a thumb in the direction of his chest.

'I didn't know you knew any farmers?' This was news to her. In all the time she'd known him, he'd never to her knowledge ever mentioned an acquaintance who was a farmer of any kind.

'Oh, aye. I've known Dick since we were kids. Anyhow, he was standing outside the pit gates when I finished work this evening and he asked me to help him, so I did.' Her husband was looking right pleased with himself now and had a twinkle in his eyes. Pulling her towards him, he whispered, 'And I was thinking...' he paused to gaze into her eyes with a look she recognised as pure lust '...after we've eaten, we can have an early night. It's a while since we've had an early night, love.'

She pulled away and nodded at him. Although utterly exhausted from work at the house, Wyn seemed to be the fella she'd fallen in love with once again. Maybe she was mistaken and he had turned over a new leaf after all?

* * *

Something awakened her from her sleep, causing her to sit bolt upright in bed with a racing heart. What was that noise? It sounded like glass smashing. Fearing for a moment it was something to do with Wyn, she turned to his side of the bed, but he was fast asleep beside her. The rise and fall of his chest and his gentle snores told her so. He'd immediately fallen asleep after their lovemaking. Although he wasn't the most romantic of men, he was able to keep her well satisfied in that direction; when he hadn't been supping the ale, that was. For when he did, he often became cantankerous with her, but these past few days since his mother's death, he'd been helpful and manageable.

Maybe things would be all right from now on and she'd been silly to ever doubt him?

Deciding the noise was probably nothing of any importance, she was just about to settle back down to sleep when she heard it again.

'Wyn!' she yelled, grabbing his forearm to shake him out of his deep slumber. This was getting beyond a joke now.

'There's someone outside the window, I'm telling you!'

Drowsily, he stirred. '*Wass* going on? I was *sshleeping...*' he said, his voice thick as he slurred his words.

'I've heard the sound of smashing glass twice now...'

'No, can't be, you must have been dreaming...' He sat bolt upright, obviously startled and somewhat disorientated.

She struck a match to light the candle in its holder by the bedside and held it in front of his face. He was rubbing his eyes. She'd rather not have disturbed him at all, but this was most unusual and startling.

'Maybe it's a cat or something,' he said.

Might it be a cat though? Knocking over something in its path. Maybe an old glass bottle that had been left on someone's wall had been toppled over by some stray tabby?

There was the sound of something smashing again, which this time caused Wyn to leap from the bed and run in his combinations towards the window, where he drew back one of the curtains and peered outside. Elin followed after him. All was in darkness through the downstairs window, which looked out onto the yard.

'There's someone out there,' he whispered. 'I can see a bulky shape. I'm going to find out who it is. Don't follow me; stay put!' he said, raising his hand.

'Here, take this,' she said, and she went to hand him the candle, but he waved her away. 'No, if I take that, whoever it is will see me coming. There's nothing like surprising the enemy.'

But how would Wyn know it was someone who wanted to hurt him? That phrase disturbed her somewhat. And who was the enemy? They had none as far as she was aware.

Watching him leave her side, she could feel her breaths becoming short and shallow; the fear was such she thought she might stop breathing altogether at any given moment.

She waited a while and then heard him unbolt and yank open the scullery door; he was shouting at someone. 'Keep away from here! I'm telling you, I'll kill you if you ever come near this door again!'

There was no response from anyone – just what sounded like more than one set of footsteps running away into the night. Then her husband bolting the door before he returned to her side. 'Give me that bloody candle!' he demanded.

Meekly, she handed it over with trembling hands. He was angry, but with who?

She followed behind him as he went to inspect the damage.

'Aye, they've kicked the back door in and smashed the scullery window,' he said, shaking his head.

They?

'But who, Wyn? Who?'

'Someone I owe a lot of money to.'

'He came here to do that to you?'

'No, not him, you silly woman! Isn't it obvious? He's sent two of his heavies to do his dirty work for him! It's a warning for me to pay up or else!'

'Oh, Wyn!' Her teeth were chattering now as her hands flew to her face. This couldn't be happening. It couldn't be real, could it? But it was real enough. As she drew closer, pulling the curtain to one side to get a better view, she could see the evidence for herself: the windowpane was smashed and the two glass panes of the back door were also broken, leaving jagged remnants behind, lodged there.

'I better board these up for now until I can get the glass replaced,' Wyn said in a sober fashion. Then, as if thinking better of it, he added, 'Or maybe it would be a good idea to keep them boarded up, just in case they return. It's money we can ill afford right now to pay for ruddy glass!'

Elin shivered as a blast of cold air blew in through the door. She wished this was all a bad dream that would disappear when she awoke.

A thought occurred to her. 'Frank! Your father!' she yelled. 'This will probably have frightened him half to death.'

The ghostly glow from the candle her husband held lit up his face, highlighting dark shadows that made him appear almost ghoul-like. 'Will you go and check on him, then?' he asked. 'I want to board this up as soon as possible. There's some hardboard and a hammer and nails in the shed that ought to do the trick.'

There was another candle on the mantelpiece, which she lit from Wyn's candle, and, shivering, she made her way up the stairs. But she needn't have worried as Frank was still fast asleep in his bed. He hadn't heard a thing by the look of it. His bedroom didn't back onto the yard like theirs did, so maybe that was why he'd not heard anything. But then again, she had noticed he was getting hard of hearing of late.

Not wishing to disturb him as he would be returning to work in the morning, she quietly closed the door behind herself and made her way downstairs, realising she'd not sleep another wink all night after this.

6

The next day, Elin related the tale to Cook who was most horrified by it all. 'But why would someone want to smash your windows and door in, Elin? Especially after all you've been through of late with the loss of your mother-in-law and all.' Her forehead creased into a puzzled frown. 'It doesn't make any sense whatsoever...'

Elin glanced around the large kitchen to ensure none of the other maids were present and eavesdropping, but there was no one else around. She and Cook were sitting at the pine table taking a glass of homemade lemonade together.

She lowered her voice. 'To be honest with you, Mrs Brightman, my husband has gambling debts. I only discovered this recently. I had no idea. I mean, he was keeping me short of housekeeping money on occasion, but I thought that was because he was spending too much of it on ale, but debts of that kind! I'm mortified.'

Cook sucked in a sharp breath as she pursed her lips and shook her head. 'Oh, I don't like the sound of that,' she said. 'So, you think it was someone who had shown up to collect money owing to them?'

Elin nodded. 'In a sense, yes. Wyn thinks it's a warning from the man himself and he sent two stooges to do his dirty work for him.'

'You don't want to mess around with people like that,' she sympathised before taking a sip from her glass. Glancing at the ceiling for a moment, she set down her glass on the table, before saying, 'The only thing I can think of is that you need to do whatever you can to clear that debt in case it all ramps up.'

A shiver coursed down Elin's spine. 'But surely now they've warned him – by damaging property – it should stop? An eye for an eye and all that.'

Cook shook her head. 'I very much doubt it, dear. I knew someone who had terrible debts and it went on for ages. The poor man was beside himself; he even considered taking his own life, as things got so bad. You see, the longer those sorts are waiting for payment, the more they can hassle and even increase what's owing to them in the long run.'

'I hadn't even considered that.' Elin blinked away the tears forming in her eyes.

'If I were you...' Cook lowered her voice, as she glanced around the kitchen in a surreptitious fashion '...I'd think of someone to ask, who you trust, to borrow the money from. Any idea how large the debt is?'

She shrugged, feeling foolish that she hadn't even asked Wyn how much the debt was.

'Maybe your father-in-law or another family member might help?' She angled her head to one side in a show of sympathy.

Elin forced a smile but a large lump had formed in her throat. In all honesty, she doubted Frank would have enough money to bail them out, especially after the expense of the funeral.

'I'll have to have a good think about that,' she said.

'Find out how much is owing first, Elin. That'll give you some idea who you can ask,' Cook said, draining her glass and rising to leave the table. She'd been resting a plate of puff pastry in the cool pantry and was keen to return to it by the seem of it. Her chicken and leek pie was a firm favourite with both her mistress and the staff at the house.

She paused for a moment and placed a hand of reassurance on Elin's shoulder. 'If I had the money, I'd help you myself.'

Elin smiled. 'I know you would, Mrs Brightman. Unfortunately, this is something we'll have to sort out for ourselves, one way or another.'

* * *

The following few hours went by in a blur of tasks that needed sorting along with interactions with the rest of the staff. There was no sign of Lawrence at the house that day. Molly was quick to inform her that he was visiting a young lady called Arabella Armitage who lived in the upper end of Merthyr Tydfil. 'Where all the posh houses are!' Molly had exclaimed. Elin struggled for a moment to think where she'd heard that name before and then it came to her: Arabella had been one of the recent dinner party guests when she'd been absent from the house following the death of her mother-in-law. She surmised the pair must have got along like a house on fire if Arabella was now reciprocating that visit by inviting Lawrence to visit her at home.

His mother, though, had been at home all day. A group of women who were friends and acquaintances had been invited to afternoon tea. Elin's services hadn't been required much, as Molly had been tending to the party, rushing back and forth from the kitchen to the drawing room with plates of sandwiches and cakes and pots of tea and coffee. From the shrieks of laughter and animated conversation emanating from the room, Elin guessed they'd all had a good time. But even that couldn't shake her out of the feeling of doom and gloom. Up until recently, she'd felt quite secure living at her parents-in-laws' home – that was until her husband had begun to raise his fists to her. But now, the episode with the smashed window and door had unnerved her. Her security and peace of mind felt violated.

When the women had departed, Mrs Langton called Elin to one side. 'I couldn't help noticing,' she said, 'that there appears to be something wrong today, Elin. I know it's not long since you lost your mother-in-law and maybe it's hit you hard... Do you need more time away from this place?'

Elin shook her head. 'Oh, it's not that at all, Mrs Langton. Really it isn't.' She feared getting laid off from work, as it was her job at this house that was keeping her going.

'Then what is it, dear?' Mrs Langton's large brown eyes were full of concern.

Elin took a deep breath and explained the whole sorry situation. Finally, Mrs Langton said, 'My dear, if you ever need an advance on your wages, let me know. It might help to tide you over.'

Elin nodded and thanked her, realising full well it was more than a sub she needed to get out of this dreadful situation. If only it were so simple. After speaking to Cook, she realised she needed to find out exactly how much Wyn owed that man and, most importantly of all, just who that man was.

* * *

When Elin arrived home from work, the menfolk still hadn't come home, so she set about removing the washing from the line in the backyard, all the while directing her gaze towards the back door and scullery window. All boarded up now, it appeared as if the house were condemned for demolition. It made her heart sink to see it looking this way. Her mother-in-law would turn in her grave to see such a sight; she'd been so house-proud.

Her heart began to pound a little faster when she returned her focus to the washing, though this time for a much different reason. She was removing the silver silk handkerchief from the clothes line to place in the wicker washing basket. She'd washed it with a view of returning it to Lawrence Langton but somehow, she'd found herself hanging on to it, maybe as it reminded her of how kind the man had been towards her. But now it was washed and dried, all she need do was give it a careful press with the iron and return it when she went back to work at the house tomorrow. It was no big issue really. Holding the handkerchief to her cheek, she savoured the moment, realising she was close to tears, then thinking no more of it, dropped it into the waiting basket.

As she hefted the wicker laundry basket inside the house, setting it down in a corner of the scullery, her ears pricked up as voices headed towards her: Wyn and Frank were home. To her surprise, both sounded quite buoyant following a hard day's graft underground and despite the present circumstances, their voices sounded jolly and upbeat.

'What's going on here?' she asked as she shot her husband a nervous smile. These days, she had no idea how he'd respond to her, even to a simple question.

'The foreman's said we're to have a slight pay increase. Won't be much but it's better than a swift kick up the backside with a hobnail boot!' Wyn chuckled.

'Oh, that's good then,' she said, feeling pleased for the pair and finding herself relaxing. She watched as both removed their jackets and caps and hung them on a series of pegs behind the scullery door. Then they made their way to the yard to have a quick wash under the pump before supper, rolling up their shirtsleeves to their elbows. They'd have a better wash once they'd eaten. She'd be ready with a clean towel for the both of them. Her role at home, as for many women in these parts, was to take care of the men.

Frank seemed to have aged about ten years since his wife's death; he appeared frail and faltering. Some might dismiss it as grief, but deep down, Elin realised, it was far more than that; the man seemed lost without Olwen. The woman had been the love of his life, one side of a pair of scissors and he'd been the other – now that blade of the scissors wouldn't work without the other any more; it was useless without its partner.

'It'll be a while until supper is ready,' she said as they returned to the scullery, the men appearing more spruced up, but their eyelashes were still sooty from the coal dust – it was hard to eradicate all traces from the pit. 'I thought it best to cook that goose out of the way. But there's some stew left over in the pan that I can heat up while you're both waiting – you can have that with a bit of bread and butter to fill you up for now!'

Frank nodded amicably but Wyn, rolling down his shirt-sleeves, scowled at her. 'You ought to have kept that goose for tomorrow when you're working a half day. You could have put it in the oven earlier for us then,' he said, raising his voice. 'That way it would have been ready as we walk in through the door. Now we'll have a long wait for our supper.'

Elin's mouth dried with anxiety. She couldn't understand why Wyn was behaving this way. It wasn't as if she had nothing to give them. In any case, he'd specifically said he wanted it this evening. 'But I just explained, you can have some stew with bread and butter!' she protested. Why was he being like this when she'd been at work all day herself?

He glared at her, his eyes as dark and hard as flint, which made her realise she was in dangerous territory now.

'That's the trouble, you never think,' he said, then he left the room abruptly. She guessed he'd gone to lie down on their bed.

'I'm sorry, Frank,' she said, meeting her father-in-law's eyes.

Now seated at the table, he waved his open palm at her. 'It's not your fault, love,' he sympathised. 'You're doing your best. Wyn's cross over his debts. Someone was waiting for him at the pit today when we left.'

Elin quirked an interested brow. 'And who might that be, Frank?'

'Someone official, it looked like. He was wearing a smart suit at any rate. The man handed him a letter warning him if he doesn't pay up soon, he'll be prosecuted.'

'Oh, my goodness!' Elin reached out to steady herself, holding on to one of the chairs. 'That all sounds rather serious.' She toyed with mentioning last night's incident to him but was saved from doing so when Wyn returned to the room, looking at her in a sheepish manner. Wyn would have to explain to his father why the back door and window were boarded up, but as Frank hadn't mentioned anything so far, she guessed her husband must have already formulated some sort of cover story.

'I'm sorry, Elin,' Wyn said softly, 'you're doing your best for us. I can see that. We'll both have that stew.' He leaned over to peck a quick kiss on her cheek.

How could he be so annoyed with her one moment and then act so placid the next? But then again, if she waited for the right moment, she could broach the subject of the man he owed a debt to.

Following supper, Frank made his way to his bed, which was usual for him these days.

Elin sat with Wyn on the couch as he rubbed his stomach. 'That was a fine meal tonight, my sweet,' he enthused. 'You roasted that goose to perfection – I'm fit to bursting.'

'Aye, and we can have the leftovers as a fry-up tomorrow evening,' she said. 'There's plenty of goose meat, taters and carrots left over. I'll fry those with some leeks, I think. It'll make for a nice meal.'

He nodded his approval, which Elin took as an invitation to speak. 'Wyn...' she began.

He turned to look at her. 'Yes?'

'About that moneylending business...' She watched as his countenance changed from being relaxed to being as stiff as a board.

'What of it?' His voice sounded strained now.

'Just how much is owed to the man?'

Wyn's face flushed. 'Fifteen shillings!'

'F... fifteen shillings?' she said. She couldn't quite believe her ears – that was enough to cover three weeks rent for most in the area, with some change left over to boot. 'B... but how do you owe that much?'

He held his hands up in an open gesture as he shrugged. 'There was a card game, weren't there. I got a bit cocky with it, as I thought I was on a winning streak. In the end there were only me and him left in it and I wouldn't back down. I made it sound as though I had more money and assets than I actually have.'

She furrowed her brow. 'How so?'

'I told him I owned this house, didn't I? So, he thought I was good for the money.'

'Oh, I see.' Her mouth gaped open for a moment. 'Might that

be why this property was vandalised then, as he believes you are the house owner?'

He nodded. 'Probably. A way to get back at me, I suppose.'

'What's the name of this guy? The one you're indebted to?'

Wyn rubbed his stubbled chin in contemplation of whether he ought to reveal the man's name. 'Believe me, he's not someone you would want to cross. You're better off not knowing.'

'No, Wyn!' she said firmly. 'I must know if I am to help you. I'm your wife.'

He blew out a hard breath. 'It's Morgan Griffin...'

She wrinkled her nose. 'And this Morgan Griffin, where does he live?'

He was silent and, for a moment, Elin didn't think he could bring himself to give away the location. Then he spoke. 'He lives in the China district of the town.'

'China?' She blinked several times as she remembered mention of a man from that area who'd taken part in that card game at the White Hart; seemed he was some big shot. 'He has to be a wrong one living there, then!'

She was feeling annoyed that he should end up mixing with that sort. Many people who lived in that area of the town were known to be crooks and swindlers. Its inhabitants for the most part were rumoured to be of ill repute.

'Not everyone who lives there is like that. There are some good folks there as well,' he added meekly, as though that improved the situation.

'So, if he's so good, this Morgan Griffin, why would he send someone to smash the house up like that?'

Wyn's face paled. 'I... I'm not saying he's any good, am I? It's just some folk living there are.'

'What does he do for a living?' She wasn't about to let him off the hook that easily.

'A bit of this and a bit of that.'

'You mean he has some sort of chequered past?'

'That sort of thing, yes...' He lowered his voice to barely a whisper. 'And he deals with ladies of the night...'

'Ladies of the night?' She gulped, unable to believe her ears. 'You mean he runs prostitutes?'

Wyn nodded slowly. This tale was getting worse by the minute.

She drew in a breath and then released it slowly to compose herself. 'So, how do you plan on paying him back?'

'That's it. I just don't know how I can. We have no house to sell and the money we have is going from hand to mouth at the moment.'

Elin could hardly make sense of what Wyn was saying to her. His poor mother, who had been an honest, hard-working woman, would surely turn in her grave to hear her son speak like this. 'But isn't there a way you could pay some back to the man, a little each week? Or even do some odd jobs for him as a form of payment, Wyn?'

Her husband's eyes widened. 'Don't you think I've thought of that? There are quite a few people who owe the man money,' he said as though that justified his debt, made it more acceptable somehow. He paused for a moment. 'I'll just avoid him for as long as I can and only pay him back if absolutely necessary...' Wyn turned his head to stare into the flames of the fire kindling in the grate.

'You have to pay the man back as soon as possible, Wyn. We have to get that money for him somehow.'

'Unless you're considering walking the streets, my love, then

I don't think we can come up with that sum of money in the next few days.'

Walking the streets? What on earth did he mean by that? Then it slowly dawned on her – he was referring to her prostituting herself to obtain that money. She shot him a sideways glance and caught him smiling to himself. Surely, he wasn't being serious? She'd never live with herself if she ever did anything like that. Tears began to well in her eyes and she rose from the couch so he might not see her getting upset. There was a stack of dishes waiting to be washed in the scullery sink, so she set upon scrubbing those, making light work of shifting those stains with a rag and soapy water, her resolute anger spurring her on.

Her eyes fell upon the wicker laundry basket by the side of the sink; Lawrence Langton's silver silk handkerchief was still on top of the pile, neatly folded. Would he loan her the money they desperately needed? Or if not, at least give them some advice on how to turn this dire situation around?

* * *

The following morning, when Elin rose from bed, she was dismayed to see the pile of laundry in the basket all jumbled up. Wyn must have been searching for something during the night; she couldn't see her father-in-law making such a mess. Now all the stuff neatly folded would need pressing with an iron for sure.

Cross that her husband was making more work for her, she silently cursed the man. She'd begun to rise earlier than usual to see both men off to work these days. It was something Olwen had done for years, banking up both fires in the scullery and living room and brewing up tea for their billy cans. On cold mornings, she'd have a pan of porridge on the go for them so they'd have something hot and hearty in their stomachs before undertaking a gruelling shift at the pit. This morning, though, as Elin had made to step a foot out of bed onto the cold linoleum, Wyn had told her to return to bed for another hour or so. He'd even brought her a cup of tea, which he'd placed by the side of the bed. Guilt, no doubt. Guilt for putting her in this position.

However, what puzzled her was that following his own breakfast, he hadn't returned to their room to plant a kiss on her cheek as he usually did. That was most odd, and she wondered why.

But now, looking at the jumbled-up basket, she got her answer as her eyes were diverted to the middle of the scullery table, the silk handkerchief lying in the middle of it like an object of crime. It was obvious her husband was trying to make some sort of a point. Now she wished she'd returned that handkerchief sooner to its rightful owner.

What could he possibly make of it though? It was just a handkerchief, even if it did tell some sort of tale.

* * *

'Good morning, Elin,' Cook said cheerfully as Elin entered via the back door. 'You're in bright and early this morning, love.'

Elin nodded at the woman. 'Aye, I managed to do what was needed at home first and had plenty of time, so I made my way over here.'

'As you're early, how about having a cup of coffee with me?' The woman's eyes sparkled this morning; she was evidently in a good mood for some reason.

'That would be lovely,' Elin said, removing her cloak and bonnet and hanging them up behind the door.

'I've just boiled the kettle so it won't take long; meanwhile, take a look in the cupboard beside the range, on the right-hand side. There's a tin in there. I made some currant buns yesterday afternoon, so we'll have those before Molly finishes her work, so we're not disturbed. Mrs Langton asked her to give upstairs a good going-over today, to strip all the beds, open the windows, that sort of thing.'

'Oh?' Elin blinked.

'Didn't you know? Lawrence is leaving later today; he's returning to London...'

Elin's heart sank. She didn't know why, but she'd been looking forward to running into him again. Still, maybe there'd be an opportunity before he departed.

She went in search of the buns and discovered the tin precisely where Cook said it would be.

'Hey, what's the matter with you?' the woman asked. 'Your face looks crestfallen...'

Elin huffed out a breath as she set the tin down on the table, while Mrs Brightman laid down a tray containing the coffee pot and two cups and saucers along with a jug of milk and a sugar bowl. She looked at Elin expectantly, awaiting an answer.

Elin nodded as she removed the tin lid, revealing the scrumptious-looking buns, though she just didn't have the appetite for them this morning. She took a seat at the table. 'You are right, Mrs Brightman. The reason I'm like this is because I had hoped to have a word with Mr Langton about the trouble my husband has got himself into.'

Cook let out a little throaty rasp. 'You mean it's worse than you previously thought?'

'I'm afraid it is. The man who is demanding his money sent

an official letter to my husband yesterday. It was delivered to him by someone at the pit gates as he headed off for home. I don't think he would have told me about it, but my father-in-law did.'

'I see.' Mrs Brightman clasped her hands together. 'It's beginning to sound rather serious.'

'But it's so much worse than that. Although it's a large sum of money, it's the man he owes it to. He's into all sorts concerning prostitutes and such. I need some legal advice about all of this...' She chewed on her bottom lip.

Cook frowned. 'That sounds bad to me! Look, I hesitate to ask, and tell me to mind my own business if you like, but might it be that your husband has been using the services of prostitutes himself, and that's why he owes this man so much money?'

Elin shook her head vehemently. 'Oh no, Mrs Brightman. It's nothing like that. He lost the money in a card game.'

Cook huffed out a breath. 'So, you wanted advice from Mr Lawrence then, did you?'

'I did, yes.'

'You don't want to tell the man the part about the prostitutes then!'

* * *

When Lawrence returned to the house, Elin summoned up the courage to speak to him while the rest of the staff were taking a break in the kitchen.

'You do look concerned, Mrs Edwards,' he said as he led her to the drawing room. 'Step inside here awhile,' he whispered. 'We shan't be disturbed in here and will be well away from prying ears.'

She nodded gratefully, and then followed him inside. He

closed the door behind them. 'Please take a seat,' he said, gesturing towards the armchair as he took the one opposite, so they were seated either end of the hearth.

Elin hesitated for a moment. She had never dared to sit in one of the armchairs in here before, though she guessed the maids probably got up to some right old high jinks when the occupants were out of the house. She'd heard them giggling behind the very same door a time or two.

Hesitantly, she took a seat and for a moment, studied her hands, which were in her lap, feeling awkward at what she was about to reveal to the man. Then it all came tumbling out: how her husband owed Morgan Griffin fifteen shillings they couldn't afford, how some men had smashed the back door and window of the property, how it was keeping her awake at night. When she had finished, she looked up to meet his eyes, fearing he'd think she was a foolish woman, but instead, all she saw was compassion and concern for the plight she now found herself in.

'What I can tell you, seeing as you've asked for my advice, Elin...'

He'd called her Elin instead of Mrs Edwards, which made her feel all strange inside, as though a thousand butterflies were fluttering in her tummy. 'Yes,' she whispered, feeling as if they were the only two people in the whole wide world.

'Your husband's debt, that is if he's telling the truth, is not all that great...'

She huffed out a sigh of relief.

'However, in my experience these sorts of small debts can eventually build up until they're totally unmanageable...'

Now she felt like crying, but she didn't want to break down in front of the man like she had that time he'd called to the house.

'What I would suggest is I give you a loan and it's paid to the man immediately,' he said, his expression serious. That's what Cook had advised too. 'But if it's not paid back, and I do know of that Morgan Griffin, who is not a nice man...' he sucked in a sharp breath and then released it '...your husband could well end up going to prison for it!'

Elin's hands flew to her face in horror. 'I... I hadn't realised that.'

'I'm afraid that is the case. He might end up at a debtor's prison.'

'Well, if you do loan me the money, I promise I'll pay you back a little at a time,' she offered.

'I'm sure you will. I can afford to give you that sum of money as a gift, as you've been so kind to my mother. She doesn't know how she'd have managed without you. But what I propose, as you've told me about your husband's drinking and gambling problems and the fact he has no intention of paying that debt as far as you're aware, is that I give you the money and you pay the man yourself without telling your husband. In fact, that's what I'd advise. If you hand it to your husband, he might find another use for it.'

Elin nodded sombrely, realising the man was correct. Wyn would probably waste the money somehow. 'I can see the sense of what you're saying, Mr Langton—'

'Lawrence, please, when we're alone...'

'Lawrence, but I wouldn't know where to begin looking for the man and I'd be afraid to approach him on my own.'

'Have no fear.' Lawrence smiled. 'I shall accompany you to China to speak with Mr Griffin, and I'll back you up in all you have to say.'

'I... don't know how to thank you, Mr... er, Lawrence,' she

said, relaxing back into her armchair as though a heavy weight had been lifted from her shoulders.

'On the contrary, I should be thanking you for all you've done for Mother. Before you came here, she was very subdued, you see. She has great concerns for my brother Benjamin...'

Elin was surprised to hear this. Not that the woman had concerns but because it was the first time a family member at the house had mentioned Benjamin's name. She figured Lawrence must trust her to bring him into the conversation.

He stared thoughtfully at her for a moment. 'You did know I have an errant brother, I suppose?'

Elin cleared her throat. 'Not until recently.' She hoped he'd change the subject as she felt embarrassed by what she did know.

'Now, I was due to return to London this evening, but I will make arrangements to return tomorrow morning instead. Tonight, you shall accompany me to the darkest recesses of that notorious area of Merthyr known as China!' he said with a wink, causing a shiver to skitter the length of her spine.

'Oh, I forgot to hand you this,' she said, standing as she dipped her hand into her pinafore pocket to hand him his silk handkerchief.

His eyes enlarged. 'Why, I'd totally forgotten about it. I have lots like that. You ought to have kept it.'

Elin couldn't tell him that keeping it might cause trouble between her and her husband, but by the look in Lawrence's eyes, she figured he might have just worked that out for himself.

* * *

That evening Wyn hadn't arrived home from work, which in a way was a blessing as Elin needed to go to China with Lawrence to seek out Morgan Griffin. Frank had given her some garbled message from her husband claiming he was helping that farmer again. Elin, though, did not believe a word of it – she was no longer that naïve young wife she had been. In fact, the naivety had been knocked out of her by her husband that night he had taken his fists to her.

After feeding her father-in-law with a simple meal of lamb cawl she'd made earlier that morning, she returned to the Langton residence, telling Frank before she left that she'd had to return there to help Cook prepare a special meal as the son of the house was leaving for London soon. She had no fears about her husband being angry about his dinner as it was already there for him to warm up. All she needed was an hour or so to accompany Lawrence in his coach to China, to pay off Morgan Griffin and then they'd be debt-free. Wyn would assume that the man had decided to drop the debt and had stopped seeking him out – but she and Lawrence would know differently. She had mixed feelings about lying to Frank though, but figured in the long run what he didn't know couldn't hurt him.

When she arrived at the property, darkness had descended like a velvet cloak sprinkled with stars. The sky above was clear and the air crisp and fresh. Her heart hammered beneath her blouse as she walked in through the already opened double wrought-iron gates of the property. It wasn't anxiety in case Mrs Langton or any of the staff saw her returning to the house, but because soon, she realised, she'd be alone with Lawrence in his coach.

With some relief, she could see the coach outside with the driver waiting on top, whip in hand, and the horse blowing out a cloud of steam as its breath met with the cold night air. Then, Lawrence emerged from the coach itself to help her on board.

'How did you explain this to your mother?' she whispered as

she glanced furtively at the house, which was in partial darkness apart from a hall light and a light upstairs in Mrs Langton's bedroom.

'Mother thinks I'm paying a visit to Arabella.' He smiled as he took her hand to help her up the coach steps.

On mention of the young woman's name, Elin stiffened. She didn't know why, but hearing the name irked her, and then a little voice within whispered, *Because you're jealous, that's why.*

Bringing herself up sharp, she settled herself against the padded leather upholstery as Lawrence closed the door behind them, then took a seat opposite. The only time she'd been in a coach before was in a public sort of hansom cab that you paid for, never a private one like this.

A sudden jolt as the coach driver cracked his whip to get the horse moving, and then they were away.

Lawrence made idle chit-chat along the way, but Elin was far too nervous to join in; she just nodded or agreed with him without offering much in return. All the while her mouth was dry with apprehension and she wished she'd taken a drink of water before setting out on this journey. All she'd had time for was a quick change of clothing and the bowl of cawl, which she'd eaten alongside Frank, and which only increased her thirst.

If her father-in-law had thought it strange she was returning to the Langton house, he hadn't mentioned it. But then again, he was in a world of his own these days. It was obvious how much he missed his wife. If only Wyn felt the same way about her, but he seemed to prefer being outside the house rather than inside it these days. She suspected this so-called farmer friend of his who needed help was a ruse so he could either get on with his gambling again or hit the bottle, or maybe both. But then again, she couldn't say she'd smelled any alcohol on him of late, so maybe he was keeping his promise on that score.

Finally, the coach pulled up near an archway.

'I've arranged for us to be dropped off here,' Lawrence explained. 'There's only one entrance into the place and one way out. Have you been here before?'

She shook her head, feeling highly apprehensive now.

'Don't worry, you'll be quite safe with me at your side,' he reassured her.

'I've heard that even police constables are afraid to step foot in this area,' she said meekly. 'Surely the place can't be as bad as all that?'

'I'm afraid what you've heard is true, Elin,' Lawrence said sombrely. 'They protect their own in this place. There are folk here who've come from near and far to work in the ironworks – not just the Welsh, but there are a lot of Irish folk here too. The Welsh resent the Irish for taking jobs from them so often fights break out. But I tell you what...'

'What?' she whispered.

'When the police enter, something magical happens because then the Welsh and Irish join forces with one another, and they become as one against the constabulary. Woe betide any young constable who dares enter this place alone; it will be at his own peril!'

'You're scaring me now!' Elin said, startled.

'I'm sorry, it wasn't my intention, but you have to understand what its inhabitants are like. Many are honest folk who have hit upon hard times, but there is a faction who are up to no good. There are pickpockets, prostitutes, pimps and others up to all sorts here. Some of the pickpockets are young children. Even the prostitutes pick the pockets of unsuspecting males. No one is safe here. It was said that some sort of boss at the ironworks at

Cyfarthfa was a regular, mixing with the likes of nymphs of the pave and other petty criminals, and even he stopped coming, because one night he got drunk out of his mind to discover the following morning that he'd been robbed. His silver pocket watch was stolen and his pockets emptied; those items were probably taken by the woman he'd paid for that night. It's not just their bodies the women sell here; some sell personal possessions like silk handkerchiefs, too.'

'A bit like yours!'

Lawrence quirked a smile. 'Yes, like mine. I'd be easy meat for their sort. That's why I've told the coach driver to drop us off here. He's going to park up the coach at a nearby coaching inn on Merthyr high street. I don't want people to realise I have money. I've dressed down a little for this evening.'

She'd noticed his lack of finery earlier in the coach but now they'd descended from it, beneath the lamplight, she could see he wore a plain shirt, tweed jacket and corduroy trousers. He still looked smart but he might have been anyone from Merthyr going about his business. His top hat was no longer in evidence, replaced now with a simple flat cap that many working men around these parts wore.

Elin hesitated as she followed Lawrence through the archway, well aware she was entering a world totally alien to her. Drawing her cloak around her shoulders as though it would somehow offer her protection, she trod carefully with only the light of the moon and that of a nearby street lamp to guide their paths. The first thing that hit her was the dreadful stench coming from the place. It was well known that people threw all sorts of slops out of their windows and doors, some of which made its way via muddy troughs when it rained towards the River Taff. Being mindful of this, she carefully lifted the skirts of her dress as they walked along.

'We're going to have to descend these steps to get there, so take care,' Lawrence warned, glancing behind to check she was all right and had remained in his wake.

'Don't worry, I'll be careful,' she reassured him, all the while wondering how people could live in the hovels in this place, which some people from Merthyr had dubbed 'Little Hell'. Her mother-in-law had told her tales about the area, saying that people lived cheek by jowl here and were at risk of serious disease, as it was like an open sewer.

Relieved when she'd reached the bottom of the stone steps, she glanced around at the higgledy-piggledy huddle of houses; some had newspapers stuffed in their windows to keep the cold out. Near the glow of a gaslight, she noticed a dwelling that seemed larger in comparison to the others.

'Here's the place,' Lawrence affirmed.

She wrinkled her nose. 'What is it?'

'It's a pub of sorts, dubbed "The Squire's Arms" by locals. Morgan Griffin owns it.'

'Strange-looking pub to me!' she scoffed. It didn't look like any of the pubs she'd seen in Abercanaid. This appeared to be a large house. 'Who's the squire, then?'

Lawrence chuckled and, tapping the side of his nose, said, 'It's an unofficial public house, trading without a licence, and the squire is Griffin himself!'

'How do you know so much about Griffin and this area, anyhow?'

'I've had dealings here a time or two. Following my training, I worked at a lawyer's office in Merthyr, so some of my clientele came from these parts. People would describe them as "the dregs of society" I suppose, but I saw a different side to some of them.'

'And Morgan Griffin? You've met him before?'

'A time or two, yes. But I have to warn you, he's not a man to be trifled with. But he does owe me a favour. So, let's get him paid off, then you and your husband can return to your business with no threats to your safety. And I suppose your father-in-law could do without what you all had to endure in the early hours of the morning when those men left their calling cards!'

She nodded. The truth was though that Frank hardly seemed ruffled by what had gone on, and she had the feeling he didn't much care about anything or anybody any longer. He'd stopped caring about things the moment his wife died.

'Come on then,' Lawrence urged. 'Follow me inside.'

Elin swallowed hard as she watched him push open the heavy wooden door. Sounds of raucous laughter drifted towards them. The sickening smell of ale hit her, an unwelcome reminder of the night she'd been beaten by her husband. The odour was the same and she wondered, in that moment, how many of those men might return home to do the same thing to their wives? Indeed, how many women lived in fear of their husband's fists, particularly when he'd had a skinful? She viewed all those men in the pub with contempt.

Several men holding pewter tankards sat on benches with a long table between them, a few smoking clay pipes. Were her eyes deceiving her? Weren't some of those young lads sat between them also supping ale and smoking pipes? They appeared no older than twelve or thirteen years of age. 'What's the matter, Elin?' Lawrence asked, taking her by the arm.

'Those lads... what on earth are they doing in a place like this? They ought to be at home with their families...' Her thoughts turned to young Thomas, who seemed about the same age as those boys. She could never imagine him in a place like this, even though he worked at the pit – his parents simply wouldn't allow it.

Lawrence shook his head. 'In China, the young lads are treated like young men, particularly if they partake of a man's job, like working at the ironworks or underground. Don't worry yourself about it,' he whispered in her ear.

But she did worry about it; it wasn't right in her book. Children should be children, shouldn't they?

Then, to her horror, she noticed a couple of women, gaudily dressed, with powder and rouge plastered over their faces, appearing quite a sight – the only time she'd seen such a spectacle was at the theatre and even then, the actors and actresses had toned things down. Those women were fawning heavily over a couple of men stood by the bar. She'd never seen such tarty-looking sorts in her life and she guessed they must be those nymphs of the pave she'd heard mention of. Were they associated with Morgan Griffin? But before she had a chance to ask Lawrence, he stopped her.

'Ah, there's the man we're looking for,' he said, pointing to a man in a brown bowler hat who was supping ale in the corner of the room. He had an air about him, making him stand out from the other men. In some respects, he appeared quite a sharp dresser, with his neatly trimmed moustache and smart attire. Elin guessed that maybe he was about forty years of age, but still a handsome fellow.

There was something about him that seemed to command respect. He was dressed differently to everyone else in the establishment, and it was obvious he was a man of some means. No blinking wonder, she thought, if he's loaning money out right, left and centre, and running girls like this!

He glanced up as they approached, and immediately, his eyes drank in Elin's form, which made her feel quite nervous; it was as though he was devouring her with those lustful eyes of his.

'Well, who do we have here, Mr Langton?' He shot her a wolfish grin, reluctantly turning his attention towards Lawrence. 'Not one of my girls, that's for sure! This one has a bit of class.'

It irked Elin that he was speaking about her as though she wasn't present. What was she to him? A piece of meat from the marketplace? Maybe he could see those silver coins dancing before his very eyes.

'Now, now,' said Lawrence. 'This lady is the wife of Wyn Edwards.'

Morgan frowned and, scratching his head, said, 'And who might he be when he's at home?'

'The man who owes you fifteen shillings from a recent card game!' Lawrence said sharply, not about to have the wool pulled over his eyes by this chancer who obviously hadn't forgotten a thing if he was prepared to send two heavies out to warn Wyn he owed him money!

'I'm not quite sure I remember!' he said in a matter-of-fact tone. He paused a moment, appearing about to say something, but then his mouth snapped shut, and he glanced at Elin. 'So... Mrs Edwards, please refresh my memory as to who your husband is?'

'I think you ought to well remember both card game and my husband, sir,' said Elin, 'seeing as you went to all that trouble to send a couple of men to smash in our back door and window in the early hours of the morning, scaring us all half to death!'

Morgan's eyes widened. Obviously, he was unused to being spoken to in such a forthright manner, particularly by a woman. Then he grinned broadly and his eyes sparkled. 'I like your spirit, Mrs Edwards!' he boomed. Then, turning his attention towards Lawrence again, he hiked a thumb in Elin's direction. 'We've got a right feisty one on our hands here!' Then he roared with laughter, which made Elin feel very uncomfortable indeed.

Lawrence exchanged a dubious glance with her.

Not knowing how to react, she made to leave, but Lawrence grabbed her by the arm. 'Please stay,' he implored.

'Yes, please do, Mrs Edwards,' said Morgan. His face had a serious expression now. He summoned the barman with a click of his fingers. 'Freddie! Fetch this pair a drink, anything they desire!'

Elin was about to protest that she hardly ever drank any alcohol, but then she thought back to that evening when Wyn had gone missing, the night of his mother's death; she'd been happy enough to partake of alcohol then and had even enjoyed the glass of brandy she'd been presented free of charge from the barman in Abercanaid.

'Thank you,' said Lawrence in a jovial manner, surprising her with how his tone of voice had changed, but then again, maybe he was playing the long game to get what he wanted. 'I'll have a glass of ale and my companion shall have a glass of...?' He raised his eyebrows in a questioning manner.

'Brandy,' she said with an air of confidence, 'and I'd like a jug of water with it as well.'

The barman took their order and within a few minutes returned with their drinks on a tray. Elin and Lawrence now sat beside Morgan Griffin, one either side of the man, at the small copper table.

'What I'm proposing is this...' said Lawrence, before taking a sip of ale and setting it down on the table. 'We pay you what Mrs Edwards's husband owes you this very evening and then that debt shall be cleared. It'll no longer be necessary for you to send anyone to damage the property or indeed to harass them in any way, ever again.'

Morgan narrowed his gaze and then stroked his stubbled chin, as Elin held her breath. 'It's not as simple as that though, is it, Mr Langton? The debt should have been paid a fortnight ago and during that time, Mr Edwards has accrued even more debt by keeping me waiting.'

'How much more?' asked Lawrence, a look of disappointment on his face.

'It's now gone up to twenty shillings.'

Elin released the breath she'd been holding. 'Twenty shillings! That's daylight robbery! You charlatan!' She spat out the words like sour pips from a lemon. 'What about the money you're going to cost us as we need to replace the glass in the scullery window and the back door?'

'Now, now.' Griffin smiled as he waved a hand at her. 'I'm sure we can come to some sort of arrangement that might suit both parties. Don't you lawyers have a name for it?' He glanced at Lawrence, who nodded at him.

'Yes, it's called "malicious damage"!' he said firmly, which obviously wasn't the answer the man was expecting. 'A door and a window at the property, which did not belong to Mr Edwards, was damaged. Two panes of glass will need replacing.'

Griffin raised his eyebrows. 'Just whose property is it?'

'His father's!' Elin chipped in, her chin jutting out in defiance. 'It's disgusting. The man is recently widowed and he hasn't the means to pay to get those repairs done after forking out for his wife's funeral!'

Morgan Griffin shook his head. 'I had no idea,' he said. 'Don't worry, we'll sort something out. It was a genuine mistake on my part.' He smiled. 'Though your husband had boasted during the card game that he owned that property!'

Elin had to admit the man was correct about that. Wyn had told her the very same thing.

She turned away, deep in her own thoughts as she scanned the bar room while Lawrence and Griffin continued to discuss the issue. A lot of the talk between them was going over her head as Lawrence spoke in legal terms. Every so often, she caught Griffin lustfully glancing in her direction as if she was a piece of meat on the hook at Merthyr market.

'What did you have in mind?' asked Lawrence.

'Well, if you have the fifteen shillings right now, I'll take it, but the other five will need to be paid too, by this time next week. I won't increase the debt any further in future if it can't be settled by then, in view of what Mrs Edwards said about it being her father-in-law's property.'

'How very noble of you,' Elin muttered under her breath.

'We can manage that,' said Lawrence confidently as he glanced at Elin. 'Can't we?'

She nodded, realising it was better to pay what they could – it should provide some breathing space, for now.

Lawrence continued, 'Unfortunately, I don't have the extra five shillings on my person right now, but I can get it for you when I return from conducting my business in London and it shall be paid by next week.'

'Or,' said Griffin as he looked Elin up and down, 'I'd take the services of your, er *companion*, to pay off some of the debt instead of those five remaining shillings.'

'Hey now!' said Lawrence. 'Mrs Edwards is a decent woman. I'll get you the rest of the money but I have to return to London first thing in the morning.' He put his hand into his jacket pocket and then slammed a small velvet drawstring bag down on the table. 'Here's your precious fifteen shillings! I'll be back in one week's time to pay off the remainder of the debt owing to you.'

'By then the price might change,' said Griffin with a salacious grin on his face that Elin didn't much care for. The man was already going back on his word, as far as she was concerned, after reassuring them that the price wouldn't change – he had them over a barrel and he knew it. Inwardly, she gasped. Five shillings was already more than a week's rent for most people. How was she supposed to come up with any more than that? But she guessed Lawrence would have that covered. It was a pity, she supposed, that the banks were all closed at this time of the night. They could have dealt with this immediately if that were the case, before Lawrence left for London.

'Come on,' said Lawrence, standing, 'we're getting out of here! This man is merely toying with us!' He glanced at Elin, who quickly necked back her glass of brandy without the water. She felt like she needed it and, wiping her mouth with the back of her hand, she rose to her feet. Then, shooting Griffin a dark look, Lawrence said, 'I don't much like dealing with people who renege on their word!'

Why was Lawrence getting so angry with the man, though? It didn't make much sense. In all honesty, she'd been expecting something like this, so why hadn't Lawrence? Was it because Griffin owed him a favour, and now it appeared he wasn't about to repay it?

Taking her by the arm, Lawrence turned to Morgan Griffin and said, 'That debt will be paid off as soon as I can pay it. All the money owed! Then no one will be in debt to you whatsoever!'

Elin stood there speechless as she watched a little smile of satisfaction creep over Griffin's face. He had the upper hand here and Lawrence didn't like it one bit.

Lawrence escorted her out of the pub as though she were a precious piece of china, as if she might be in danger of breaking into a million little pieces at any given moment. For some reason, Morgan Griffin seemed to bring out his protective instincts towards her.

* * *

On the way back to the coach, Elin could sense that Lawrence was seething with anger, as he barely said a word, except to warn her occasionally of where she should step to avoid various pitfalls in her path, such as a pile of rubbish, or guiding her around a pool of water to save soaking her feet. Occasionally, he brought the flat of his hand to the small of her back as though protecting her, and she had to admit she liked that as it made her feel cared for. Wyn never did that; indeed, he often strode ahead whenever they walked together, rarely remaining by her side.

It wasn't until they were both settled in the coach, where the driver had been patiently waiting for them and she rested her head against the padded leather, that Lawrence spoke. 'I can't believe the cheek of that fellow!'

Elin reached across to where he sat and touched his hand. She hated to see him consumed like this over a problem that was not of his making but of her husband's. If only Wyn hadn't got himself involved in that ruddy card game. There were a lot of 'if onlys' though – if only he'd not started drinking in the first place, if only he'd remained at home with her, if only he hadn't gone to that particular pub... The list went on and on.

'Please don't concern yourself so much, Lawrence,' she said kindly. 'The man now has his fifteen shillings returned to him. It should be enough to keep him sweet for—'

'For now,' said Lawrence, finishing her sentence for her. 'Don't worry, I'll visit the bank and get the rest of the money to pay him by this time next week, then we'll be rid of him for good.'

An idea began to form in her mind of maybe visiting Mr Griffin on her own, to see if she could pay off that remaining debt herself before Lawrence returned from London. She hated being beholden to anyone, not just to Mr Griffin, but to Lawrence himself because, in her experience, when people granted a favour, they expected something in return.

* * *

When she returned home, Wyn was waiting for her in the scullery with an empty bowl and spoon in front of him, as though he'd just eaten. With a serious look on his face, he rose from his chair, the legs scraping on the flagstone floor. 'Why weren't you here when I got home, Elin? I had to warm that up myself!' He pointed towards the large pan of cawl sitting on top of the stove.

'I would have been!' she said, removing her cloak and tossing it over a chair, then she fiddled with the ribbons of her bonnet and placed it on the table. 'But you weren't here yourself, were you? I had your food ready to dish up with your father's. Where were *you*, Wyn?' She was in no mood to be trifled with and was spurred on by the alcohol she'd consumed. Morgan Griffin had already wound her up a treat with his stubborn behaviour and his way of keeping her on the hook.

'I told my father to tell you I was helping that farmer again.'

'Were you really?' she said in a mocking tone, not believing a word of it. 'Sheep escaped from those ruddy broken fences again? Thought you helped him to fix those?'

Wyn shook his head. 'I know where I was, but where were *you* until this time of the night?'

'I had to return to the big house to help Cook prepare for a dinner party. Didn't your father mention it to you?'

He shook his head. 'How could he? He went to bed early again. Well, I hope you get paid for your time and trouble.' His tone changed now, as though he believed her. She felt a sliver of guilt for lying to him, but it was the only way. He'd be so angry if he knew she'd arranged to pay his debt off for him. In Wyn's mind, he'd got one over on Morgan Griffin by not paying back what was owed to him, and no doubt he thought the broken windows were enough of a payback for the man. Hopefully, he wouldn't seek further retribution now and maybe when this debt was fully sorted, they'd never have to set eyes on Morgan Griffin or his ilk ever again.

7

Elin and Cook had time to speak privately the following morning. They were talking to one another in the pantry while two maids were clattering around outside, banging pots and pans as they stacked them in the kitchen.

Elin related what had happened the previous evening and how she planned to return to Mr Griffin alone to pay off the remainder of her husband's debt.

'Oh, I don't like the sound of that at all,' said Mrs Brightman as she covered her mouth with the palm of her hand.

'It's not as bad as it sounds,' said Elin. 'I figure if I do some bar work or cleaning for the man, I can pay off the remainder of the debt that way and Mr Lawrence won't have to cough that up as well. I feel guilty as it is that he's offered to take the debt on.'

Cook touched Elin's shoulder. 'Oh, do take care though, dear. I reckon you'd be better off allowing Mr Langton to pay off the remaining five shillings. He can well afford it.'

Elin lifted her chin in a prideful fashion. 'I don't like to be in debt to anyone though,' she said. 'This way when he returns from London, I can tell him he'd needn't bother. In any case, it might turn out to be more than five shillings owing, Griffin did threaten to put up the price at one point, then said he wouldn't, and then changed his mind again. So, who knows how much the final sum will be!'

'Sounds like the man is a contrary character to me, but your mind is obviously made up,' said Cook, reaching for a tin of mustard powder on a high shelf. Noticing the woman's efforts to reach it, Elin, being a good four inches taller than Cook, reached up to grab it.

Elin released a breath. 'I was thinking of going to see Mr Griffin early this afternoon. I'm supposed to be working a full day, but I could nip out and make up the extra hour later, if Mrs Langton doesn't mind.' She guessed Wyn wouldn't be home from work early, so she'd be able to get away with it.

Cook nodded. 'But even if Mrs Langton approves, don't you think you'd be better taking someone with you? That place is a hellhole!' She spat the words out like venom.

'No, I'll go alone. I have my bearings around the place now and it will be daylight; no ill will befall me.'

'What if that Mr Griffin isn't around though?'

'I have a feeling he will be, or at least someone can inform me of his whereabouts...' She hesitated for a moment.

'Now just what are you thinking, Elin?' Cook blinked.

'That I shall have to use my feminine wiles to get around the man.' She shot Cook a crafty smile. 'I have a feeling he'd have been a lot more affable if Lawrence hadn't been with me last night. You know how that old saying goes...'

'Er, what's that?'

'*You catch more flies with honey than with vinegar!* I shall just have to sweeten him up!' She laughed.

* * *

Although Elin was granted an hour's grace by Mrs Langton, by the time she came to leave the property she wasn't feeling as confident as she'd felt while speaking to Mrs Brightman. Maybe this was all a mistake? Perhaps she'd be better off waiting for Lawrence to return from London? He'd left before she'd arrived for work that morning. Now her stomach kept churning. *Don't be so silly,* she chastised herself. *You're doing this to help your husband, to keep that man and his cronies off your backs. And most of all, you're doing this for Frank. He can do without all the hassle at his age.*

Taking a deep breath, she left the house via the back entrance and made her way towards the canal bank, heading towards the town of Merthyr.

As she passed the bustling high street where the outdoor market was in full swing, she watched as folk hurried about their business, wondering if any of those had any debts to settle. She guessed many did. It wasn't uncommon for a person to owe someone else something in these parts, whether it was simply a few pennies, a loaf of bread or cup of borrowed milk. It was a way of life, she supposed, but never had she owed anyone money in her life; it just wasn't in her nature. What really annoyed her was that it needn't have come to this. All of them might live comfortably in that house with three wages coming in. Granted, she didn't earn as much as the menfolk; women were paid less than men, something she thought most unfair when occasionally they carried out the same sort of work, grafting much harder in some cases.

When she reached the arch leading to China, she realised it didn't seem half as threatening in the daytime. The difference this time of day was that there were more people around, mainly children playing outside what she assumed were their homes. A few ragged-looking boys ran past her – the boys appeared to be trouble, she thought to herself. Mrs Brightman had warned her about the pickpockets in the area, so she was mindful to have hidden her reticule in her wicker basket beneath a tea cloth. Oh yes, she had a firm grip on that basket.

The pub door was wide open when she arrived, the smell of stale ale wafting towards her as she entered. This time, the pub was silent. There were only a few men supping ale quietly and her eyes scanned the room for Mr Griffin. Foolishly, she'd assumed he'd be seated in the corner just as they'd left him last night, but he was nowhere to be seen. The barman looked busy behind the counter, setting up for his shift by the look of it, stacking the shelves behind him and occasionally polishing the odd glass with a cloth.

As she approached the bar, the men who had been quietly supping turned their heads. One let out a low whistle, which bristled her spine.

The barman turned to face her. 'Can I help you, madam?'

'You can indeed!' said Elin with a confidence she didn't feel. It was no use acting like a quiet mouse when she was a woman on a mission. She set down her basket on the bar. 'I'm here to see Mr Griffin. I've brought him something.'

'The lady's brought him something!' One of the men behind her tittered and she turned to glare at him. His face flushed red and his neck appeared to shrink into his collar.

'He didn't mean no harm by it, missus,' his companion said. ''Tis his sense of humour, that's all.'

Elin smiled at the man. 'No offence taken,' she said brusquely. She couldn't afford to upset the regulars here, feeling the need to keep everyone sweet. She turned her attention back to the barman. 'Well, is Mr Griffin around or not?'

The barman nodded. 'He doesn't rise until late but he should be awake by now. I'll just go and have a word...'

Elin couldn't understand how someone could rise past this hour. She'd been up since the men set off for work before six o'clock that morning. It was gone noon; the day was already half over in her book.

It wasn't long before the barman returned. 'He'll be down in a moment. He told me to pour you a drink while you wait. What's it to be?'

Now she didn't know what to say. Should she partake of another alcoholic drink or not? Would it give her more courage than she felt right now? On the other hand, it might well impede things. 'I'll just have a glass of lemonade if you have any, please,' she said.

The barman nodded and went to pour her a glass from an earthenware jug. She supposed they had lemonade in stock as sometimes people added it to drinks like port or brandy. And by the appearance of some of the women she'd seen hanging around here last night, they probably had it to dilute their drinks while working. They wouldn't want to get too inebriated in their line of work; they had to keep themselves very sensible and sober if they didn't want to get taken advantage of. Though, they probably encouraged their male companions to drink as much as possible. The more those varmints drank, the less likely they'd be able to perform and then, to their relief, if the men were high as kites, the women might be able to pilfer the odd wallet, silk scarf or silver fob watch.

Mrs Brightman had given her all the information she needed to know about this place. The woman loved to read the court cases in the local newspaper when she was having a little break, and more often than not, she'd find something tasty involving the area and would read it out to Floss and Molly who would sit there and listen, mouths open wide.

While she waited for the man, she seated herself at the table they'd found Morgan Griffin at the previous evening, causing some curious glares from the men she'd spoken to. When the barman arrived with her glass of cloudy lemonade, she whispered to him, 'Why are those men looking at me in that fashion? I have to sit somewhere.'

After setting her drink down on the table, he whispered in her ear, 'You see, no one in this establishment dares to sit at this table, not unless invited by the man himself. It's an unwritten rule.'

'I understand,' said Elin as the barman moved away. She purposely spoke loud enough for the men to hear. 'I am staying put here as I have business to conduct with Morgan Griffin himself.'

If he was surprised by her stance, the barman didn't say so. Instead, he smiled and nodded.

She had almost finished her drink when Griffin himself appeared through a doorway behind the bar. Surely, he hadn't been sleeping all this time? His appearance didn't show any signs of tiredness. He was well spruced up, even more so than last night – freshly shaven, in a navy jacket with a crisp white cravat adorning his neck, held in place with a gold pin. His hair was gelled down with what she suspected was pomade. Indeed, he looked even more handsome than she remembered – there was a roguish charm about him.

'Mrs Edwards.' He beamed as he approached her as though he were some long-lost friend, which caused the men's mouths to gape open in astonishment. 'I knew you'd return to see me.'

'Then you were right, Mr Griffin.' She smiled at him. 'I wanted to bring a cake I baked for you.' Oh goodness she was being forced to lie. It was another coffee and walnut cake that Cook had baked – she hadn't minded sparing it, anything to help Elin out. In any case, it was her baking day and she'd been up at the crack of dawn and had made two coffee and walnut cakes, two trays of scones and had used her bakestone to bake Welsh cakes.

'That sounds lovely,' he enthused as he took a seat beside her. He snapped his fingers at the barman and then, glancing in her direction, asked, 'Would you like another?'

'Yes please, that lemonade was delicious.'

'This time, I'll ask the barman to add a little port for you?'

Deciding to throw caution to the wind, she said, 'I'd prefer a drop of brandy...'

He winked at her. 'Then a glass of brandy you shall have, my dear.'

Morgan took a tankard of ale as she slowly sipped her drink. They chatted amicably with one another for a while, discussing everything from how it had always been his ambition to run a pub, to her life in Abercanaid; she was surprised at how amicably they got along with one another now that she wasn't being chaperoned. He told her how he now owned the property they were seated in and she'd joked, asking him if he'd won it in a game of cards. This had set him off roaring with laughter and the men opposite stared at them again, wondering no doubt what on earth was going on in that corner.

Elin drew back the tea cloth on her basket to reveal the rich coffee and walnut cake. It was covered in butter icing and adorned with several walnuts around the edges, with the largest one placed in the middle. It did look tasty and all, and she could see Morgan salivating beside her. 'My dear, you are wasted with that husband of yours.' He took her hand and lowered his head to plant a kiss on the back of it, surprising her with his intimacy. She removed her hand from his reach and he carried on. 'I know I asked you to do some work for me to pay back the rest of the debt. How would you feel about cooking at this pub for a couple of weeks with a view to clearing it?'

Now she was in trouble! Although being a perfectly adequate cook at home, Elin was not a baker like Mrs Brightman who could turn her hand to anything.

'Don't look so concerned,' he chided. 'I'd only be asking for plain old home cooking for the lads: beef pie and a few spuds with carrots or a tasty stew, that sort of thing. We haven't put on any grub here before, but as I've started taking in lodgers, they need feeding up three times a day, as to their requirements.'

'I understand,' said Elin, feeling better now about the whole idea. The trouble was there was no way she could get that amount of time off from work unless she pretended to be sick, but that wouldn't be on, especially as Mrs Langton had allowed her leave of absence when her mother-in-law had passed away. 'Although I'd like to help you out, Mr Griffin, I wouldn't be able to do so as my employer needs me.'

He narrowed his gaze. 'Your employer? Doesn't that husband of yours support you then?'

'It's not a question of that.'

'What is it a question of then?'

'I was already working for Mrs Langton, Lawrence's mother, before I wed my husband and I wanted to carry on working at the house, although we didn't seem to need the extra income at the time. I've since discovered that my money is helping those ends to meet!' She hadn't intended to be forthright with her explanation. Indeed, did she owe this stranger any explanation at all?

He was reflective for a moment before speaking again. 'I think that's admirable of you, I really do. But your husband, on his wages as a collier, ought to be able to keep you while you keep home and hearth. I don't abide by women having to work.'

'Oh, don't you?' She folded her arms and angled her head to one side as if amused he was saying so.

'Hey, what do you mean?' he said, frowning.

'Those garish painted ladies I glimpsed here last night, they work for you, don't they?'

'Aye, they do, but those are single ladies, not married ones.'

Sighing, she said, 'So, from what I've just explained to you, how on earth could I possibly work for you? I just don't have the time because as well as working at the big house for the Langtons, I have to cook and clean at home.'

He shot her a disarming smile. Then he peered at the cake. 'But you are able to bake cakes?'

'Oh yes, I bake at home.'

'Well then, how about you bake some things for the pub for a few a weeks, and I will write off the remaining debt owed to me?'

She looked at him vacantly and then frowned. 'But that will cost me even more money.'

'Not at all. I'll supply whatever you require. You just give me a list of what you need. If you could, say, bake a few large pies for the lads to share, then Aggie – she's a charlady what works here – she could put on a pan of spuds to go with them, and warm up the pies or stews or whatever you choose to make.'

'Can't this Aggie bake pies for you, then?'

'I dare say she can but it's you who needs to repay your debt, not Aggie.'

She had to admit he had her there, though she had a feeling Morgan Griffin didn't really require the extra five shillings from her. What he was really after was her servitude and making her beholden to him. But what choice did she have?

None whatsoever, a little voice inside her chided.

8

The sunlight filtering through the bedroom window caused Elin to stir. Feeling startled for a moment, she wondered what day it was. Then with relief at seeing her husband beside her snoring gently, she realised it was Sunday morning. Today there was no work for either of them – well, not in the usual manner anyhow. Wyn reckoned he had to go and help that farmer again, so she decided that today she'd bake a few pies for the pub. She'd explained the situation to Dilys next door about how they needed to get out of debt and the only way to do so was to do a few favours for Mr Griffin. Dilys had agreed to take in the ingredients from the man and not to breathe a word of this to anyone – except Joshua, as she lived with him, so it would be difficult to hide her involvement here.

Mr Griffin delivered to Dilys a sack of flour, blocks of lard and butter, beef stewing steak, and a string of onions. If Elin stored that lot under their own roof, there was a high chance that Wyn or Frank might stumble upon them, causing questions to be raised. She had thought of leaving the supplies in the shed outside but couldn't risk any rodents nibbling away at them; it was just too much of a risk. So she'd taken a chance confiding in Dilys.

Frank had said he'd be attending chapel and then walking over to the nearby village of Pentrebach to visit an old friend, so it gave her the opportunity to get cracking on those pies. Dilys had also kindly offered her services with baking them, which she'd gladly accepted.

Dilys Evans was in a jovial mood about the whole situation, making light of it as she rolled some pastry on the pine table in her scullery with a floured rolling pin. 'Now don't you go worrying, Elin.' She smiled. 'It's a while since I've done anything like this, but I'll soon get into the swing of it again. How's the steak and onions looking?'

Elin stooped to open the oven door and when she did so, a blast of hot air hit her full in the face, a wonderful odour permeating the air, causing her mouth to water. She'd been a little off her food of late since Wyn had got himself immersed in trouble, and even though she was taking measures to rectify that, she still tossed and turned in bed at night, fretting feverishly at the situation. Sometimes she found it difficult to eat anything at all. But now, for some reason, she felt ravenous.

'It's all cooking well.' She nodded with appreciation, so grateful for her help.

'When we've baked our first batch of pies, we shall have to taste a little here and there just to check we've seasoned them properly and that the steak is nice and tender.' Mr Griffin had insisted they make small individual pies as well as the larger ones, so he might sell them at the pub to customers as well as to his lodgers.

Elin chuckled. 'I can't wait!'

Before too long a batch of twenty-five small pies were ready to bake along with four large ones. Dilys had insisted on preparing an uneven number of small ones so they might taste and test one, leaving a round two dozen to hand over to Mr Griffin. When they sampled that spare pie, Elin closed her eyes to savour it. It tasted even better than she'd ever imagined: the onions complemented the steak, and the filling was well seasoned with salt and pepper. 'Mrs Evans, you're a marvel!' she said, and then she kissed the woman's soft powdery cheek.

'Please don't thank me yet; we don't know what the men at that pub will make of them!'

'I reckon they'll love them! Mr Griffin said he'll pick them up from you at about two o'clock this afternoon. Please though…' She hesitated a moment. 'Will you tell him not to call to see me next door when he's here?'

Dilys knitted her eyebrows. 'Oh? Why not?'

'It's Wyn, you see – I don't want him to know I'm doing any favours for the man.'

Dilys nodded. 'Very wise indeed. You don't want to risk him finding out about this pie-making venture before it's even got started! It's best he doesn't know.'

Elin sighed. 'You see, Mr Langton paid off most of Wyn's gambling debt, but there's still some owing to Mr Griffin.'

Dilys smiled sympathetically at her. 'You've got yourself into a right pickle indeed, due to that husband of yours!' She shook her head. 'And it would only make trouble for you if he ever found out.'

Elin nodded. 'That's about the sum of it. I know I told you I needed to bake pies to help clear the debt but I hadn't mentioned the deceit behind it all. I feel dreadful about it.' Tears were close to the surface now as Elin swallowed a lump in her throat.

'Aw, I do understand, you know,' said Dilys as she patted Elin's hand. 'Believe me, if this is the only way to deal with your husband's debt, then you must do what you see fit, my lovely. But what you must do now is not allow Wyn to run up any more debt in the future.'

Elin nodded. 'I know. At the moment he maintains he's keeping away from the pubs and I've not smelled any alcohol on his breath lately, but he's helping out some farmer now and staying away from the house. I have my suspicions...'

Dilys folded her floury arms and narrowed her gaze. 'Who is this farmer?'

'Dick Constable is his name apparently. He lives in that farmhouse up the mountain overlooking the village.'

'Dick Constable? Now that does sound odd to me.'

'Why do you say that, Mrs Evans?'

'Dick has two sons, strapping lads they are an' all. I can't see why he'd need to ask anyone for any help with that pair around.'

The tears that were near the surface finally emerged as Elin began to cry. 'Oh, Mrs Evans, what on earth is going on and why am I always the last to know?'

'I can see my words have upset you, dear. It wasn't my intention, believe me. I could have lied to you, but I can't see the sense of that. Now, after I've put the next tray of pies in to bake, we can have a good chat about things. All right?'

Elin nodded gratefully. She could see now why her mother-in-law always said that Dilys was such a good friend to her. The woman was someone Elin felt safe to confide in.

* * *

Elin held up the lace curtain to peer outside onto the street while a horse and cart drew up outside Dilys's house. She watched as Morgan Griffin clambered down from the driver's seat, and then he took a couple of covered trays of pies from the woman who was already waiting outside to greet him. Then quite unexpectedly, after loading them onto the cart and nodding at Dilys, he glanced at the window, prompting Elin to loosen her grasp on the curtain and step away into the shadows. She knew he'd seen her as he'd tipped his hat in her direction.

Morgan took his seat back on the cart and she watched him ride off.

Breathing a sigh of relief, she flopped into a nearby armchair. Whew! That was a close one. Frank and Wyn might potentially arrive home at any moment.

Her heart pounded profusely. All this stress wasn't good for her – she realised that – but in some sort of way Morgan Griffin brought an excitement into her life that she'd not experienced in a long while.

By the time her husband and father-in-law returned home, she'd managed to get dinner on the go. It might have looked suspicious that she hadn't put a roast in the oven but now there was a whole chicken cooking away, and she'd prepared the vegetables beforehand. Frank had returned home before his son, and she had to admit, it was the best mood she'd seen him in since Olwen's death. He seemed quite buoyant so she guessed that the visit to his friend had gone very well and helped to lift his spirits.

When Wyn returned, he approached her, pecking a quick kiss on her cheek, causing her to stiffen at the thought he'd been lying to her. Dilys had confirmed something that had niggled her for a long while; the farmer had more than enough help, so it was unlikely he'd need Wyn's too. 'My, my, something smells good, my sweet.'

She closed her eyes, feeling a strong urge to make an accusation regarding his whereabouts, but instead, took a deep composing breath and let it go. She flicked her eyes open. 'I cooked a roast chicken dinner, that's all.'

'Let's be having it, then!' he said, rubbing his hands with glee. There was something about him that told her he was in too good a mood, and considering that he ought to be thinking he owed Morgan Griffin a great deal of money, he should be dispirited. She couldn't forget how he'd seemed to be taking pleasure in thinking he had one over on the man, which she didn't much care for. Griffin wasn't the nicest of fellows from what she'd heard about him, but he had a kind side to him too. After all, most people were a mixture of light and shade – though some like him were shadier than most.

'Anything for afters?' Wyn grinned with a gleam in his eyes. Did he mean dessert or was it a dessert of a different kind? He had seemed a little fruity of late, which unnerved her. But thankfully, as yet, there'd been no more violence. It was almost as though it was all too good to be true.

Sidling away from his grasp, she went over to the hob and lifted a saucepan of potatoes to drain them in the sink. The table was already laid with a pristine white cloth. Something her mother-in-law had taught her was to have it laid ready for the men as soon as they came in through the door – that way, even if their food wasn't already dished up on the table, it appeared as though wheels were in motion for it to be served. Olwen had been quite canny in that respect. Frank was a mild-mannered sort of man, though Olwen had said when he was younger, he'd had a bit of a temper on him, so maybe that's why she'd liked to keep things steady in the home. The woman must have been a calming influence on her husband. If only Elin could have the same effect on Wyn.

During the meal, Wyn spoke animatedly with his father about business at the pit and their recent pay rise. Maybe that's what had put both men in such good spirits, Elin thought. As they ate and chatted, she found her racing heart calming down to a steady rhythm. Perhaps they'd finally turned a corner. As soon as this debt was settled, they could go back to normal. No more needed to be said about it, as Morgan would be paid off, both with the original sum and in kind for the rest. There was no sign of her husband drinking alcohol and his mood had lifted somewhat.

Frank had gone upstairs to bed, and Elin stood in the scullery drying the final dish. She planned on retiring early too as today with the baking of the pies had all but worn her out. She needed to be up early for work in the morning. She stacked the final dish with the others on the shelf and closed the cupboard.

But then she felt a presence behind her. Her husband's warm breath was on her neck.

She turned sharply, but he was invading her space. The look in his eyes was different now; they bore a look of sheer contempt for her.

'And whose silk handkerchief was that in with our washing in the basket the other day?' he asked in a taunting manner. 'Taken in washing for the gentry now, have you?'

Elin felt her face grow hot and she hoped it hadn't gone red – the thought of that handkerchief only evoked those feelings that she was developing for Lawrence of late. It served to remind her of the day after her mother-in-law's death when he'd called to the house to check on her. It had been highly embarrassing the way she'd broken down in front of him like that, but he'd been so kind to her, being a proverbial shoulder to cry on and in loaning her his handkerchief. Now she wished he hadn't, as then Wyn wouldn't be accusing her now of this. How could she reply to him?

'I… I…' She swallowed hard. 'I found it at the big house when I was tidying up. I'd been crying over your mother dying. I thought they wouldn't miss one handkerchief, but when I got home with it still in my pocket, I felt guilty. So, I washed it and returned it to the house without anyone knowing about it.' She hoped he wouldn't realise she was lying to him because, of course, someone had known she had the handkerchief and returned it and that person was Lawrence himself, though she'd got the impression he wouldn't have minded at all if she'd kept it.

Wyn smiled and then he glanced at the ceiling, tapping his fingers on his chin. 'That's got me thinking,' he said. 'You know what…'

'What?' She frowned, having the feeling she wasn't going to like this at all.

'I reckon doing the job you do getting up close to Mrs Langton, you could easily pocket a few items without the old girl cottoning on. We might get a good price for a few silk handkerchiefs and some small pieces of jewellery… though don't take anything too obvious – things that would be missed, of course. The old biddy might think she's losing her marbles instead of one of her brooches!' He threw back his head and laughed.

'But I couldn't do anything of the sort, Wyn!' She'd raised her voice, feeling mortified he would suggest such a thing. 'Mrs Langton trusts me implicitly. The woman has been good to me too, allowing me time off when I had the flu and following your mother's death.'

'Look, think of it this way,' he said, his voice gravelly now. 'It's what you're owed for all the work you do there. Just imagine it, we could enjoy ourselves if we sold off a few of her belongings. You could claim you know nothing about them and make out she's becoming forgetful. Even if anyone believed her, there's enough staff at the house to throw the finger of suspicion on instead.'

Elin opened her mouth, about to say something, but then she closed it again. Wyn seemed to be getting high on thinking of such a thing and before she knew what was happening, he was pushing her against the counter.

'Come on, live a little, Elin. You're so uptight these days.'

Then roughly he tugged at her hair, pulling her head backwards, and he began to plunder her mouth forcefully with his tongue. She didn't like it. He'd never done anything like that to her before and she felt violated. Where had he learned to do such a thing?

As his tongue invaded her mouth without her permission, she felt him lift the skirts of her dress as his hands roamed freely, and then he withdrew his mouth from hers.

'Y... your father...' she said breathlessly. 'He's only just gone to bed. He might hear something or return to the scullery.' She hoped to appeal to her husband's better nature. He'd never normally touch her in such a fashion – especially not in this part of the house; their marital life was for the bedroom only – but he seemed to be taking pleasure in making her feel uncomfortable. It was obvious he wasn't about to stop until he got his own way.

To her horror, he turned her around roughly, so she was facing the counter, and began dragging and pulling at her underwear. It was then she realised he was about to take her and there was nothing she could do about it. If she cried out, Frank might hear and she'd be mortified if he came into the scullery to catch her in such a position with her husband.

There were the sounds of Wyn unbuckling his belt and loosening his clothing as she realised just what was about to happen to her. All she could do was hold on to the counter top, grit her teeth and close her eyes.

Tears rolled down her cheeks. Her husband's grunts and groans told her what enjoyment he was taking from having her in this manner. It was his right in his eyes, even without her consent. Indeed, it was as though he had all the power by taking hers away in a brutal, forceful fashion, causing her such discomfort. There was nothing loving about the act whatsoever.

When it was all over, he kissed the back of her neck and said, 'Thank you, sweetheart. I enjoyed that.' All the while, she stood motionless, unable to respond. 'Well, I'm off to bed. Don't be too long. Tidy yourself up!'

Then he left her standing there, her underwear tossed into the corner of the room as she cried her heart out. She was still clinging on to the counter, and trembling from top to toe. If his mother had been alive, Elin very much doubted he would have treated her this way. But now with the woman gone, a new version of him had been unleashed. One she hated with a vengeance.

9

Elin felt as though her hands were glued to the counter worktop, unsure of how long she remained frozen to the spot before she realised she needed to do something to make herself feel clean again. She felt completely violated, never expecting in her life to ever endure a sexual act like that. The matter of consent aside, it was commonplace for married couples to make love in the missionary position. What had happened to the loving man she'd first encountered on the canal bank before they'd wed? It was almost as though giving her a gold ring and signing a certificate of marriage had given him licence to behave as he wished, as though her feelings, wishes and desires mattered not one jot – it was all about him.

Hands trembling, she filled a few saucepans with water from the pump outside and set them on the hob. When those had boiled, she dragged the tin bath from outside into the scullery and after pouring some cold water into it first from a large jug, she added the hot. Then quietly, she crept to their bedroom to fetch some clean underwear, her nightdress and dressing gown. Wyn was spark out asleep, but still she moved quietly as she began to remove her clothing. They'd need to be washed tomorrow as well, now they were contaminated. Contaminated by her husband's filthy lustful urges.

Elin made her way to the scullery with the bundle of clean clothing beneath her arm, and as she did so, she passed the spot in front of the hearth where Wyn had taken his fist to her face. That had been a warning of things to come. Glancing in the mirror above the mantel, she caught sight of herself. The shadows beneath her eyes gave her a haunted, hollow look that she hardly recognised as the woman she was. She'd hoped in her heart that would have been the first and last time he'd hurt her, but evidently not. A feeling of utter despair took hold of her as she walked through the open scullery door, placed her night things on the table and stared at the bath full of water.

Gingerly, she placed one foot into the water and, satisfied with the temperature, she immersed her body, proceeding to lather herself up with a bar of soap and a long-handled back scrubber. Vigorously, she scrubbed away, so much so that her skin began to smart and tingle. She knew she was being too rough but it was the only way to absolve her feelings of being sullied by him, wanting the scent of him removed entirely.

When satisfied she'd washed all the dirt of his actions away, she lay back and closed her eyes. The bathtub was only brought out occasionally and most definitely not at this time of the night, but she'd not have felt right going to bed as she was.

She dried herself and dressed, then got rid of the dirty water and hung the tub back on its nail on the outside wall of the house. Back inside, she put a pan of milk on to boil. The warm drink should help her sleep.

As she sat at the table sipping it, her mind turned to Lawrence. She'd bet everything she had that he wouldn't treat a woman this way. He was kind and considerate towards her and even if he hadn't been, she'd have been aware of his compassion from the way he treated his own mother. Lawrence would never raise a hand to a woman; she was sure of that. And his lovemaking would be warm and tender. After what happened tonight, she no longer felt any guilt for having such thoughts.

No wonder those ladies of the night did what they did for a living. There was some form of empowerment there, she supposed, and they got paid for it into the bargain, even if they had to endure all sorts of positions to earn their money.

* * *

It was a few days later when Molly beckoned Elin towards the back door of the house. 'There's some guy out there asking to speak to you, Mrs Edwards,' she said with a dubious look on her face.

Elin blinked. 'To speak to me? Who is this fellow?'

'Said his name is Mr Griffin.'

At the mention of the man's name, Elin swallowed hard. Oh no! This was all she needed, him turning up at her place of work. And how did he know she worked here anyhow? She was certain she hadn't mentioned the address of her workplace to the man, but then she guessed maybe he'd put two and two together at Lawrence Langton's involvement in all of this.

Taking a deep composing breath, she patted down her hair and said, 'Thank you, Molly. I'll attend to him right away.'

Molly stood still for a moment as though expecting Elin to provide her with some sort of an explanation as to why some strange man requested to see her at the back door – it was most unusual for someone unknown to turn up at the house like that requesting to see a member of staff; most callers at the back of the house were either tradesmen or hawkers, not handsome men with a vested interest in a female employee.

Elin forced a smile. 'You can go about your business now, Molly. I don't need a chaperone,' she said sharply, dismissing the girl. She wasn't usually as curt with junior members of staff but the last thing she needed was the girl earwigging and passing on her business to others.

She walked purposefully along the corridor to the back door of the house, the skirts of her dress swishing as she passed the walls adorned with family portraits, until she arrived at the back door. Through the frosted glass she could make out the outline of Morgan Griffin who, at around six feet, was taller than most men she knew. He was a few inches taller than her husband but only marginally taller than Lawrence.

Gingerly, she drew back the door to be faced with the grinning face of Mr Griffin.

'My dear,' he said, stepping back as if to appraise her. 'You did me proud with your fare the other day. They've been selling like hot cakes, or should I say hot pies!' He chuckled as though pleased with himself for his attempt at humour.

Elin returned the smile. 'That's good to hear!' she said, thinking maybe now he'd let her off the hook.

'So, I was thinking...' He drummed his fingers on his stubbled chin. 'How would you like to make some more for me?'

'B... but I don't have the time, Mr Griffin. As you can see, I work here during the day and the rest of the time I have to look after my husband and my widowed father-in-law as well as run the home.'

'But I'd pay you handsomely for your efforts!' He dipped his hand into his pocket and dangled a black velvet drawstring purse in front of her eyes, jingling the coins inside. She wondered whether it was the same purse that Lawrence had given him the other night.

Elin opened her mouth to say something and then snapped it shut again.

'My dear, you seem at a loss for words.'

'Look,' she said, breaking from her reverie, 'I've already explained to you the position I'm in at home and here working at this house.'

'But you don't understand how well those pies are selling. Lots of folk have been back to the pub asking for them. I could have sold them several times over! Total strangers who've never set a foot in the establishment before have been badgering my staff to buy one. Word has got around! When people eat, they get a thirst for the ale, so it's a winning situation all around for the both of us. If you bake them regularly for me, it will be good for my business and good for your own!' He held up the purse and shook it again.

She had to admit it was a tempting offer, but she didn't want to leave her job at the house. It just wasn't an option for her at the moment, and anyway, this pie business might be just a flash in the pan. She couldn't risk leaving a good job for something that might fizzle out.

'Look,' he said, lowering his voice, 'I'll give you time to think about it. And maybe there's some way you can carry on working here. You could just take on a few extra hours a week for me on top of it? I'm sure there must be a way around the situation?'

The more she thought about it, the more she liked the idea. Wyn was hardly at home these days and her father-in-law's mind seemed elsewhere.

'Let me consider it, and I'll let you know.' She glanced behind her to ensure no one was listening, and found no one there. It was too risky to speak to the man for much longer. She didn't want any of the staff asking awkward questions of her – though she did think of one member of staff who she felt safe to confide in.

He nodded as she made to close the door on him.

'Don't take too long about it,' Griffin said.

Taking a deep breath, she made her way to the kitchen.

* * *

'You want to use the facilities here?' Cook's eyes widened with disbelief. 'I don't know about that.'

Elin realised how territorial Cook was about 'her kitchen' and knew it would be a big ask of the woman.

She hesitated before saying, 'What I was thinking was that if I came into work a couple of hours early, like you do to begin work in the kitchen, I could prepare the pastry and put a few trays of pies in the oven to pass on to Mr Griffin later.'

'Oh, I don't think so, Elin.' Mrs Brightman looked dubious as she shook her head. 'It wouldn't be fair robbing stuff from the house.'

'It wouldn't be theft though, as Mr Griffin will supply all the ingredients – that's what he did for me with the last batch of pies. All I had to do was prepare them and bake them, then hand them over to him.'

Cook wrinkled her nose. 'You mean you've already made some for him? But how did you have the opportunity to do so?'

'Sunday last. My neighbour helped me; we baked them at her house as I didn't want Wyn to know. It's a way for me to pay back the debt he owes the man. Apparently, according to Mr Griffin, the pies went down a storm at the pub and he says he will pay me handsomely.'

'I get that, honestly I do,' Cook carried on, 'but you would still be stealing in a sense.'

Elin frowned. 'How do you make that out?'

'Because you'd be using the mistress's oven, wouldn't you?'

'I know that, Mrs Brightman, but you have the oven going in the morning to cook breakfast for Mrs Langton and the staff, anyhow. It would only mean popping a few trays of pies in at the same time. I can even bake a few to leave for the staff lunch later. You can make out you baked them yourself!'

By the look on Cook's face, Elin thought there'd be no leeway whatsoever, but then she smiled and said, 'All right then, we can try it this once – or twice – as long as the staff benefit from those ruddy pies!'

Elin beamed at the woman. 'That's that then, all sorted out,' she said, smacking her palms together with purpose.

* * *

It worked out very well with Elin working at the big house so early in the morning to prepare the pies and then later, while Mrs Langton was having one of her 'afternoon naps', Griffin would call to the back door of the house to collect them. Of course, Elin realised this would all have to change soon, as Lawrence would be returning to the house for a few days, and she guessed he'd be most annoyed to hear she'd been paying her husband's debt off to the man in such a way.

In a strange sense, she took a sort of satisfaction in getting one over on Wyn after all he'd put her through of late. As soon as he and Frank set off for the pit in the mornings, she'd have those dishes washed, dried and put away in double quick time. The only thing she felt bad about was the fact she had to involve Cook in this, who was also allowing her to use the pantry to store the sacks of flour, salt and blocks of lard, along with the chunks of beef. But the staff weren't complaining, oh no. They were enjoying those pies in the belief that Cook herself had baked them as a special treat. Even Mrs Langton had inadvertently tried one before Mr Griffin had a chance to collect them. She had entered the kitchen unexpectedly and inhaled the delicious aroma wafting towards her, noting the pies stacked on trays on the counter.

'The mistress was drooling at the mouth!' Mrs Brightman explained later. 'I had to cut one in half and give her a nibble right then and there!'

'And?' said Elin, lifting her brow.

'She ruddy well loved the taste and asked for one for her supper later that evening! So, sorry and all that, as a result, there were a couple of pies short for Mr Griffin's order.'

'That's all right.' Elin shrugged her shoulders. 'We don't have a firm arrangement as to exactly how many to supply him with, other than four trays a day.'

Mrs Brightman nodded sagely. 'Best keep it that way.' She chuckled. 'That way we can hold a couple back.'

'Cook, I never had you down as a petty thief!' Elin laughed.

'Look, people like Mr Griffin don't do things by the book, do they? So why shouldn't we be canny and resourceful ourselves?' She tapped the side of her nose with a knowing look.

'You're absolutely right. Perks of the job and all that.'

'What does your husband think of you doing this?'

To her horror, Elin felt her face grow hot and her bottom lip began to quiver as she blinked back tears threatening to fall.

'I didn't mean to upset you, dear.' Cook approached Elin to lay a reassuring hand on her shoulder. 'I'm guessing you still haven't told him, then?'

Elin sniffed and then she shook her head. 'No, I haven't. He hasn't been treating me too well of late.'

'Come on,' said Cook. 'Take a seat at the table and tell me all about it. A problem shared is a problem halved.'

At that moment, Molly barged into the kitchen with a tray stacked up with crockery, having collected Mrs Langton's used dishes from the drawing room. One warning look from Cook as she deposited the heavy tray on the counter was enough to set her marching back out the door again, muttering under her breath as she went.

'That girl knows me well enough,' said Cook as she took a seat opposite Elin. 'She understands when I don't want her in my presence.'

Forcing a smile, Elin sniffed again, prompting Mrs Brightman to stuff her hand into her pinny pocket to give her a clean white handkerchief. When she'd composed herself, Elin began to relate the tale of how Wyn had taken her by force a couple of evenings ago.

When she'd finished, Mrs Brightman looked at her with compassion in her eyes. 'That's dreadful, Elin,' she said, patting her hand. 'You can't go on putting up with that sort of behaviour. He has no right to do that without your consent.'

Elin nodded slowly, her tears blurring her vision. 'But what can I do about it? It's obvious Wyn views me as being his property now that we're wed. He sees it as his conjugal right, whether I consent or not, I suppose.'

'There's no suppose about it,' said Cook, pursing her lips with disapproval. 'It's tantamount to rape in my book, married or not. You should check out what the law says about it.' She rested her elbows on the table and then glanced at the kitchen ceiling for a moment as though the answer lay there. Then she straightened, raising an index finger as though she'd just come up with an idea. 'I have it,' she said, looking at Elin, 'why not have a quiet word with Mr Langton when he returns from London on Friday? He can advise you legally on the matter.'

'Oh, I couldn't...' She shook her head. It wasn't just that she'd be mortified to discuss such personal matters with him because he was a man, it was more to do with the growing attraction she was feeling for him. What on earth would he think of her discussing things of that nature?

'Look, Elin.' Cook shook her head. 'You can't go on living with a man who treats you like that. He's already brought trouble to your door with his drinking and gambling...'

'There's something else, too...' Elin stared at the wood grain on the table, following the swirls and the small knots that made intricate designs on the pine table, avoiding the woman's gaze.

'Yes, go on,' Cook said gently. 'You'll not shock me, I promise.'

'The night his mother died, in the early hours of the following morning to be precise, he came home drunk and he hit me...' Her lower lip began to tremble again and this time those tears flowed freely. Grief for all she'd endured these past couple of weeks, now everything was in the open. Lawrence knew Wyn had hit her – he'd seen the evidence of the bruises that time he'd called to the house – but Mrs Brightman hadn't as Elin had been given a few days' leave. By the time she returned to work at the house, the bruising had faded and she'd carefully applied powder to hide anything left behind. She'd been a good actress during those first few days back at work too, pretending everything was all right, but she and Lawrence had known differently. Mrs Langton didn't have a clue and she hadn't intended telling the woman either. Even her own father-in-law hadn't seemed to notice much was amiss. He'd been so wrought with grief that he wouldn't even have noticed if a pink elephant had set up camp in his house. Thankfully, now though, he seemed to be more his old self.

Elin brought her gaze to meet with Cook's, who was about to say something when the kitchen door burst open. Molly had returned and she shot a sideways glance at Cook as though to ask, *Am I allowed in here now?*

Cook just smiled and nodded at the girl. Elin took this as her cue to leave. Now that Mrs Langton had finished breakfasting, she needed to see if there were any chores the woman wished her to do. Sometimes those chores involved letter writing in the form of replying to various invitations or letters from friends and relatives. In which case, once written and placed in envelopes, she'd need to take them to the post office for dispatch. Other tasks included sorting out items the woman wished to send for repair or simply accompanying her in the coach to the bustling town of Merthyr, or sometimes farther afield to places like Pontypridd or Aberdare.

Mrs Langton had her own favourite costume stores she liked to visit. They were always ones where she might have her gowns and hats made to order, attended to by ladies who had their tape measures to hand. There were no thrift stores or pawn shops for Mrs Langton, oh no. Only the best for her. But Elin didn't begrudge the woman one tiny bit. Although she could never afford such luxuries herself, she felt the woman's husband had worked hard for the success of his confectionery business, so why shouldn't she enjoy the fruits of his labour now he was no longer with her? And to be fair, she was a good employer who saw to the needs of her staff. Yes, Elin was fortunate indeed to work for Mrs Langton. Most fortunate.

10

The following morning, when Elin had a little time to herself after baking the pies and before Mrs Langton rose from her bed, she perused some of Lawrence's law books in the library – all thickly bound volumes with gold lettering that appeared to be stacked alphabetically on the shelves. She guessed they'd be worth a bob or two.

One dusty old tome spoke of something called 'the rule of thumb' when it came to domestic violence. This intrigued her and she was shocked to read an account of a judge, who in 1782, supposedly said it was permissible for a man to beat his wife with a stick providing the stick was no wider than his thumb. Apparently, there was no evidence for such a thing ever being said by the man, but it hadn't stopped him being the subject of cartoons depicting him as 'Judge Thumb'. Maybe that was where the saying 'rule of thumb' came from? But to be honest, Elin wouldn't have been surprised if such a thing were true, as after all, it seemed to her that it was a man's world. There was also some literature about a social reformer called Caroline Norton, who campaigned over child custody and the conditions of divorce for women, which helped bring about a change of the law. As Elin read with interest, she understood that Caroline had been born into a wealthy family and her own husband used to beat her. The woman had fought for the rights of women and Caroline's campaign efforts were influential in the passing of the Divorce and Matrimonial Causes Act of 1857.

Elin couldn't help feeling enormous respect for the woman, discovering she'd even written to Queen Victoria herself. But sadly, from what she could tell from Lawrence's books, there was basically no rape in marriage as the law stood. A divorce for someone of her own standing would be difficult to procure, though there might be grounds for her to petition for a legal separation, but that wouldn't even leave her free to remarry. The only items that could petition a divorce were: if Wyn had committed bigamy, bestiality, incest or maybe if he hadn't consummated the marriage, none of which were true. She closed the book with a slam, sending a cloud of dust into the air, causing her to cough.

Feeling annoyed, she vowed to instruct Molly to dust in here later. But while Molly's cleaning skills might not be the best, it did cause her to wonder how often Lawrence opened these precious books of his.

* * *

Elin was beginning to realise she'd better stop operating her pie business from the house, as soon Lawrence would return from London and she had no idea how early he rose in the mornings. For all she knew, he might rise at the crack of dawn and get his head stuck into all those legal books – though somehow, she doubted that going by the dusty condition of some of them.

Then again, he probably had a decent library at his London office to reference something regarding one of his clients.

But whatever he did in the mornings, there was a good chance that he'd be up and at it before his mother was. Elin decided to ask Mrs Brightman later about the matter but, right now, as she walked along the corridor, she noticed Molly was headed towards her, a feather duster in her hand. The girl was wearing her grey apron, the one used for menial tasks around the house – it would be an ideal moment to ask her about dusting those shelves.

'Molly,' she said with a smile, 'when you're dusting around this morning, would you take care to clean Mr Lawrence's books and the shelves in the drawing room?'

Was she imagining things or was that a scowl on the girl's face? For a moment, she feared Molly was about to snap, 'No, I ruddy will not do as you say!' back at her but instead, she returned the smile.

'Yes, Mrs Edwards,' she said meekly as she headed towards the drawing room.

My mind must be playing tricks on me this morning. I was expecting a sharp retort there!

Thinking no more of the incident, she made for the kitchen.

* * *

Cook informed Elin that yes, Lawrence was up and around expecting his breakfast most mornings by around a half past seven, unlike his mother who rose at nine o'clock. But Cook reassured her that he hardly ever set a foot in the kitchen anyhow. But that wasn't enough to allay Elin's fears. It was too big a risk that he might encounter her and question why she was in work so early. That surely would compromise Mrs

Brightman's involvement in all of this – she'd been complicit in her silence. What was that legal term now that sprung to mind? Ah yes, aiding and abetting. She'd aided and abetted her by allowing her to make use of the Langton kitchen to run a business that supplied someone of nefarious character.

When Elin had been thumbing through those legal books, she'd found mention of the Accessories and Abettors Act of 1861, which mentioned that someone who had been a party to such a thing could be liable to be tried, indicted and punished as a principal offender. So, in other words, treated in the same manner as if they had committed the very offence themselves!

When Elin mentioned this to Cook later, the woman simply laughed. 'You have a strong moral streak running through you, girl, you really do,' she said, giving her a gentle push.

Elin blinked, astonished at Cook's cavalier attitude considering it had been hard to persuade her to have use of the kitchen in the first place. She'd had to cajole her a little. 'But I wouldn't want to get you into any trouble where you might get dismissed from this house, Mrs Brightman,' she said as she watched Cook carefully transport a saucepan of potatoes over to the hob to set it on to boil.

'Look,' Cook said firmly, when her task was complete, 'all of this is hardly a ruddy hanging offence!' She gestured towards the trays of pies cooling on the counter. 'The mistress has already seen and tasted them, so will think no more of it if she sees them in the future. She highly regards my work at this house, so she'd hardly dismiss me anyhow. Good cooks are hard to come by!' She picked up a wooden spoon and began to wag it back and forth in front of Elin's nose as though reprimanding a young child.

Elin sighed. 'It's not the mistress I'm concerned about.'

Cook ceased wagging the spoon and her forehead creased

into a soft frown. 'Who then? Just exactly *who* are you concerned about, Elin?'

'Mr Lawrence. He's very tied up with all sorts of legal stuff. I'm worried in case he discovers *who* the pies are for. Because Morgan Griffin has a previous criminal record.'

'Oh, I see,' said Cook, now making sense of the situation.

Elin continued. 'And the fact you told me he rises around half seven – if he were to catch a glimpse of me here at that time, he will question his mother about my presence at the house. And that simply wouldn't do.'

'You're such a worrier,' said Cook with a smile. 'If you feel that way but you wish to continue with your pie business, then why not think about setting up properly? Either run it from home with your husband's knowledge and approval, or find someplace else.'

Elin slowly nodded, all the while realising Wyn wouldn't like her to have something for herself. Something she might be praised for by others. Oh, he was happy enough for her to bring in a small wage for 'skivvying at the big house' as he put it, but he would never stand for her being in charge of her own business.

'I shall have to give it some consideration,' she said, chewing on her bottom lip.

'Maybe Mr Griffin would set up some cooking facilities for you on his premises?' The woman arched an eyebrow as Elin's stomach somersaulted. Now that would be a very big risk indeed. And in any case, how could she work there and at the Langton house at the same time? It was a dilemma.

* * *

Elin laid her wicker basket down on the scullery table back home. She'd been to one of the local shops to fetch some potatoes and carrots, as there was hardly anything in the house. She planned to make beef stew with dumplings. That shouldn't take too long as she had kept back some of the braised beef from her earlier pie-making venture. She had borrowed one of the tin bowls from the kitchen to transport it home, which she'd return discreetly tomorrow.

As she removed the covering cloth, she was surprised to see Frank at her side, lowering his head. 'My, my, that smells tasty.'

'Cook braised some beef earlier and it's in a rich gravy. She gave me some to take home,' she said. 'There was plenty left over.' Feeling bad now about lying to the man while realising she could hardly tell him the truth, she changed the subject. 'I'll make you a cup of tea while you're waiting. I just have to prepare the veg and make some dumplings.'

'Allow me to make you a cup of tea instead, Elin,' offered Frank as he laid a comforting hand on her shoulder. 'You work hard at that house all day and for us here, too. When our shift is over at the pit, we hardly lift another finger, but your work is ongoing.'

She smiled at him and nodded. 'Thank you. I'd appreciate that,' she said, all the while wondering why Wyn wasn't more like his father. If only...

* * *

By the time the meal was prepared, there was still no sign of Wyn.

'We've waited long enough for him,' said Frank with a sigh. 'Come on, let's eat. It's his loss. Otherwise, it will go cold.'

The pair ate in silence. All that could be heard was the tick of the clock on the mantelshelf and the occasional sound of their metal spoons clinking against the crockery. Elin ate without relish; she couldn't enjoy it as she had a sickening feeling in the pit of her stomach that all was not well. Wyn was being so secretive lately that it unnerved her, alongside his abusive behaviour. Frank, though, ate with gusto, and it was nice to see as he'd been off his food since Olwen's death.

Finally, when they'd both finished, she opened her mouth to say something but Frank said it for her. 'I know what you're about to ask, Elin. Where did Wyn go to this evening?'

She nodded at him.

'I'm sorry, but this time I really don't know. By the time I'd reached the pit gates, he'd gone. I asked a couple of people if they'd seen him but no one had.'

'Oh,' was all she managed to say. This time there was no excuse about helping some farmer who already had plenty of help in the form of his own sons. This time there was no excuse forthcoming. It was almost as though he was rubbing her nose in the fact he could do what the hell he liked with no repercussions. All those promises he'd made after he'd hit her seemed empty now. She had to conclude he was spending his time at the pub again and possibly frittering away the finances on a dubious card game.

She went to bed realising that Wyn wouldn't be home before she turned down the light of the oil lamp in their bedroom. The last time that had occurred was before he'd laid hands on her. Still, there was no use waiting up for him, as who knew what sort of a mood he'd be in on his return home; that's if he did return home before morning.

Sighing to herself, she slipped into her night gown and slid into bed. The sheets were cold, particularly as her husband's body wasn't there to keep her warm as it usually was. But then again, she'd been on tenterhooks of late, wondering if he'd take her by force again, yet for some reason since that fateful night, he hadn't. Nor had he even mentioned it to her. It was almost as though it had never happened in the first place, except she knew it had and was still living in the aftermath.

* * *

Elin had no idea what time it was when she heard raised voices outside the bedroom door. They appeared to be coming from the living room. One was her father-in-law's, who was yelling now, which was most unusual for him, as he was a mild-mannered sort of man. The other, of course, was Wyn's, whose tone of voice sounded defensive.

'You come back here at this time treating this place like a dosshouse! Where have you been, man? You're disrespecting your wife and me, your father who has put a roof over your head!'

'I'm sorry,' said Wyn. His voice wasn't slurred at all, so maybe he hadn't been at the ale.

'And by the sight of you...' Frank continued, then he lowered his voice so that Elin had to strain to listen to what was being said '...and the smell of you...'

She couldn't hear the rest so she got out of bed, padded along the cold floorboards, and put her ear to the door. Certain words she picked up on but the rest were missing. She heard the words, 'perfume' and 'chasing something'.

There was what sounded like a big apology from Wyn, and then Frank said, 'I'm off to bed and so should you be. We both have work in the morning.'

'Aye,' said Wyn with a tone of resignation, 'don't I ruddy know it.'

Fearing he might come crashing into the bedroom and take things out on her, she leapt into bed and shut her eyes tightly. Her plan was to pretend to be asleep, but he must have headed off to the scullery to see what there was to eat, as she heard the door going and footsteps as Frank undoubtedly headed off for bed.

Where on earth had Wyn been all this time? It must have been in the arms of another woman if perfume was mentioned. But who and why? She'd never left him short in that department and, to begin with, their lovemaking sessions had been good, but then she had noticed sometimes when he'd been drinking, he'd failed to perform. She'd never taken issue with it though, but maybe that night he'd raped her was a way to prove to her that he was a man who could have her whenever he wanted. One thing was for sure: there was no way he was going to have her this night, particularly if he'd been with another woman. She felt sick to the stomach at the thought of it.

It was a good twenty minutes or so later when the door opened and he climbed into bed beside her. She reckoned he must have had a wash before changing as she smelt no perfume on him.

There was a part of her that longed for the Wyn of old to take her in his arms and cuddle her as they once used to do, but since his mother's death, he seemed different somehow.

He wasn't the man she'd married – that was for sure.

* * *

The following morning, Elin rose early having kindled the fire in the hearth as she always did, so as not to arouse suspicion. Wyn would have no idea that she often left the house not long after he did to begin work on those pies at the Langton house.

Considering he'd arrived home late last night, he was full of the joys of spring this morning. And though he and his father barely exchanged a word with one another over the breakfast table, the tension between them was palpable. She wondered what they'd be like walking to the pit together. Probably Frank would have another dig at him or they'd walk some distance apart.

Before leaving and taking his snap tin from her, Wyn said, 'I am sorry about last night...'

She waited, expecting him to say more – some excuse about him helping his friend on the farm again – but he gave none. 'I wasn't drinking or gambling, just wanted to break loose for a night, that was all.'

She nodded at him. What could she say? If she was antagonistic towards him then he might turn that against her later, and by heaven she didn't want that – no, not at all.

She'd aim to keep the peace at all costs, for Frank's sake.

* * *

Later, when all her baking was complete at the Langton house and she'd finished her morning's work, Elin was about to take a break when there was a soft rap at the back door. She drew it open to see Morgan Griffin stood there.

'I wasn't expecting to see you so soon, but the pies are ready if you want them?'

He nodded at her. 'I've not come for the pies. Well, I have, I suppose, but I needed to speak to you first, as I've an idea.'

She glanced anxiously behind her. Mrs Langton was around somewhere and she didn't want to arouse suspicion. 'We can't talk here,' she said. 'I'll step out the back with you. Meet me by that gardening shed in the corner. Wait behind there.'

He grinned as though finding high old amusement in the situation. 'It's like that, is it?' Then he nodded with understanding.

Elin waited a little while before following him to the shed. They were well shaded by trees and bushes from the side so obscured from view from the house itself, but as a precaution, she spoke quietly as she rubbed the palms of her hands on her pinafore, which were perspiring profusely. Whatever happened she had no intention of jeopardising her job at the house.

'It's like this, see,' said Morgan, drawing closer to her. 'I've had an idea, as I realise these aren't easy circumstances working from this house as a base, especially when Lawrence returns.'

She drew a sharp intake of breath and nodded, then let it go. 'Yes. What do you suggest?'

'I'm taking charge of a large oven this afternoon. It's from an old pub what's being pulled down. The landlord said I could have it for a good price. Thought if I install it at my pub, then you can do some of your baking there.' He hesitated for a moment. 'If it suits, that is?'

The tension she'd been feeling began to ebb away. It might be the answer to her prayers. 'Yes, it will suit indeed. But how shall we work things out?'

'My suggestion is this... from what you've been telling me, you work on the pies here in this kitchen from about half past six in the morning until around eight or half past eight, before your usual time to begin work at the house, right?'

'That is correct.'

'What I could do is send a coach to pick you up from your house at around six as your husband will be beginning work by then so won't be around, then the coach will bring you to my pub where you'll have a couple of hours to prepare the pies and bake them ready for the lunchtime trade. The girls can warm them and serve them up later.'

'What girls?' She blinked. She'd seen no female staff behind the bar, only one or two barmen, and one young lad who collected the tankards and glasses.

'The working girls. They're up out of their beds by noon; it shall all fit in nicely for the lunchtime trade.'

Elin almost choked on her own saliva to think of some of those good-time girls serving up her bill of fare.

Noticing her shocked expression, Morgan said, 'Of course, if you'd rather return and dish them up yourself?'

'No, no,' she said rather too quickly. 'That would be pushing things. After nine o'clock I need to remain at the big house. Questions would be asked.'

They would too as she was only allowed twenty minutes for her luncheon break.

'So, you'd be happy for my girls to dish up those pies to customers?'

She exhaled. 'Yes.'

What did it matter to her? She wasn't the one who'd be consuming them, and as far as she was concerned, once those pies were baked – as long as all was satisfactory with them – what happened after that was none of her concern.

'That's good.' Morgan nodded approvingly. 'I'll wait here for them, then?'

She wrinkled her nose in puzzlement. 'For who?'

'For the pies you baked this morning of course!' He chuckled.

Thinking of working at the pub had made her completely forget why he was here in the first place. She returned to the kitchen and handed the trays of pies over to him. 'I'll nip back in and fetch the sacks of flour and everything else,' she said. 'Now that we shan't be needing to store them here any longer.'

'Aye. Good idea! Get rid of the incriminating evidence!'

She wondered how many times he'd said that before.

Once she'd handed everything over to Morgan and watched him loading them up on his cart, she breathed a sigh of relief. Now there was no need to ever worry about wrongdoing at the house ever again.

Morgan took his seat on top of the cart and, taking the horse's reins, said, 'The coach will arrive at exactly six o'clock to your house in the morning!' He tipped his hat at her.

'Oh, not to the house, please!' Her hands flew to her face.

He smiled. 'Where then? Where's the best place to pick you up so you'll not be seen climbing aboard?'

She thought carefully for a moment. 'There's a pub on the canal bank – make it near there. If it's seen, people might assume either something's being delivered or it's picking up someone who's been there overnight.' She realised her reasoning was daft, but it would be better than the coach drawing up in her street.

'Very well,' said Morgan, looking thoroughly pleased with himself.

'And one more thing,' said Elin, looking intently at the man.

'Oh?' He quirked a questioning eyebrow.

'Please promise me that you won't slip up and tell Lawrence I've been paying off my debt to you this way, until I've had a chance to explain myself when he returns home.'

'You have my word!' said Morgan, tipping his hat to her and then replacing it on his head.

Watching him steer the cart away, Elin wondered what the heck she was doing. How had it come to this? Working for a man like Morgan Griffin and feeling beholden to him.

As she made her way towards the kitchen, she failed to see someone quickly rearrange one of the lace curtains upstairs.

11

Elin stamped her feet, blowing on her gloveless hands in an effort to keep warm. She'd catch her death while waiting for Mr Griffin's coach to arrive if she wasn't careful. She wished now that she'd worn her cape instead of her shawl, and was in two minds on whether to run back to the house to fetch it when she heard the familiar sounds of horses' hooves and the rattling sound of a coach pulling up beside her.

To her surprise, Griffin himself was leaning out through the window. He raised his bowler hat to her. 'Good morning, my lovely!'

'Haven't you got the sense you were born with?' Elin scowled at him because he was causing a scene and she hoped there was no one awake at the pub to see this spectacle. Surely it would sport idle gossip in the village.

Just fancy that! Wyndham Edwards's wife getting into a coach with a nefarious character from China!

He smiled and, raising an index finger to his lips, said in a hushed tone, 'I'm sorry, I didn't think. Don't concern yourself though, as it shan't happen again. It's only this morning I thought to accompany you to make you feel reassured on your journey, and I intend to show you where everything is.'

Now she felt dreadful for chastising him – he was only thinking of her welfare after all.

'That's all right then,' she said, her chin jutting out. Then he opened the coach door. She stepped up, raising the skirts of her dress as she did so, so she wouldn't stumble. He took her hand, escorting her safely inside, and she closed the door.

Easing herself into the padded leather seat, she exhaled and then gazed out of the window. That was good: there was no one outside the pub and no twitching curtains either. She decided there and then that she was going to give the man the benefit of the doubt as to what his motives were.

A sharp crack of the coachman's whip and a sudden jolt as the horses pulled away from the pub, and they were on their way.

* * *

When the coach pulled up outside the archway leading to China, Elin glanced around. 'Why has it stopped here?' Her forehead creased into a concerned frown.

'Because, my dear, there is no way a coach is going to be able to descend those steps leading to that huddle of hovels!' He threw back his head and laughed, making her feel very silly indeed. Of course, this is where Lawrence's coach must have pulled up the night he'd brought her here, though it had been too dark to see much. She'd forgotten that there was only one way in and one way out of China. Mrs Brightman had told her that at one time there were even men keeping watch over that entrance arch to send word of any intruders.

Griffin left the coach first and escorted her down the steps, where he tipped his hat to the coachman and then dipped into his pocket to hand the man what appeared to be a sovereign. Elin gulped. She wasn't used to seeing such large sums of money. She guessed that sovereign wasn't just payment for today's trip though – maybe it would cover her journey to and from the pub for some time to come.

'Come along,' he said, linking arms with her.

Elin shivered. What if her husband or someone she knew were to see him escorting her? That would surely cause ructions at home and malicious gossip around the village. As they descended the stone steps leading to the dwellings, Griffin keeping an eye she didn't trip on her way down, she inhaled deeply and instantly regretted it as she felt her stomach heave. The stench was like rotten eggs and cabbages!

Noticing her distress as she fought to keep the contents of her stomach in place, Griffin said, 'Don't worry, this is the worst part when the wind is blowing across from the river. It's all the sewage, you see. Around these parts, a lot of people throw their mess out of their doors and windows and then, when it rains, it all gets washed down to the river.'

'No wonder there's been outbreaks of cholera in the area over the years, then!'

'I won't deny that,' said Griffin. 'One day there'll be a proper way to keep Merthyr clean. But for the time being we have to learn how to live in a cesspit. Though...' he paused for a moment as he rubbed his moustache as though in contemplation '...we do have standards at my pub.'

Standards? thought Elin. *What sort of standards?* For she didn't notice any the times she had visited the pub.

Griffin chuckled. 'I wasn't referring to any shenanigans going on at the pub itself. I meant the people who work in it. They keep it as clean as possible. You won't find any bodily fluids thrown out of its windows. Anything like that is taken in buckets and thrown directly into the River Taff itself, not to stench the place up.'

She didn't know if she was satisfied with that answer or not, as to her, it was a filthy practice. And that sort of stuff floating around in the river, it didn't bear thinking about. Children played in that area and she'd seen people bathing in the waters on hot summer days. On its path to Cardiff, the river flowed beside the village she lived in, so no doubt it brought all that waste in close proximity to the local community, but thankfully their house wasn't on the riverbank itself.

Elin was surprised at how quiet the area was this time of the morning. No doubt many were sleeping off the excesses of drink from the night before. Griffin pushed open the pub door, which she was shocked to see wasn't even locked. Immediately, the aroma of stale ale and tobacco smoke hit her hard, but at least it was better than the stench of rotten eggs and cabbages.

It was dark inside the bar room itself, but there was enough light filtering through some chinks in the heavy drapes to illuminate their way.

'Aggie, who helps out here, will open the curtains when she arrives for work,' Griffin said.

'Is she one of your girls, then?' Elin asked.

'Good gracious, no!' He threw back his head and chuckled. 'Aggie's almost old enough to be my grandmother! She's a salt-of-the-earth sort of person who has been with me and this pub for a number of years – she's part of the fixtures and furnishings now. She comes in and cleans up after the night before, ready for the pub to open its doors again at midday. She washes up all the tankards, cleans the tables too and sometimes cooks for me. She also arranges things for my girls.'

Elin frowned. 'How'd you mean?'

'Well, she takes any bookings from the punters, if you get my drift.' He tapped the side of his nose.

'You mean she's a bit of a madam, then?' Elin was incredulous with disbelief.

He nodded. 'In a manner of speaking, yes. Though she's getting a little old for that sort of caper, I suppose.'

Elin didn't know what to think. At least he was being honest with her, she assumed. She followed him over to the bar and watched him raise the wooden hatch, to allow her access, and they walked through behind it past the bar itself and into a little corridor, which led to a large room.

'Now this is the kitchen where I've recently installed that new cooker.' He gestured with a flourish towards a black cast-iron cooking range that sported a brass pot rail and a couple of doors. 'It's fuelled with coal. I lit it earlier before going to fetch you, so it ought to be nice and hot by now.'

She frowned. 'Where are all the utensils I need, though?'

'Over there!' He pointed to a long wooden counter behind them, which had a stone sink attached to it. 'There are all the bags of flour, the lard, the beef and everything else that I picked up from the Langton house.'

'Yes, but what about the cooking tins?'

He stroked his chin. 'Oh dear, I hadn't thought of those.' Looking at her distressed face, he chuckled. 'Of course I had. I went to the ironmonger's yesterday to get the pie tins and other things and managed to obtain some other stuff for you from the marketplace; they're in that cupboard above the sink.'

A feeling of relief flooded through Elin. She couldn't afford to waste any time as she needed to get back to the house no later than nine o'clock or her presence would be missed. 'You seem to have thought of everything, Mr Griffin.'

He nodded. 'But if there's anything else you need, I can

easily get it for you and quickly too as there are many folks around here what owe me a favour. They'd even loan their own stuff until I can buy it for you.'

Elin placed her wicker basket down on the counter and went to inspect the cupboard, and was relieved to see all she needed was there, complete with rolling pin.

'I'll just show you how to use the range and then I'm off to bed,' he said with a smile.

'Bed?'

'Aye, once you get to know me, you'll understand why I usually sleep in until the pub opens at twelve o'clock. It's because I'm up all night! I made an exception for you today, it being your first day here and all. I'll ask one of the girls to light the stove ready for your arrival tomorrow morning instead.'

Now she was beginning to understand. He must be up all night involved in gambling games and such, though she daren't think too much about what the 'and such' really meant!

* * *

Following a few mishaps, which involved almost burning a whole tray of pies, Elin settled down into a routine. She discovered this cooking range Griffin had purchased was far fiercer than the one back at the Langton house. She managed to scrape a few black burnt bits off the pies' crusts and was able to persevere with it all. The task consumed her so much that it wasn't until Aggie arrived, puffing on a clay pipe, she realised how late it must be.

Aggie was one of the oldest people she'd ever met and never before had she seen a woman smoke a pipe. Her weather-beaten face had so many wrinkles ingrained in it, anyone would be hard pressed to place a pin between them.

'So yewse the new girl I've heard so much about,' she said, taking another puff from her pipe, filling the air with acrid smoke. To Elin's relief, the woman rested her pipe on a saucer on the counter and now appeared to be chewing on something, which Elin guessed might be tobacco, reminding her of a cow chewing the cud.

'Yes. I'm Elin Edwards from Abercanaid.'

'My name's Aggie Dunbar.' She smiled, revealing there was hardly a tooth left in her mouth.

'Do you have any idea of the time?' Elin asked anxiously.

'It's not long since turned the hour, my lovely. I heard the bells chime as I passed the parish church on my way here.'

Elin's hands flew to her face. 'Oh, my goodness! I ought to be back at the Langton house by now,' she said, undoing the strings of her apron, then tossing it into her basket. 'I better get a move on; the coach will be waiting for me near the archway.'

Aggie nodded. 'I did notice a coach there when I passed by, but thought it was waiting for His Lordship!'

'Lordship?' Who was the woman referring to? Elin wrinkled her nose.

'Otherwise known as him upstairs, The Squire!' She pointed to the ceiling and threw back her head, cackling with glee.

Then the penny dropped. Of course, Aggie meant Mr Griffin.

Elin smiled nervously at the woman. 'I'd better make tracks. I'll see you tomorrow and hopefully, I'll be more organised by then.'

'If yewse more organised by then, then you shan't see me at all,' said Aggie in a sage fashion. 'Though we might encounter one another by the arch or I'll see yewse getting into that fancy coach.'

Elin wrapped her shawl around her slim figure and placed

her bonnet on her head, carefully tying the ribbons beneath her chin. 'Hopefully,' she said. She bit her lower lip and fixed her gaze on the woman. 'There are six trays of pies covered with tray cloths cooling on the counter over there. If you can ensure that no one from the pub pilfers them, I'd be most grateful to you.'

Aggie nodded. 'Don't worry, missus, there's a room just off this kitchen where they'll fit nicely and be out of harm's way. No one's getting their filthy mitts on those until after midday when they'll have to pay a penny a piece for 'em.'

Elin smiled appreciatively at the woman. 'I'll best be off!' she said as she whisked past her, thinking so far it had been an eventful sort of morning. Now she worried in case her absence from the house would be noticed, but then again, Cook had promised to cover for her if anything went wrong.

* * *

Apologising to the coachman for keeping him waiting for her for so long, Elin climbed into the carriage. He simply smiled and said it mattered not a jot to him as Mr Griffin was paying him by the hour each way. Still, she reassured him that it shouldn't happen again. After using that cooking range this morning, she had more of an idea now how it worked. But nevertheless, she would have to speed up preparing the pastry and cooking the meat ready to place inside the pies in the future.

Flustered and breathless, Elin arrived at the house. Cook was in the middle of kneading a batch of dough as she entered the kitchen. The woman turned around; her reddened face had a fine dusting of flour dotted over her nose and cheeks.

'So, time was a bit tight for you this morning, I take it?'

Elin blew out a hard breath. 'Yes, it took a long while for me to get used to that cooking range after this one.' Then she frowned. 'I suppose Mrs Langton is up and about and waiting to see me?'

'I've just checked with Molly. She said as she couldn't find you, she helped Mrs Langton to get dressed and I sent her breakfast into the drawing room about fifteen minutes since. She ought to have finished it by now. If you just pop in to see her and explain I sent you to the shop. Say I'd run out of yeast to bake the bread.'

'But I haven't been there,' Elin protested.

'I know that and so do you, but Mrs Langton doesn't, does she?' Cook quirked a supercilious eyebrow.

Elin smiled as she removed her shawl and bonnet and hung them on a peg near the pantry. 'But what about Molly? What does she think?'

'I told her the exact same thing. But tomorrow, please ensure you return here before nine o'clock as I can't keep covering for you.' She turned back towards the dough on the counter and began to pummel it with some force. It appeared as if she were taking her frustrations out on it. Elin hadn't a clue who it might be, hoping it wasn't herself, but she guessed it could be Molly, as the girl had a tendency to wind Cook up.

Elin brushed down her skirts and patted her hair – she was feeling a little windswept after this morning's ordeal – then she headed for the drawing room where she found Mrs Langton seated on a high-backed velvet chair behind a low-level table. The woman chose not to eat her food in the dining room unless she had company, she'd explained to Elin once, as sitting at one end of that long mahogany table by herself made her feel very lonely indeed.

Initially, Elin hadn't noticed Molly attending to the fire, as she knelt by the side of the hearth to stoke it up with a poker, but when she did, the girl glared at her, making her feel quite uncomfortable.

Elin stiffened as she walked past her towards her employer.

'Good morning, Mrs Langton,' she greeted as she glanced down at the remains of a hard-boiled egg and some crusts of bread.

Mrs Langton, who was in the process of taking a cup of coffee, placed her cup down in its saucer, looked up and smiled.

'Good morning, Elin. Molly said you weren't around as you'd gone to the shop on an errand for Cook.'

'Yes, I returned about ten minutes since. I've been with Mrs Brightman, helping to sort out the kitchen.'

'Did you manage to purchase any yeast?'

Elin nodded. 'Yes, I did.'

What else could she say? If Cook was in the middle of baking, then she had to have had some yeast already, so it was a necessary lie on her part.

Molly laid down the poker, obviously now satisfied with how the fire was kindling, and stood, turning her attention to Elin. 'That's strange.'

'What's strange?' Elin made eye contact with the girl.

'You having to pop out to get a packet of yeast for Mrs Brightman. There was plenty of it here last week.'

Elin laughed nervously. 'You know what Cook is like – she's always baking something or other.'

'Aye, like those pies she's been baking lately. Right tasty they are an' all!'

Molly had a gleam in her eyes now and Elin felt like she was toying with her. She knew! She had to know, the way she was taunting her.

'Yes,' Elin continued. 'She needs a lot of yeast as she bakes bread on a daily basis along with yeast cake and tea bread. You can never have too much yeast!' She cast Molly a hard penetrative stare, as if to say, *Hey, what's your game, missy?*

Silenced now, Molly dismissed herself in front of Mrs Langton and left the room. It seemed obvious to Elin that the girl had become suspicious of her whereabouts that morning. Elin was just going to have to hope she didn't slip up.

A cold chill ran the length of her spine when she thought of Molly's reaction and a familiar saying came to mind: *Keep your friends close and your enemies closer.* She'd made an enemy all right; that much was certain. But what puzzled her most was how did Molly realise she was doing something she shouldn't have been doing at the house? She'd done her very best to hide her pie-making activity from the staff – only Cook knew and had made out she was the one baking them – and as far as Elin was aware, she hadn't slipped up either.

12

Lawrence was due home, so the staff were busy preparing things for him. This time he would be staying a while longer, so his bedroom was well aired and Molly was dispatched to light the fire in the hearth. His bed linen was changed too. Mrs Langton had a thing about giving him clean bedding on his return after being amongst 'all those filthy London germs' as she put it.

Cook was busy baking something special for Lawrence, which appeared to be some sort of game pie with a selection of vegetables, to be followed by a bread-and-butter pudding with fresh cream. Elin had to smile at the thought of game pie being served up to the regulars at Griffin's place. They were happy as things were and she guessed game pie wouldn't suit their salacious palates. They were satisfied with beef pies and plenty of ale to wash it down with. Still, she thought maybe she ought to experiment with a selection of fillings to provide a bit of variety. Maybe chicken and ham and corned beef and onion?

The main thing was, she didn't want Lawrence to discover she'd been doing any sort of favours for Griffin, nor that she'd been paid for them. As far as he was concerned, he was going to pay the man the remainder of the debt on his return. If he hadn't been expected in London the following day, he'd have visited the bank to get the remainder there and then, but as it was, he'd had to leave the house at the crack of dawn. Now, though, she realised it was imperative she explain things to Lawrence on her own terms – a necessary withholding of information on her part, until the right time emerged. He'd express his disapproval – of course he would; she was well aware of that – but these days, she was prepared to be her own woman, having come to realise that the only person she could really rely on was herself.

She'd already warned Griffin not to let on, but then again, wouldn't he now be accepting payment under false pretences as the debt was already paid off? More than the debt really, with all the work she'd put in lately. She supposed she could walk away from it all right now but deep down she didn't want to. She quite liked Morgan Griffin, deciding he wasn't as bad as depicted by folk. From what she could see of him, he would do people a favour or a good turn and even loaned them money when they were in dire need, so he couldn't be all bad. What she'd had trouble reconciling with, though, was the thought he was housing prostitutes at his pub – *that* she had an issue with. But at least those particular ladies were being paid for their services and from what Aggie told her, they were treated well too. They were clothed and fed, paid a wage and had decent accommodation, which meant they were better off than many in Merthyr Tydfil.

Elin wondered whether Lawrence's friend, Arabella, would be invited to dine at the house again over the following few days. With that thought came a sudden pang of jealousy, full force. She'd developed feelings for him of late, and although he wasn't of her class or creed, she'd felt close to the man. It was strange; the two men who treated her with respect and admiration were like chalk and cheese. Lawrence was a man of strong morals and principles and Griffin was shady and broke the rules. Yet, both had a similarity to one another in that they liked to help people out – one was a rule maker and the other a rule breaker. Both were so different to her husband, though, who treated her with utter disdain at times and who ill-used her, yet he was the one she'd expected to treat her well in this life, cherishing her until the day she died.

As the day wore on, she became so excited at the prospect of seeing Lawrence again that her heart began to pound profusely and her palms became moist. What if she finished her shift before his arrival and she might not see him then until tomorrow morning? What if his coach was delayed on the journey home? She'd never felt so keen to see a man in all her life. With some regret, she recalled how, when she'd first met Wyn, she'd experienced a similar sensation – those little butterflies fluttering away in her stomach at the prospect of seeing him again. Now she had butterflies of a different sort in her stomach when she thought of him – the feeling of anxiety and dread that he might hurt her in some way again.

Molly had been shooting her strange looks all day. She'd dismissed them as sour grapes to begin with, as the girl was obviously miffed at the way Cook had been so sharp with her. She also couldn't have been happy with the way she'd had to undertake Elin's duties that day she'd returned late to the house. But all Elin had done was be nice to her. Earlier that day, she'd even summoned her to the kitchen to take a cuppa together, but Molly had refused, saying she had far too much to do to take a break. Later, she'd spied the girl from Mrs Langton's bedroom window, which overlooked the back garden, seated on a low wall drinking something from a cup – she'd taken her time too, so obviously she'd had time for a break after all. It was becoming increasingly obvious the girl would no longer take orders from her or even speak civilly, so she worried and fretted about what to do.

She discussed the matter with Cook that afternoon.

'From what I can see, she's annoyed with you about that pie business, maybe because you never let her in on it?' Cook shrugged her shoulders.

'It could be that, I suppose,' said Elin as she watched the woman stir the custard on the stove in preparation to pour over the prepared slices of bread and butter.

'It might be the best thing if you take her to task about it to clear the air,' Cook suggested, raising her eyebrows.

'Aye, maybe you're right.' Elin gave an approving nod. 'It might not hurt to do that, as we can't carry on like this. By the way, is Miss Arabella likely to be dining here over the weekend?'

'Nope,' said Cook. 'Why do you ask?'

'Er, no reason really.' Elin's face grew hot and she hoped she wasn't blushing. She didn't want to give Cook the impression she liked Lawrence in that respect, so she changed the subject. 'Anything I can help you with?'

'Yes, can you take over from me here, please, until the custard thickens. I just want to check that game pie in the oven.'

Elin nodded and she took the silver whisk from the woman's grasp and began to whisk up the custard – slowly at first and then more vigorously.

'Don't take your eyes off it for a moment, mind,' Cook warned. 'Don't want no lumps in it or for it to burn and catch in the pan. There's nothing worse than lumpy, burnt custard!'

Elin had just removed the pan of custard from the stove on Cook's orders when there was a commotion out in the hallway.

Floss, the laundry maid, popped her head around the kitchen door. 'The master's home!' she shouted to the pair.

'Oh, my goodness!' yelled Cook as she patted her brow with her handkerchief and then proceeded to wave it around as if it were the white flag of surrender. 'I'm most unprepared for this – I wasn't expecting him back for some time yet. He must have left London earlier than he'd planned.'

Although Elin's heart was silently racing beneath the bodice of her dress, she took a deep composing breath and let it out again. 'Don't worry yourself, Mrs Brightman. Lawrence, er, I mean Mr Lawrence is not like that. He'll understand.'

Mrs Brightman, who had seemed all of a fluster at the announcement from the young laundry maid, appeared to calm down. 'You're quite right of course, Elin.'

'In any case, if he's hungry meanwhile, you can offer him some other sort of refreshment like a sandwich and a cup of coffee, can't you?'

'Quite right,' said Cook as she made to open the oven door to check on the pie, the crust of which was beginning to brown nicely by now.

'I'll just go and check what he needs,' said Elin. Her mouth was dry with apprehension, and she hoped it wouldn't be evident to him.

Leaving the kitchen, she closed the door behind her in time to see Molly open the front door. The girl glared when she glimpsed her approach but she did not move away to attend to her duties.

As Lawrence stepped over the threshold, his dark hair tousled and windswept, making him look even more handsome than usual, Elin felt as if her heart had stopped beating. Then he stamped his long leather boots on the doormat to ensure he didn't bring any muck into the house and her breath hitched in her throat. He caught sight of her, his blue eyes sparkling mischievously, and he opened his mouth to say something, but Molly beat him to it.

'Mr Langton,' she said. 'I need a word with you, please.'

'Yes?' He turned sharply towards her and Elin could tell he was slightly annoyed by the girl's presence. Maybe he wanted to greet Elin alone without having the annoying maid by his side.

'There's something I need to tell you...' She stared at Elin.

Lawrence's forehead creased into a soft frown. 'Can't it possibly wait? I've only just set foot through the door here. You haven't even closed it behind me yet!' He sported a smile now, trying to make light of the situation.

'No, sir. It can't.' She closed the door and then turned to face him.

'Go on, then,' said Elin. 'Tell Mr Langton what you're bursting to say!'

This had the effect of removing the wind from Molly's sails and now she seemed speechless, but Lawrence, who appeared intrigued, gently cajoled her. 'Yes, please do tell me. It must be something of importance to you.'

Molly's face reddened at the attention and finally she found her voice. 'I can't, sir...' She shook her head.

'Then I'll say it for her,' said Elin. 'She's been annoyed with me for days now. I might as well tell you. I think it's because I've been making pies and selling them. I made use of the kitchen here for a few days, though not using any ingredients from this house. Now I've found an alternative premises to work from, so it's no longer a problem. I am sorry, Mr Langton. It didn't interfere with my work here at all as I was doing it very early in the mornings before my work at the house began. Only one day I was a little late and Molly here had to help your mother get dressed; that was all. Other than that, the staff did well from my little pie-making venture as all of them got to taste the fruits of my labour. Even your mother tried one. Though I have to confess, I didn't explain to her what I was up to.'

Lawrence's face broke into a wide grin, appearing bemused by the situation. 'Is that all?' He chuckled and, looking at Molly, said, 'Off you go now, you silly thing. It was hardly a hanging offence, was it?'

Molly lowered her head in shame as she slowly made her way up the staircase.

'Is there more to it than that?' he asked, looking Elin in the eyes.

She nodded as she bit her lower lip. 'I'll explain all later. But for now, would you like a pot of coffee and something to eat after your long journey?'

Without breaking eye contact, he whispered, 'Yes, I would appreciate that, Elin. I missed your company very much when I was away.'

She yearned to say the same thing back to him but was prevented from doing so in case anyone was eavesdropping. Instead, she just nodded and said, 'Sit yourself down, sir. I'll attend to things for you.'

She needed to put some space between them as her feelings were racing out of control. She imagined him taking her passionately in his arms and kissing her tenderly. The thoughts she was having just weren't respectable at all; they were thoughts no decent married woman ought to be having. And if Wyn were to find out, what would he do to her? It wasn't worth taking the risk, no matter how she felt about the man. Still, she reminded herself, Lawrence was only here for a couple of weeks and then he'd go back to London for a long time and her life would return to normal once again.

* * *

'Look,' said Lawrence later, 'I'm pleased for you for having the nous to set up your own pie-making venture, really, I am. What I'm not so keen on though is that you've done it as a way to repay Mr Griffin. That simply will not do.' He shook his head as though trying to dismiss all thoughts of her being connected to the man. 'I've been to the bank to get the money to pay him off, but obviously, that's not necessary now!' She could see the hurt expression on his face and now his eyes appeared guarded.

Elin frowned. 'But it's all working out very well for me.'

His eyes flashed dangerously. 'That may be so at the moment, but what would happen if your husband were to run up more debt from the fellow? You might be forever and a day trying to pay it off and be indebted to Morgan Griffin for life. Do you really want that?'

'Well, er, no.' She had to admit he had a point.

He relaxed now and smiled at her. 'Then what we shall do is ensure to provide you with suitable premises to work from. Somewhere you can rent. Meanwhile…' he stroked his chin '…I shall have a word with Mr Griffin myself about the situation.'

Elin nodded but, in some ways, she felt a pang of regret at having to part company with Morgan Griffin and she didn't know why. But maybe it would be all for the best.

She was still mulling things over when she returned home, astonished to find her husband waiting for her as she walked in through the door. This was most unusual as lately he'd been keeping late hours again.

'Where on earth have you been?' he demanded, his eyes widening, expecting an answer.

'I'm not late coming home, am I?' she asked cheerfully. Then she glanced at the clock on the mantelpiece, gulping as she realised it was an hour later than her usual time to arrive home. She figured it must have been because she'd been enjoying chatting with Lawrence so much. What she'd thought had delayed her for ten minutes had turned into one hour. But that was how time felt in his presence – it seemed to fly past.

'I am sorry,' she said, now placing her basket on the scullery table and removing her shawl before draping it over one of the wooden chairs. 'I'll get on with supper now.' She untied the ribbons of her bonnet and tossed it on the table. 'I thought about making a corned beef stew; that shouldn't take too long. There's a tin of corned beef in the cupboard.' She made to open the kitchen cupboard but felt a strong arm around her neck, gripping tightly as he dragged her away. His lock on her was so tight, she felt herself struggling for breath, but his arm only tightened as she desperately tried to claw it away with her fingernails.

'You think corned beef stew is good enough for me and my father when we've toiled for twelve hours in the bowels of the earth, do you?' A spray of spittle hit her cheek as she struggled to break free from his grasp. Then as if coming to his senses, he loosened his grip.

She rubbed her sore neck. 'S... sorry, Wyn,' she gasped, her voice sounding croaky now. 'Of course I'll make you something else. A... anything you want at all.' Tears filled her eyes. How had it come to this? She'd been walking on air coming home and now she felt in the depths of despair.

Wyn released her from his grasp and roughly, he shoved her so that she fell on the flagstone floor, striking her head on the cupboard. Then she heard him unbuckling his belt, reminding her of the night he'd raped her. Dear Lord, please, no! But then she realised he was about to belt her instead, and she didn't know which would be worse.

'Please...' she yelled as she held up her hands to protect her face. The silver buckle end of the belt, like a whip, flew towards her. It was obvious he intended to disfigure her. The buckle slapped hard against one of her hands, delivering a stinging blow, and she cried out in pain. But at least it did not make contact with her face. And then to her relief, she heard another voice from behind him.

'Wyn! What the hell are you doing? I didn't bring you up to lay a finger on anyone, never mind a woman, your wife!'

Through splayed fingers, she peeped to see Frank stood beside his son, with such a look of horror on his face, she could have wept for the man. It must have been a tremendous shock to witness the sight before him. Her fingers were warm and wet as she realised her hand was bleeding. And when she looked up again, Wyn had gone, the back door banging behind him, obviously annoyed that his father had witnessed such a despicable act, making himself look bad both as a husband and a son.

'I'm so sorry, Elin,' Frank said, crouching to help her to her feet. 'I'll get a bowl of water so you can wash your hand, shall I?'

She nodded at him and then burst into tears. Oh, how she hated for her father-in-law to see her in this mess, but none of it was any of her doing. She sat at the table while Frank bathed her hand with a wash cloth dipped into an enamel bowl of fresh water, gently patting it dry with a clean towel.

'You shouldn't have to do this for me.' She sniffed, looking at him through glazed eyes. Why couldn't Wyn be as tender and compassionate as his own father was?

'Of course I should,' he said, smiling at her. 'Many a collier has had an injury like this underground and I've tended to them from time to time, though this was no accident.' He shook his head. 'I can't believe my own son has done this to you, Elin. He's no longer welcome in this house.'

'Oh, Frank...' Tears began to spill down her cheeks. 'You can't banish him from here; he's your son. He's missing his mother.'

'I'm missing her too, Elin, but I don't go around treating people like this. I'm guessing this isn't the first time, either? That time you had a black eye when you claimed to have tripped over, Wyn did that?' He arched his eyebrows.

She nodded. 'Yes, that was the first time. Wyn and alcohol just don't mix. Do you think he's been drinking already this evening?'

'He might have had the opportunity, I suppose, though I thought he'd gone home straight from work, not via the pub this time.'

A thought occurred to her then: she'd always blamed the booze for her husband's actions towards her, so foolishly had thought if he gave up the drink then he'd treat her much better. But if it were the case that now he seemed to be entirely sober, then alcohol couldn't be blamed at all – it was Wyn himself responsible for his actions, and that thought chilled her to the bone.

* * *

Wyn did not return home that night, even though she had lain awake for many hours straining to listen for his key in the lock, her stomach feeling unsettled with fear.

The following morning at breakfast, Frank was unusually quiet. Before leaving for the pit, he pecked a kiss on her cheek. 'There's always a home for you here, Elin,' he said, laying a hand on her shoulder, 'though I quite understand if you'd prefer to get away from here, given the circumstances.'

She nodded gratefully at him. 'I'll have a think about it,

thank you.' She forced a smile as he made to leave, closing the back door behind him. The truth of the matter was she felt caught between the Devil and the deep blue sea. If she remained where she was, there was a good chance Wyn would return home and maybe strike her again, worse this time, when his father wasn't around. If she left and asked to stay at the Langton house, then she knew she'd find it difficult to curb her feelings for Lawrence. So, what could she do?

Maybe she ought to have let her parents into the fact that her marriage was not all honey with roses around the door, but she hadn't wanted to concern them. Her father suffered badly with his chest after years of working underground and Mam had enough on her plate right now, taking care of him and the rest of the family. No, she couldn't inflict any of her personal torment on them right now; it just wouldn't be fair. In any case, it would be the first place Wyn would seek her out and maybe he'd cause trouble for them all.

There is somewhere else you could go... a little voice from within herself whispered.

Of course, she could ask Morgan Griffin if she might lodge with him, but then she'd have to go through the humiliation of explaining what Wyn had done to her. There was no love lost between either of them after that gambling debt business. Morgan despised the fact that Wyn hadn't paid off his debt to him, and Wyn didn't like the fact the man had sent two heavies to their home to cause damage.

But if she went to the pub to ask Mr Griffin a favour, then she'd be even more indebted to him than she already was. Lawrence's warning about that rang in her ears.

She was toying with the idea when the back door burst open. Fearing it was her husband, she had the overwhelming urge to vomit yet she remained rooted to the spot. But then she relaxed, letting out a little sigh of relief, when she realised it was Frank, and not Wyn.

'I'll forget my head one of these days.' He chuckled as he approached the table to get to his snap tin. 'I won't last the shift without my cheese butties and Welsh cakes.'

'Oh no, you don't want to leave those at home. Though when I'd noticed, I would have taken them to you.' She smiled, realising she'd not been herself of late. The way she felt just then when Frank returned unexpectedly, fearing it was Wyn, was enough to make her decide she just had to get away from this place – it was no longer a safe sanctuary for her.

'See you later, Elin!' Frank said cheerfully, and she nodded at him with some regret.

When her father-in-law closed the door once again, she knew in her heart that Frank wouldn't be seeing her later that day. She couldn't remain here a moment longer. She felt a modicum of guilt for abandoning the man who had been like a father to her since she'd moved into his home, but she had to think of herself now.

Quickly, she flew around the house stuffing clothing and small possessions into two carpet bags that she'd brought with her when she married Wyn. No, what she'd do was leave Frank a letter, placing it on his pillow so her husband was unlikely to see it, and take the coach as usual from outside the pub to prepare the pies for Griffin. Then when she saw him later, she'd explain, asking if he could put her up for a while. In the meantime, she hoped Lawrence hadn't already been to see him about looking for alternative premises to work. She didn't want to cause any umbrage with him.

* * *

When Elin arrived at the inn, she was surprised to see Aggie already there with her pipe in her mouth, puffing out clouds of tobacco smoke.

'Good morning, Aggie. How are you here so early this morning? I usually see you on my way home or not at all.'

Aggie ceased puffing on her pipe to study her. 'You obviously ain't heard then, 'ave you?'

'Heard what?' She frowned.

'The coppers were called here last night. One of the girls upstairs was badly beaten up by a punter. Looks like he left her for dead...'

Elin gasped. 'And is she dead?'

'No, thankfully,' Aggie said, then she removed her pipe from her mouth and placed it on a nearby saucer. 'Mr Griffin sent word he wanted me in early to clear up the room. There's blood everywhere.'

'And the girl?' To Elin, it was the young woman's welfare that was paramount, not the amount of mess in the room.

'Mr Griffin got a doctor in to examine her and he's cleaned her up. She has a nasty head wound though, lots of stitches to stop her brain from oozing out.'

Elin shook her head, realising that Aggie sometimes had a propensity to embellish facts and it was unlikely the girl's brains were being held in by a few surgical stitches.

'Where's Mr Griffin?' She fixed her gaze on the woman, realising that maybe now wasn't the best time for her to explain her own predicament and ask for a room at the inn.

'He's in the back room speaking to a couple of detectives. Apparently, there's some bloke been going around the China area attacking prostitutes and talk is one of these days he's going to kill one!'

A shiver coursed down Elin's spine. This was too close to

home – sometimes she felt her own husband was capable of doing that to her! And what about that recent Jack the Ripper headline? Might the press be right that the monster had left London for pastures anew? After all, Merthyr had many similarities to Whitechapel, especially in the China district of the town where there were pimps, prostitutes and pickpockets in abundance!

'Look, I'm going to take a mop and bucket up to that bedroom and clean it up as best as I can. Meanwhile, if I were you, I'd carry on as normal baking your pies; it will help to lift spirits around here.'

She nodded meekly, knowing the woman was right.

Aggie glanced at her carpet bags – Elin still had one in either hand – as though she was only now seeing them for the first time. 'What's them?' She pointed.

'I, er…' She was about to make up some cock-and-bull story about how she was going to give away some clothing to someone when she decided to tell the truth. 'I've just this morning left my husband and I'm looking for somewhere to stay, to be honest with you.'

Aggie hiked a thumb in the direction of the back room. 'Have a word with Mr Griffin. He'll help you out. He put me up here many moons ago until I got back on me feet.'

'Oh?' Elin arched her eyebrows with surprise.

'Yes, I hit rock bottom. Was one of those ladies of the night meself back in the day, though you'd hardly believe it now looking at me. I came a right cropper and hit the gin bottle hard, so Mr Griffin took me in and cleaned me up, and I've been as sober as a judge ever since. Only vice I got now is this ruddy pipe.' She laughed.

'It's good to know Mr Griffin is so caring,' said Elin thoughtfully.

'Aye, he is. No matter what folk say about him, he wouldn't want one of his girls injured at all. Not for all the tea in China he wouldn't, pardon the pun!' She cackled.

Elin watched as Aggie waddled off to fetch a metal pail and a mop and then left the room to make her way upstairs. The woman had obviously seen a lot of life and maybe had witnessed this kind of thing previously. To Elin it was simply shocking though.

No more shocking than what your husband is doing to you, a little voice reminded her.

* * *

It was just after Elin had placed the final tray of pies in the oven that she heard voices. It sounded as though the policemen in the room next door were leaving through the back door. Mr Griffin was showing them out.

All went silent for a while and then he entered the kitchen. 'Good morning, Elin,' he greeted, but his face looked sombre. There was no light-hearted twinkle in his eyes as there usually was. 'I suppose you've heard all about what happened last night?'

She nodded. 'Yes, Aggie just filled me in. Dreadful business.'

'Yes, it is. That was the police I was talking to.'

Of course, she already knew that but didn't comment on it. 'What did they say?'

'She's not the first, er, lady who has been attacked by the same man by the sound of it. They're going to issue a description to the local newspapers today, to warn women in these parts about him.'

'Which girl was it?'

'Gwenda. I don't think you'd have encountered her as yet;

she only started here last week. She's a bit naïve. That's the problem, see.' He stroked his chin as though contemplating something. 'The older ones are tough as nails and they can spot if there's trouble brewing. They know how to protect themselves. Need someone to keep an eye on some of them. I don't have the time myself with all of my other business activities. Now, I was thinking...' He was studying her hard now, so hard she was wondering just what was going through his mind. 'Someone like yourself who's not too young and not too old and has a bit of class, you might be good for my girls. You could watch out for them. Fix them up with the right sort of customer...'

Elin gasped. She'd never heard anything so preposterous in all her born days. Lifting her chin, she glared at him. 'Mr Griffin, I am here to cook pies and pies alone. I don't much care for what you're suggesting! It makes it sound as though you wish me to become the madam of a whorehouse!' Her face was flushed with indignation and it didn't help that she was standing near a hot oven either.

'Calm down!' he said as he waved a hand. 'It was merely a suggestion, that was all. I didn't mean to offend you, Mrs Edwards. I wouldn't be expecting you to get up to the same shenanigans as that lot upstairs, now, would I? I just need someone with a bit of mettle to take care of their welfare, is all.'

Elin took a deep breath in an effort to calm herself down. 'Well, although you have offended my sensibilities, I shall tell you where I stand... I have just left my husband this very morning, as he has been violent and raising his fists to me. I had been planning on asking if I might stay here out of harm's way for the time being, but not if you intend to turn me into a bloody brothel keeper!'

On hearing her say this, Griffin threw back his head, roaring with laughter. 'Oh, I'm sorry, my dear. It sounds so comical when you put it like that.'

This man was unbelievable; he was making light of her misery with her husband. 'So, you think it's funny that I suffer at the hands of my husband, do you?'

'No, not at all. You misunderstand me. It wasn't that making me chuckle; it was the way you called yourself a bloody brothel keeper!'

She smiled and found herself stifling a laugh. 'I suppose it does sound funny. Look,' she said, serious now, 'I can carry on cooking pies for your clientele but I might be seeking new premises to work from.'

He frowned. 'But I thought you liked working here?'

'I did. I do…' She bit her lower lip, unsure what to say.

He narrowed his gaze. 'It's Lawrence Langton, isn't it? He knows you're working from here and he's warned you to stay well away.'

What could she say? There was no denying it, so she simply nodded.

'I get why he might say that and particularly now if he hears of what occurred here last night, but you'd have to pay rent on a property, with money you don't have. And even then, you'd need a good oven like this one.' He tapped his hand on its cast-iron casing, then quickly withdrew it, forgetting it was so hot. 'And one of these isn't cheap.'

'You do have a point, I must say.'

'So, you'll consider stopping on here?' he asked, hopefully.

'I will indeed,' she said as she folded her arms to show she meant business. 'It might be an idea to take a few of these pies to the police station as a gesture of goodwill towards those policemen. After all, you need to keep them onside.'

He nodded, and now the glint in his eyes returned. 'Elin Edwards, you're a woman after my own heart!'

* * *

It was decided that Elin would be allowed to stay at the inn for the time being, so before setting off to perform her duties at the Langton house, she decided to pop upstairs to see how Gwenda was doing. Gingerly, she tapped on the bedroom door, which caused her to wince. She'd forgotten about her sore hand for a moment. It was only a superficial injury that would heal in a few days' time, but her other wounds from her husband were etched far deeper.

'Wh... who is it?' asked a nervous-sounding voice from inside.

'It's Elin Edwards. I make the pies for this pub; you might have heard of me?' Elin said softly from her side of the door. 'Is it all right if I come in to see you? I thought you might like a hot pie and a glass of ginger beer after your recent ordeal.'

There was a long silence and for a moment, Elin feared the young woman was ignoring her, but then she heard a scuffling sound on the linoleum, a key being turned in the lock and then the door swung open.

The scene before her would have caused her to bring both hands to Elin's mouth, but one was occupied holding the tray.

The young woman appeared around eighteen years of age, her blonde wavy hair spread loose on her shoulders. On top of her head was a reddened patch, which Elin guessed was where she'd been struck by something, and now there were stitches in place from the doctor. Below one eye was a purple bruise, and there was swelling on the other side of her face. Elin's heart went out to the sorry sight trembling before her.

'My dear, you've been through so much. Here, take this pie and the drink. I'll be back in a tick as you need some ice for that swollen cheek of yours.'

The girl nodded gratefully as she accepted the plate and glass. 'Thank you. I'm going to lock the door again when you leave, so please knock again and say it's you.'

Elin forced a smile. Of course she'd feel nervous and apprehensive as hadn't she, herself, felt the same way the first time Wyn had done something to her? The difference was, though, this girl had been injured by a stranger, not her own husband. She didn't know which was worse really.

When she returned to the kitchen, Aggie was standing there with her sleeves rolled up. 'I take it you've just been upstairs, then?'

Elin nodded. 'I felt I had to take her something; she's been through so much.'

'Aye,' said Aggie, who appeared to be chewing on a piece of tobacco. 'She's had it tough. I knows the family, I do. Her father's a drunkard and a good-for-nothing. Kept the family short for years. She's gone the same way as her mother.'

'How'd you mean?'

'She was selling her services to men too, if you get my drift.' She tapped the side of her nose with her index finger.

Elin knew all too well to what the woman was referring. How sad that Gwenda felt she had little choice other than to spend her young life servicing customers in the upstairs bedroom of a pub!

'Shouldn't you have left here by now?' Aggie frowned.

'Yes, I should have. I'll be late getting back to the big house now, but I want to take some ice up to Gwenda for that swelling on her face.'

'Yewse go now. I'll chip some ice off the block in the cellar and wrap it in a tea towel to take up to her.'

'Aggie, you're a marvel!' Elin enthused.

How on earth was she going to explain to her employer the reason for her lateness back at the house though? And not only that, she'd have to face up to Lawrence, knowing he'd be none too pleased she'd agreed to remain working at Griffin's pub and would be boarding there as well.

13

Elin glanced up at the house as she made her way along the driveway, gulping when she noticed Lawrence's coach parked outside. So, he'd evidently not left the house that morning as yet and now she'd be taken to task for being late and for her continued association with Morgan Griffin.

Flustered, she turned the knob of the back door to enter, closing it behind her, and then she walked along the corridor, where she spotted Molly headed her way.

'Hello, Molly,' she greeted, but the girl didn't offer a reply, instead appearing stone-faced as she made her way towards the laundry room. No doubt she was changing all the bedding again and annoyed there was such a fuss when the master was at home.

Shrugging her shoulders at Molly's attitude, Elin entered the kitchen to find Cook in a tizzy.

'Thank goodness you're here at last!'

Elin surveyed the mountain of food the woman appeared to be in the midst of preparing. On the counter, freshly prepared pastry was rolled out; on the hob, a couple of saucepans were bubbling merrily away; and, in the corner of the room, Beatrice was chopping up carrots, while Floss was frantically whipping up something in an earthenware bowl.

Elin smiled tentatively, having no idea of the reason for all this unexpected activity.

'Hello, Mrs Brightman. I'm so sorry I've been delayed; I'll fill you in on the details later.' She hiked her thumb in Floss's direction. 'What on earth's going on here?'

Cook raised her brow. 'Molly's busy getting some guest rooms prepared. There's to be a party here for Mr Langton this evening.'

'Party?' Elin removed her cape and hung it on a hook along with her bonnet, then she removed her gloves and placed them in her basket.

'Yes, today's his birthday and his mother thought it would be a nice idea.' She rolled her eyes as though it wasn't a nice idea at all. 'Of course, Miss Arabella's been invited along with others just to make more work for us, as if we haven't got enough to do in the kitchen already!'

Elin felt her heart plummet to her boots. The thought of Lawrence being in such close proximity to that good-looking young woman unnerved her somewhat. 'Who are the rooms being prepared for then?'

'One is for an elderly aunt, his father's sister, and the other for his brother.'

'Brother? Not Benjamin?'

'Yep, one and the same!' Cook said, rolling up her sleeves and heading over to the floured table. The pastry and rolling pin lay awaiting her deft hands to shape it into some sort of fantastic creation for that evening's fare.

'What can I do to help you out?' Elin asked, realising this wasn't her usual role at the house, but she didn't mind helping if they were short-staffed. 'I'll just check in with Mrs Langton and see if I'm required as yet; if not, I'll return and make a nice pot of tea as you all look like you haven't got a moment to live!'

Cook nodded gratefully. 'Yes, thank you, Elin, a brew would be most welcome! Then, after that, I'll give you a list of jobs to do.'

Elin marvelled that working at the house, no two days were ever the same.

* * *

Much to Elin's surprise, Mrs Langton asked her to stay on that evening to help with the dinner party. It wasn't usually in her remit of work at the house but she agreed to do so as the extra money would come in useful for her, now that she had left her husband.

Wyn, though!

Any moment now he might return from work to discover she was no longer living at the residence – that's if he chose to return there. Poor Frank would realise it too when he noticed that letter on his pillow. But from now on, she decided, the only person she needed to take care of was herself.

It became so busy that she had little time to reflect on her position with her husband. Things needed doing. The long mahogany table in the dining room required laying out properly. Molly, so far, had made a right hash of it. She'd placed the knives and forks on the wrong sides of the waiting plates and confused the soup spoons with the dessert spoons. And the table arrangement she'd prepared was a paltry affair – just a few wilted blooms in small vases, hardly showpieces! Instead, Elin went to have a word with Dewi Price who was tending the garden, and he showed her where she could pick the best blooms from. So she made a large stylish arrangement from those as a centrepiece for the table, along with two smaller arrangements for each end. She also swapped the washed-out linen tablecloth that Molly had seen fit to cover the table with for a fresh white cotton one edged with lace, along with matching napkins. She knew this would upset the girl, but so be it. There were standards to maintain at the house and Molly's were not high enough. She wondered who had taken it upon themselves to allow her to do this. Maybe Cook in an effort to save time?

She hadn't encountered Lawrence today so far, but later, when she called Dewi in from the garden for a cup of tea with her and Cook in the kitchen, she noticed the coach had disappeared from the side of the house.

She was pleased to hear from Dewi that Mrs Langton had paid for him to see a doctor, who had sorted out medication for his chest infection, and now he was able to speak without his conversation being interrupted by bouts of harsh coughs.

As he and Cook maintained idle chit-chat, Elin's thoughts returned to the missing coach. Lawrence was conducting business in Merthyr town, no doubt. Something occurred to her and she gulped. *Has he gone to see Morgan Griffin to warn him off?*

She'd had no time to forewarn the man, and Mr Griffin was likely to be in a bad mood after all that had occurred overnight. Still, she reminded herself that Lawrence was perfectly capable of taking care of himself and had no doubt seen it all in London, what with some of the people he represented. He'd be well used to conflict arising, she was sure.

She changed into a grey work apron to rake out the ashes from the grate and set the fire in the dining room, so it would be warm enough for the party. As she worked, she tutted to herself – this should have been Molly's job. She was well used to tending to the fire at home of course, but her role at the house was to take care of Mrs Langton and her requirements. Today the priority was this evening's birthday party, for which Elin would be expected to help the woman dress.

By the time Elin returned to the kitchen, the air was blue with Cook's curse words. Throwing her hands mid-air, she said, 'I don't know how I'm expected to conjure up a birthday cake on top of all of this work I've got on here today! How can Mrs Langton expect me to perform a magic act at such short notice?'

Elin smiled and she let out a little sigh. 'Now don't you go worrying none, Mrs Brightman. I'll help you. You just concentrate on the cake and I'll watch whatever you have in the oven.'

Cook smiled at her. 'I just don't think it's possible for me to ice this cake and for it to set in time for the party.'

'Then how about you don't ice it at all?'

'Huh?' Cook wrinkled up her nose as though she'd suggested something most distasteful.

'Do you really need to ice it?'

'Of course I do, otherwise it will be just an ordinary jam and cream sponge cake!'

'One of the nicest birthday cakes I ever saw didn't have icing sugar on it. It was covered with whipped cream and decorated with fresh fruit. A gentleman at the chapel, who was a great baker, made a cake to celebrate Mr Probert's eightieth birthday a few months ago. It went down very well with everyone.'

'Now that's an idea!' said Cook, her face breaking into a large grin. 'The master loves fruit.'

'There you go then. And we can still add a few candles to it and light it up. In fact, you could make that the dessert too, instead of whipping something else up that's quite unnecessary. Most people would be too stuffed to eat a dessert and a slice of birthday cake, anyhow.'

'Elin, has anyone ever told you what a bloomin' marvel you are?!' said Cook, and then she planted a kiss on Elin's cheek.

'All the time.' Elin laughed, feeling pleased she'd resolved some of Cook's stress.

* * *

That evening, the sound of chatter and the odd burst of laughter emanating from the dining room unnerved Elin. She'd still not set eyes on Lawrence that particular day but could hear his resinous tones as he no doubt charmed Arabella, and it irked her somewhat. She couldn't help imagining them being quite intimate with one another. Nervously, she hovered outside the door, holding a tray containing a covered dish of potatoes and another of mixed vegetables, while Cook stood behind her with the pièce de résistance: a silver salver containing salmon en croûte, a French gourmet dish of fresh salmon seasoned with dill and cream cheese, wrapped up in a golden-brown pastry. To Cook's delight, the pastry had puffed up like she wanted it to.

All appeared to be going well, apart from Molly throwing Elin stinking looks every so often. She guessed the girl had discovered that she'd removed all the table settings and replaced them with her own version. But imagine, though, if that lot in there had turned up to a table looking more in place at a cheap chop house in Cardiff docks than an upmarket home in Merthyr Tydfil. Cook had reassured her though; she'd done the right thing even if the girl was miffed by it. There were standards that needed to be kept at the house, she'd said.

Elin hoisted the tray onto her shoulder and, with her free hand, gave a sharp knock on the door with her knuckles. Floss, who had been keeping an eye on things, opened it for them from inside, to allow access. Elin laid down the tray on a serving

table near the window and then Cook placed the baked centrepiece in the middle of the table, removing the lid to much applause as the guests appreciated her effort – she'd even managed to craft the dish to look like the shape of a salmon, complete with a head, tail and intricate scales on the pastry. Elin marvelled at the woman's skill. What a spectacle it was to behold. All the while, Elin sensed Lawrence's eyes on her, watching her every move. She made no eye contact with him, but noticed he was seated beside Arabella who appeared to be hanging on to his every word.

'Whew! Thank goodness for that,' said Cook after they'd left the room, standing with her back to the closed door. She blew out a breath.

'Well done, Mrs Brightman!' Elin enthused as she laid a hand of reassurance on the woman's shoulder. 'You're doing amazingly well. It can't be easy to produce all of that at short notice.'

Cook shook her head. 'No, indeed it's not! I just have to whip up that cream now for the cake and add the fruit as decoration, then that's me done for a bit. We can both have a little break then. You've been on your feet all day too, Elin.'

'Yes, I have, and I had the shock of my life when I arrived at the pub to work this morning. I'll tell you all about it when we have that break. Meanwhile, there's someone I need to speak to.'

Cook nodded and she watched her walk away towards the laundry room in search of Molly.

As the door creaked open, Molly looked up from where she'd been in the midst of folding a pile of sheets. The girl quickly averted her gaze, returning her focus to her task, acting as though Elin was not in the room.

'Molly,' Elin said softly, 'I feel there has been some bad

blood between us lately and I don't really understand why that is?'

Molly turned to face her. 'Oh, don't you, Miss Perfect Drawers!'

Elin stiffened, quite shocked by the way the girl was speaking to her. It just wasn't on – a junior member of staff speaking to a senior one in such a manner – and it could be a dismissing offence, were Mrs Langton to overhear.

'Why are you speaking to me in such a derogatory way? I don't deserve this!' Her voice trembled as she spoke. She couldn't understand such antagonism – she'd had enough of that at home – and all she ever did was try to help people. 'Is it because you don't like it that I have authority over you at this house?'

'No, it's not that, even though you changed my table settings earlier. That's not why I dislike you so much.' She folded her arms as if it were a form of self-protection.

Baffled, Elin persisted. 'Could it be because I didn't explain to you about my pie-making venture, then?'

'I couldn't care less about your ruddy pie-making business!' The girl spat the words out, and then threw her arms in mid-air.

'Then what is it?'

'If you really want to know it's because...' Was it her imagination or did she see the girl's lower lip tremble as she spoke? 'You keep hanging around Mr Lawrence, drawing his attention all the time.'

'Whatever do you mean? I have to answer him when he speaks to me.' For a moment, she wondered if Molly somehow realised she had feelings for the man, but how could she? Unless... she had feelings for Lawrence herself! That's exactly what it was! Poor little Molly had one big crush on the master of the house! Of course, why hadn't she noticed this before? She was at such a young, impressionable age that her emotions were in turmoil over him. He was a handsome man.

Elin let out a little sigh. 'I'm sorry. I didn't realise you liked him so much. You know that he's not of your class or station in life, don't you?'

Molly lowered her head and she began to sob. 'It was just the other day, I felt you were both taking the mickey out of me.'

Elin angled her head to one side in a show of sympathy for the girl. 'Aw, that's simply not true, Molly. I wasn't at any rate. I was upset that you seemed so off with me, but now I quite understand. And let's be mindful of one thing – Mr Lawrence would never want to marry the likes of you or me, would he?'

Molly glared at her through glassy eyes and there was a catch to her voice as she spoke. 'B... but you're already married so he couldn't marry you anyhow!' The girl sounded affronted as she held her head in a determined fashion.

Elin had obviously touched a raw nerve there and made a huge mistake by including herself within the reference of marriage. 'I just meant that people like us who are working class rarely mix with the upper echelons of society, the upper classes. There have been a few marriages of that sort, granted, but those rarely work out for the best, not with the opposition they receive from family members and others. We're best sticking to our own kind, you and I. We were both born the wrong side of society for Lawrence Langton, I'm afraid.'

Molly nodded and then sniffed. Elin proffered the girl a clean handkerchief from her dress pocket. 'I know you're right...' she sighed deeply '...but I've had dreams about it.'

If anyone understood about that it was Elin. She too had had dreams about being with Lawrence, but she knew in her heart it was not to be. Arabella had designs upon him and the pair would make a good match. A union between the pair of them would suit both families down to the ground. Though from what she'd been able to ascertain at the table tonight, it was increasingly obvious that Arabella had more of a thing for Lawrence than he had for her – he seemed at times uninterested in her conversation, while Arabella, on the other hand, appeared to hang on to his every word with stars in her eyes. Yes, she was in love with him too. It wounded Elin deeply to picture the two of them together while her own heart bled for him. But in all truth, Lawrence didn't seem all that interested in the young woman and for that, she was supremely grateful – it was the kind of gratitude peppered with a sprinkling of guilt, while realising he only had eyes for her.

* * *

By the time Elin and Cook had the chance to settle down in the kitchen for a break, the word coming from the dining room via Floss and Molly was that the evening had been a resounding success. Cook smiled when they heard the guests sing 'Happy Birthday' to Mr Lawrence as the appearance of the cake had gone down well with everyone.

'Now then, Elin,' Cook said, patting her hand across the table, 'what was it you said you'd tell me later?'

Elin explained how she'd left her husband and was now residing at Morgan's pub and what had occurred there the previous evening.

Cook shook her head and tsk-tsked. At first, Elin thought she was being disapproving of the place being run as a brothel, but then she realised the woman was exhibiting a show of sympathy for young Gwenda.

'You know,' said Elin thoughtfully as she laid her cup down in its saucer, 'when Mr Griffin asked me would I help the girls, I immediately turned it down. I was outraged that he'd asked such a thing of me!'

Cook stared at her intently as she tilted her head to one side while she listened with interest. 'Well, I expect I'd be the bloomin' same!'

'But now when I think about it, maybe the girls at the pub do need someone to take them in hand as it were, to take care of them and watch over things.'

'Aren't there any older prostitutes working there, well-seasoned sorts, who could give them some tips on how to take care of themselves?'

Elin shook her head. 'From what I can see, they're all around twenty years of age, apart from a couple who might be in their mid to late twenties.'

'I expect Mr Griffin likes to keep a stable of young fillies!' Cook raised her eyebrows.

'Aye, maybe. There is one elderly lady there though...'

'Good grief! She's not at it as well at her age?'

Elin chuckled. 'No, she told me she worked at the pub many years ago, probably well before Mr Griffin took it over, but he employs her now as a charlady.' She hesitated before adding, 'But of course, by taking this new role at the pub, I'll have to leave my work here and I'll miss you all, the Langtons and the staff too, but particularly you, Mrs Brightman.'

Cook's eyes were beginning to fill with tears and she smiled at Elin, nodding at her. 'And I dare say I'll miss you too, Elin.'

'We can keep in touch though,' said Elin brightly. 'I don't know whether this role will turn out to be a long-term thing or a flash in the pan, but one thing I do know, after recent events, those girls need someone to keep a watchful eye on them, and I'll have a roof over my head so, even if it turns out to be temporary, at least I'll be away from Wyn.'

'I'm wondering,' said Cook, 'what's your motivation in all of this?'

Hearing the woman say those words brought Elin up sharp. She hadn't honestly considered that – the reason she wanted to help. 'I... I suppose it might be after seeing young Gwenda in that sort of state with a black eye and highly traumatised too...' There were tears welling up in her eyes now and a lump had formed in her throat.

'You saw something of yourself in her, didn't you, Elin?'

Slowly, she nodded. 'I'd like to do something to help if I can.'

'Then what you must do is inform Mr Griffin of your intention as soon as possible, before someone else steps in. You'll have more understanding than most and you're very good with people too.'

'I don't know about that. I've messed things up with Molly here.'

'No, you haven't. I had a word with the girl earlier and she told me how good you'd been about things and how you'd had a word with her. I guessed she had a big crush on Mr Lawrence about a month ago, to be truthful.'

'You did?' Elin arched her eyebrows with surprise – she'd not noticed anything herself.

'Oh, yes. Whenever she spoke about the man, her cheeks flushed bright red, prompting her to turn away. Also, she seemed to mention him rather a lot in conversation, any chance she had. I should have told you about my suspicion but to be honest, I didn't realise she felt so strongly about him. I thought it was a passing fad.'

'I think Molly must be going through so many emotions right now. It can't have been easy for her seeing him sat beside Arabella this evening.'

'No, it can't have.'

'By the way,' Elin said, 'what happened to Mr Benjamin? I thought he was supposed to be attending the party?'

'He was. No one has said a word to me. But then again, he was never the most reliable of men; perhaps he's forgotten all about it. If you ask me, everyone is better off without that scallywag being here!'

Elin was still reflecting on Cook's comments when she was preparing to head off for the pub, where she would be spending her nights for the time being. At least she'd be on the premises first thing in the morning to begin baking, which would save her some valuable time. She reflected on what Wyn might be doing right now. He was probably in some pub or another having gone there straight from work again, and wouldn't notice she was missing until he got home in the wee small hours. Or maybe he'd not return home at all after how he'd treated her in front of his father – he'd incurred his father's wrath, that was for sure. And poor Frank, he didn't deserve any of this, particularly after his recent bereavement. Had he read the letter yet? she wondered. And who would prepare his evening meal for him now? A vision of a lonely man sat at an empty table with just a piece of bread and cheese before him flashed through her mind.

She must have been deep in her thoughts as the sound of someone clearing their throat behind her caught her off guard. She turned to see Lawrence stood there, his eyes sparkling.

'Thank you so much for helping out this evening, Elin,' he said with great warmth. She was aware Cook had left the kitchen, so she was alone when he arrived, and maybe he'd noticed the woman leaving himself, so had taken this as his opportunity to speak to her.

'That's all right. I've enjoyed myself.' She hesitated for a moment as she gazed intently at him. 'There's something I need to tell you though...'

His eyes darkened for a moment. 'Oh, that sounds ominous. Don't tell me you're never going to be working here again as we've run you ragged today?' He forced a chuckle that sounded hollow to her. It was almost as though that's what he feared.

'Well, sort of in a way. I mean, I'll carry on working here for a while until you find someone else, but I intend carrying on baking my pies at the pub and I've been offered another role there. That's where I'm headed now as I'm living there.'

'You're living there!' His eyes flashed dangerously. 'But why would you do that? Especially as I told you I'd find other premises for you to work from.'

Her eyes began to fill with tears and then she heard herself telling him all that had occurred with Wyn, and the next thing she knew, she was in his arms. He was holding her close to him and she felt so safe there, in her own private world. It was as though all the hubbub outside the kitchen was turned down. His lips were dangerously close to hers and she had such longing in her that it was positively indecent, these feelings she was having for him.

Coming to her senses, she pulled away. 'I think I'll be safer staying at the pub than I will with my husband in Abercanaid!' She sniffed.

'I can see that,' said Lawrence. 'But you could stay here instead. There's plenty of room.'

'No, I've made up my mind.' She donned her cape, bonnet and gloves and lifted her wicker basket. 'I need to set off now as it's a fair walk to the pub.'

'Let me take you in my coach,' Lawrence yelled after her as she walked away, not caring who heard him.

'No, you must return to your guests. They'll wonder where you've got to otherwise. I'll be back here mid-morning tomorrow.'

'Then at least allow my driver to take you home. You must be shattered.'

She smiled gratefully at him. 'I am rather tired, thank you. I'd like to take you up on your very kind offer, but you must return to your guests, else you'll be missed.'

He nodded. 'I'll just ask my coachman to take you and I'll return to them, but we must speak tomorrow.' His dark blue eyes had a longing in them that she recognised. He wanted her and he needed her badly. She longed for him too, if she cared to admit it.

14

By the time Elin settled herself in the coach, her heart had ceased racing. What on earth was that with Lawrence earlier? She'd felt the need to put distance between them and thanked her lucky stars she was on her way to China. A gentle jolt as the horses pulled away down the drive and she laid her head against the padded leather upholstery, closing her eyes. In truth, it all seemed like a dream. She no longer felt in full control of her life. She was, after all, a married woman, and many a woman would put up with a drunken husband who raised his fists to her, as long as he was keeping a roof over her head and food in her belly. The only other options were the street or the workhouse.

But she wasn't just any woman, was she? She was Elin Edwards, who from now on would take no messing from any man. She realised that, yes, even though everything felt out of her control, she was in the driving seat of her life, just like the coachman was in charge of the coach. She could do anything she wanted to. It felt scary, but thrilling at the same time.

'Where on earth have you been?' Morgan Griffin grilled her as she entered the pub. There were still a few stragglers supping near the bar, but most seemed to have been turfed out of the establishment. Griffin had his favourites though, those whom he trusted, and he was happy they stay behind for a quiet drink or a card game in the back room.

'Sssh!' She waved her gloved hand at him. 'Let's speak in the kitchen.'

He nodded, allowing her to take the lead as he followed in her wake.

When they both entered the room, she closed the door behind them as she didn't want anyone to overhear their conversation.

'I would have been back sooner,' she explained, 'but Mrs Langton asked me to stop on at the house, as she wanted to throw a surprise birthday party for Lawrence and it needed all hands on deck.'

'Oh, I see.' He sighed. 'I was concerned about you, though.'

'Why's that?' She frowned.

'In case that husband of yours turned on you again.'

'I haven't seen him at all since I left,' she said curtly, laying down her basket on the counter and removing her gloves and tossing them onto the counter too.

'Yes, but you will take care, won't you?'

'I promise, cross my heart!' She licked her index finger and made a cross shape over her heart, which made him smile. 'Being serious now, though, I've been thinking about what you said to me.'

'Oh?' He furrowed his brow, almost as though it were a bad thing she was about to say to him.

'About that proposition you made to me, about looking for someone to take care of the girls.'

'Oh, I see!' he said, smiling now. 'You'd like to take charge of them?'

'Yes.' She removed her cape and bonnet, and placed them neatly on the table. 'Providing—'

'Providing what?'

'Providing you're not expecting me to be in their line of business! That's what!' She tossed her hair back over her shoulders and stood with both hands on her hips.

'My dear, I wouldn't dream of it. You are far too lady-like for that line of work. Though I expect you'd fetch a pretty penny with those looks of yours.'

She felt herself blush. 'And don't think I approve of what you're doing either. I just feel if those girls are going to work in that line of business anyhow, and there's no stopping them, then someone needs to watch out for their welfare, especially as you have your fingers in a lot of pies, so to speak!'

'My dearest Elin, the only pies I'd like to dip my fingers in are yours.'

Elin gasped. Was she imagining things, or was he overtly flirting with her? But then he threw back his head and laughed. 'You should have seen your face there! I respect you far too much to try any funny business with you, Mrs Edwards!' he said, throwing her a cheeky wink.

* * *

First thing the following morning, Elin went to check on Gwenda, realising she was in the bedroom beside hers. She'd not heard a pip from that room overnight, which disturbed her somewhat. No sounds of creaking floorboards or the door opening and closing. There'd been plenty of activity emanating from the room across the landing though; that belonged to another working girl called Bridget. Bridget had come over to Wales with her family from Cork in Ireland a few years ago. Back then, her father had found himself a job at the Cyfarthfa ironworks, but the family had become destitute when he'd got killed in a horrific accident in one of the blast furnaces. And hence, the young woman, as the eldest child, had sought to help her family. Her mother had ended up working at the washhouse in China, but that too had a reputation for the seedy and sordid side businesses, so likely she'd found herself on the game too.

Gently, Elin tapped on Gwenda's bedroom door.

'Gwenda, it's me, Elin,' she said softly, but there was no reply. She slowly turned the brass doorknob to be faced with the back of a winged armchair that was set up in such a way that its occupant might look out of the window. From what Elin could make out, the young woman was sat in it, but Elin swallowed down a lump in her throat. She feared that – by the still form and lack of forthcoming reply from Gwenda – she might be dead. Had she taken her own life overnight?

But as she drew closer, she could see the bodice of the girl's dress move up and down – thank goodness, she was breathing. Elin knew from her own experience that Gwenda was likely still in shock.

'Gwenda, are you all right?' she whispered, not wishing to startle her. It was almost as though she were in a hypnotic trance.

Gwenda turned her head towards her; tears were streaming down her swollen face, which appeared more bruised than yesterday. But Elin realised that was perfectly normal as it all took time to heal. The swelling and bruising needed to come out first, and then it would all settle down.

Gwenda opened her mouth as though to say something, but

nothing emerged. It was as if she was frozen. Elin knelt beside her and took her hand.

'Have no fear, Gwenda. I'm here now to help you,' she said. 'Mr Griffin has asked me to take care of you girls and I promise I will. Believe me, I do understand a little of what you're going through right now, as my husband was knocking me about. What you need to do is to feel safe again and for things to seem as normal as possible, establish some sort of routine if you can. Work has helped me enormously.'

Gwenda nodded at her. Finally, she found her voice. 'But how will I be able to work here looking as I do?'

'Well, you'll not be doing that sort of work for a time yet, not until you're fully healed and feeling up to the mark. And that's only if you want to.'

'Thank you.' Gwenda sniffed.

It seemed incredible to Elin that the girl was still considering that line of work after all that had happened to her. But then again, maybe she, like Bridget, needed the money for her family.

'I tell you what you can do for the next couple of weeks or so: you can help me in the kitchen, making those pies. That should keep you busy and you won't have to see many people either.'

Gwenda nodded gratefully at her.

'Come on, let's go there right now and have breakfast together, and then we can crack on making those pies.'

* * *

It had worked out very well having Gwenda as a help in the kitchen. It meant that Elin could speed up the process and return to the big house for her work on time. She did realise, though, she would need to speak to Mrs Langton about the whole situation as she now had made a choice between working at the house and working at the pub. The pub won hands down – it was some sort of calling for her, a vocation of sorts – those girls needed her help and she could enhance her pie-making business at the same time. She had regrets about leaving Mrs Langton in the lurch, but the woman would find a replacement for her. Even Molly could help her until she did. The girl lacked maturity, Elin knew, so Mrs Langton wouldn't find her as easy to make conversation with when she got dressed of a morning or needed a companion to accompany her for a shopping trip to Merthyr town, but she was more than capable.

The other good thing about working at the pub was it would create enough distance between her and Lawrence. If she were left alone in the man's company, she couldn't be certain of her actions. Being alone with him did crazy things to her emotions; they consumed her – a feeling she'd had with no other man, ever.

'A penny for them?'

Elin turned to discover Morgan Griffin standing behind her.

'I was just thinking, I need to set off for the Langton house or I'm going to be late. Gwenda here has been a great help to me in the kitchen this morning.'

Morgan smiled. 'That's good to hear,' he said, then, turning his attention towards Gwenda, added, 'You won't go far wrong allowing Mrs Edwards to take you under her wing. How are you feeling today?'

'A little nervous, Mr Griffin, but it's helped me assisting in the kitchen this morning and I'd like to do it again, if I may?'

'Then carry on doing so as long as you like. There's no rush for you to return to the other business. No rush at all.' He turned his attention back to Elin. 'Have you thought about how you'll help the girls to keep themselves safe in future?'

'Yes, I have,' said Elin, releasing a breath. 'I'm going to set up their appointments for them and vet each and every man who comes to visit them upstairs. No one shall get through who does not have my seal of approval. I shall take their names and addresses too!'

Griffin's eyes widened. 'But you can't do that! Many are married men who wouldn't want that sort of information privy to all and sundry.'

'But it won't be available for all to see. I'll keep the book locked away in a drawer. No one else shall see it. In fact, I can use a numbering system instead of names, to keep their identities safe. The customer will be assigned a number that will be recorded in the book but his address will be kept under lock and key.'

'Oh, I see,' said Griffin as he rubbed his stubbled chin in contemplation. 'That might work I suppose. A few might provide you with false information though.'

She sighed. 'They might indeed, but it's better than the system you have right now.'

He frowned. 'What system is that?'

'Precisely,' she said, folding her arms. 'What ruddy system!' She sighed. 'From what I can see, there is no system in place here other than the girls fawning over men in the bar, some of whom have been introduced to them by Aggie. Then they're bought a few drinks and they lead them upstairs to their rooms.' She pointed to the ceiling.

Griffin's face reddened, but a smile crept over it as he said, 'You're the boss, Mrs Edwards! Maybe get the girls together later to fill them in on this new system of yours.'

She nodded approvingly. 'Now I really must go! I'm needed

at the house. I'll be informing Mrs Langton of my intention of leaving there this morning.'

* * *

When Elin returned to Mrs Langton's, she encountered Molly and Floss in the hallway. Floss had her hand over her mouth as though relating some sort of secret to Molly.

'What's going on here?' Elin frowned at the pair. She hated secrets. She'd had to put up with enough of those from her husband.

'It's something that happened here late last night after the party,' related Floss. 'I was just setting off for my bed when I heard a commotion from downstairs, right here in the hallway.'

'What happened?' Elin blinked.

'It was Mr Lawrence and Mr Benjamin, Mrs Edwards...' Floss said with some excitement to her voice. 'They were fighting here in this very spot.'

'Fighting?' Elin could hardly believe what she was hearing.

'That's right,' confirmed Molly. 'I was in the kitchen, putting the last of the plates away before going to bed myself when I heard a lot of shouting. Mrs Langton was most upset by it all and she tried to part them, but instead ended up falling to the floor.'

Elin's hand flew to her mouth. 'Oh no!' She understood all too well how unsteady her employer could be on her feet at times, and thought how distressing that sight must have been for the woman. 'What were they fighting over, do you know?'

'I think it was something to do with the state Mr Benjamin turned up here in, as he was very drunk,' said Floss quite knowledgeably. Elin guessed the girl had a bird's-eye view after peeking from the landing.

Elin let out a little sigh, realising it would be impossible now to tell Mrs Langton today of her decision to leave the house. 'I'd better go and check on Mrs Langton. Where is she?'

'She's having a lie-down on her bed. I don't think she'll be leaving her room today,' said Molly.

'I'll just go and check on her and let you know if she requires her breakfast be sent to her bedroom. That's of course if she can manage any after all that's gone on. Where are Mr Lawrence and Mr Benjamin right now then?' Those pair needed their heads banging together, as far as she was concerned, causing their mother emotional upset like that.

'Mr Benjamin was thrown out of the house by his brother,' said Floss. 'Not sure what's happened to Mr Lawrence. I haven't seen him this morning. Have you, Molly?'

Molly shook her head, looking entirely despondent. Of course, Elin realised the girl would be quite forlorn about it all as she was head over heels with infatuation for the man.

'Thanks for keeping me posted,' Elin said to the pair. 'I'm going to see how Mrs Langton is. Hopefully, she won't need to see the doctor, though the whole situation is very troubling indeed.'

The bedroom curtains were still drawn and Mrs Langton appeared to be fast asleep when Elin entered the room, but then the woman stirred and sat up. Blinking in the semi-darkness, she said, 'Good morning, Elin. I suppose someone has filled you in on what happened here last night.'

'Yes, they have, ma'am. How are you feeling now? I hear you were caught up in it all?'

'I'm all right, thank you. I managed to drop off eventually, and I'm more rested now.'

'How do you feel about getting washed and dressed and taking a little breakfast in the drawing room as usual, then?'

Mrs Langton forced a smile. 'I suppose I'd better.'

Molly had obviously given up on the woman and would have left her in bed all day if it was down to her, but Elin had a way of cajoling Mrs Langton that no one else at the house had.

'And can you cope with a couple of pieces of toast and a pot of coffee?'

'Yes, that would be lovely, thank you.' Mrs Langton nodded.

'I'll just open the drapes and let them know downstairs what you'd like, then I'll return to help you wash and dress.' She made her way to the window and drew back the long jacquard curtains, allowing a stream of sunlight into the room, and then left for the kitchen. At first glance, there seemed no sign that the woman had been injured physically, but she reminded herself to check when she helped her dress later.

Cook was pursing her lips with indignation when Elin found her. 'I suppose you've heard about last night?' she said as she turned away from where she was in the midst of frying several rashers of bacon and a few eggs in a large pan. The sizzle of the hot fat and the smell of the bacon frying was making Elin's mouth water. She'd not eaten since rising early at the pub and then it had only been a piece of toast with Gwenda for company.

Elin sighed. 'I did, yes. Do you know what it was all about, Mrs Brightman?'

Cook flipped a couple of bacon rashers over in the pan before turning her attention back towards Elin. 'From my understanding, Mr Lawrence was most upset with his brother turning up drunk at around midnight. Seems he'd been out on a bit of a bender. In fact, it's a wonder you didn't bump into him last night!'

'Me? Why would I bump into him?' Elin could hardly believe what the woman was saying to her.

'Because by all accounts, he tends to frequent the pubs of China.'

'Oh!' Elin gasped as her hands flew to her face. 'Why on earth would he choose to go there? A man of his means.'

'Because there's all sorts to tempt a man in that place, as well you know, especially where you're living right now!'

'You mean you think he's paying for women there?'

'I've no doubt about it, whatsoever. You watch you don't run into him where you are, my girl.'

'I shall take care. I can't say I've seen him at the pub or with any of the girls, as I'll make it my business now to find out who any strangers are, but then again, I've never met the man before. I was going to have a word with you after you've finished doing that.' She glanced at the frying pan. 'Who's it for?'

'For the staff of course. Who did you think it was for?'

'I assumed it was breakfast for Mr Lawrence or that aunt of his...'

'Oh, he's well gone from here. After sorting out his brother, he left me word to keep an eye on his mother, saying he'll return tomorrow.'

A sense of crushing disappointment engulfed her. Despite all that had gone on and the realisation she would need to leave the house, part of her had wanted to see him; yearned to, in fact. But maybe it was all for the best.

'As for the elderly aunt, she didn't hang around...' Cook continued. 'Oh no, she left here early this morning. Most upset by the brothers' brawling in the hallway last night, she was!' Cook paused for a moment before asking, 'Does Mrs Langton want her breakfast now?' She removed the large frying pan from the hob, placing it on a cast-iron griddle beside it so that its contents should not overcook.

'Yes, she thinks she could manage a little bit of toast and a pot of coffee, please.'

'Well, you get back up to her and I'll get Molly to do the honours. Once you've settled her in the drawing room for breakfast, we'll all eat together here. I'll keep this warm until you're ready.'

'Thank you, Mrs Brightman.' Elin smiled at her.

It didn't take long to get Mrs Langton washed, dressed and seated in the drawing room with two pieces of buttered toast and a pot of coffee in front of her. Elin had taken her time dressing the woman, carefully checking her over for any significant bruising after last night, without telling her so. There were no significant bruises on her body as far as she could see right now, apart from a small one on the woman's left arm, which might have occurred at any time. She realised some bruising might emerge later, and if it did, she still had some of that balm Dilys Evans had given her when she'd needed it.

Elin would have liked to stay with the woman to find out more of what happened last night, but that wouldn't have felt right as what she needed right now was peace and quiet to eat her breakfast. She guessed she'd only manage one piece of toast, but Cook had insisted on preparing two pieces. It wouldn't go to waste though – no doubt Floss or Molly would polish off the remaining slice in secret, when the woman was through.

During staff breakfast in the kitchen, Cook related to them how she'd never heard Mr Lawrence so angry in all his born days and that when she'd peeped through the kitchen door into the hallway, she'd witnessed him punch his brother to the ground. Then he'd dragged him outside to the coach where the driver had been given orders to take him somewhere. Where, Cook hadn't a clue, but the coach had returned within the hour, so she guessed it wasn't somewhere that far away.

'What if he returns though, Mrs Brightman?' Molly said anxiously. 'Maybe he'll still be off-his-head drunk.'

'Now don't any of you girls be worrying about anything like that. If he comes here and plays merry hell, he'll have me to deal with!' She began to roll up the sleeves of her dress, looking like she meant business. Elin guessed she'd be a force to be reckoned with. The woman was well built with a robust constitution.

'We could always bash him over the head with that frying pan!' Molly joked, which caused Floss to stifle a giggle.

'Now, there'll be none of that caper!' Cook chastised. 'If it's necessary, I'll send one of you to fetch a local bobby to take him to the police station. I don't know if he would turn up here like that, anyhow. His brother left him in a bad way last night.'

'Maybe he sent him to see a doctor then?' Elin offered.

'Possibly so,' said Cook. 'Doctor Bridges from Pentrebach is the family physician – he might have been taken to his house, especially if stitches were required. The man lives in a house that has a surgery attached to it.'

'I know of it,' said Elin. From her understanding, only the wealthy of the area could afford his services.

Cook paused, laying her knife and fork down as though something had just occurred to her. 'Mrs Langton, was she all right physically this morning, Elin? I know she stepped in between the brothers at one point and was knocked to the floor. Once that happened, Mr Lawrence came to his senses and ran to her aid and then he ejected Mr Benjamin from the house and sent him away.'

Elin nodded. 'Yes, she seems fine. I could only see one small bruise on one arm – the poor woman is so slight and slim, she'd bruise easily I suppose. At least there are no broken bones. Imagine how her sons would feel then.'

'I suppose Mr Lawrence feels bad about it, though,' remarked Cook. 'He'd never intentionally hurt his mother for all the world.'

And at that, the four of them fell silent for a while, the thought of what might have happened to Muriel Langton that night hanging over their heads like a big black cloud.

15

When Elin arrived at China, she descended the stone steps to make her way to the pub. The area was dimly lit by the glow of a gaslight and a mist had rolled up from the nearby river, shrouding the area in an eerie, grey haze. With each step she took, she had the sensation of there being a presence behind her. Her chest tightened and her mouth became dry, and then a shiver coursed her spine.

Someone was following in her wake, she was sure of it. She quickened her pace, but the faster she walked, the closer she felt the presence, somehow being unable to shake it off. It was him – Wyn! It had to be. He must have found out she worked here now and was coming to get her. She'd scream if she ruddy well had to.

Then she felt it, a hand clamping down on her shoulder, thinking she'd faint from the sheer shock of it all.

'Elin?'

That wasn't Wyn's voice though, and a shot of relief coursed through her veins as she turned towards the person. She was relieved to see it was Freddie, one of the barmen at the pub.

Elin let out a breath she hadn't even realised she'd been holding. 'Oh, Freddie! I'm so relieved it's you!' she said, almost laughing with hysteria now.

'Who did you think it was then?' He sounded surprised.

'Oh, just someone I'd rather not see. I thought you weren't working this evening?'

'I'm not. I've just finished my shift, but I left my scarf behind at the pub and decided to return to get it. I wouldn't bother but it's perishing and I've a long walk home to Cefn Coed. I'll think twice before walking so closely behind you in future though, if it's going to scare you so much,' he said.

She deliberated for a moment and, deciding honesty was the best policy, said, 'The person I thought was following me was my husband. You see he's been very violent towards me...'

'Oh, I see. Well, I shall watch out for you should anything untoward happen. In fact, let me escort you safely inside.' He proffered his arm for her to take, making her feel reassured as he guided her to the pub.

Elin thanked Freddie, leaving him to locate his scarf so he could set off home. Some of the girls were already in the bar buzzing around a group of men like bees making honey. Oh no, this wasn't what she intended at all. She was going to have to keep an eye out for them right now and she was utterly exhausted. The aftermath of what had occurred at the big house had all but worn her out, and she'd felt unable to tell her employer of her plans to leave.

Feeling on a knife edge, Elin's eyes searched the bar room for Mr Griffin, but there was no sign of him anywhere. She gritted her teeth. Surely this couldn't be happening to her? Why hadn't Mr Griffin prevented this arrangement from occurring tonight in her absence, following all that had gone on for poor Gwenda? Thankfully, the girl wasn't in the bar with the other young women. She had to admit, she felt safer when Morgan Griffin was on the premises, rather than when he was away from the place.

'Where's Mr Griffin?' she asked the barman. She'd not actually been introduced to this particular man before, but he looked as though he could handle himself, going by his broad shoulders and muscular arms.

Glancing up from where he'd been pulling a pint, the man made eye contact with her. 'Mr Griffin's out on business, won't be back until the early hours,' he said as he placed a foaming tankard for a customer on the bar. 'Anything I can help you with?'

'Unfortunately not,' she said, 'but thanks for the offer. What's your name by the way?'

'Jim, Jim O'Connor,' he said, stretching out his hand for a polite shake. She took it and felt he was someone she could trust. Of course, she'd seen him here before, along with other bar staff, but hadn't a chance to encounter him properly until now. 'And you're Mrs Edwards, I've been told?' He shot her a disarming grin.

She nodded and thanked him, and then headed towards the girls, who were in a quiet corner of the pub. One was actually seated on a gentleman's lap, whispering in his ear. The man looked old enough to be her grandfather, never mind her father, which disgusted Elin.

The other three were sitting chatting to the men, who were gazing lustfully at them. Elin recognised some of the men – they worked at the ironworks, and might be managers and foremen – and in that moment, she wondered what their poor wives, if they had any, would make of this.

The girls exchanged glances with one another as she approached.

'You looking for Mr Griffin?' asked Bridget, with her broad southern Irish accent.

'Er, no.' Elin felt her face flush as now the men were looking at her too and she wondered if they thought she might be one of them. 'It's you girls I need to speak to right now.' She pointed to the back room.

The ensemble nodded at one another, and then Bridget said, 'Well, yer heard the lady, didn't you? To be sure, there's a good reason she needs to speak to us.'

'We'll be right back,' Bridget reassured the men as she rose to leave the table. The small party looked astounded that Elin had broken up their little rendezvous. After all, going by the number of tankards and glasses on the table, they'd already bought the girls a few drinks. In Elin's experience, men like that always wanted some payback for their money; only decent men bought a woman a drink expecting nothing in return.

When they'd all gathered in the back room, Elin closed the door behind them – what she had to say was for their ears alone.

'Now then, girls...' she began. 'I don't know if Mr Griffin has told you this, but from now on, I'll be taking charge of you after what happened to Gwenda the other night.'

The girls exchanged glances with one another and then nodded. 'To be sure, Mr Griffin did mention something in passing,' admitted Bridget.

'What you are not to do from now on is just to pick up random men in the bar room. It's far too dangerous – you could be risking your lives. From here on in, I shall be vetting any potential customers and trying to find out exactly who they are, but for obvious reasons, I'll be discreet. We need to promise discretion or they won't come here at all.'

'But how do you aim to do that?' a dark-haired beauty called Dora asked.

'What I plan to do is to keep a register of their addresses, fixing a suitable time they can visit you. From now on, there'll be no complete strangers going up that staircase!' She pointed to the ceiling.

'Makes sense I suppose,' said Bridget, and the girls nodded their approval. 'I feel uncomfortable with that brute being on the prowl.'

'You mean the man who attacked Gwenda?' Elin blinked.

'Yes. Any one of us might be next,' said Dora, causing the girls to murmur amongst themselves.

'Did any of you see him that night?' Elin wanted to know.

All the girls shook their heads. 'Unfortunately, no,' said Bridget. 'That night, Gwenda was the last one to leave the bar. The man must have entered the pub and propositioned her while the rest of us were entertaining upstairs. 'T'wouldn't be a good idea if I knew what he looked like either. If I ever set eyes on him I'd pulverise the bugger!'

'And I'd get my brothers to beat him to a pulp!' Dora held up her fist.

Elin had no doubts that in some respects the girls could handle themselves, but what she had to ask herself was: if any one of those had encountered the man that night, what chance would any of them have had? They were only slight sorts, with petite frames. What chance would they have against a hard, muscular fella? There was only one girl, Cassie, who was very well built, standing around five feet nine inches tall. She had arrived in Merthyr from a neighbouring valley, thinking the streets were paved with gold. But instead, she had experienced a hard, nasty shock when she realised they were paved with all manner of muck and filth.

The press had compared Merthyr Tydfil to a gold rush town in the earlier part of the century when there had been a population boom, where it had been flooded with people to work at its heaving ironworks, of which there were four in the town. They arrived from farming communities, Ireland, and as far afield as various Eastern European countries and Spain. Although people had arrived in their droves back then, their families still remained – it was a cosmopolitan sort of place. The lure of employment at the ironworks had brought all manner of folks to the town. But from what Elin could tell, the only people growing rich were the ironmasters themselves, like the Crawshay family who lived in that castle specially built for them. They even had a room there where lavish balls were held, such was their wealth.

'Now what about those fellas you've been sitting with, ladies?' Elin asked. 'How well do you know those?'

Dora smiled. 'We know them all; they're regulars here, have been for some time! They're harmless enough.'

'That's all right then.' Elin gave a nod of approval. 'Just one thing before you all return to the bar room,' she continued. 'I'd like to learn how much Mr Griffin is paying you for your services?'

There were several raised eyebrows at this, as though some were thinking, *Just who does she think she is?*

'It's all right,' she reassured them. 'I'm not being nosy, but if I am to run things properly here, I want you girls to get what you deserve.'

At that remark, the girls perked up and she discovered that each girl received twenty per cent of what was paid to them by a punter. Trying to stifle her shock, Elin swallowed, but she made no comment that she thought that was very little. Even if they got lodgings at the pub and food in their bellies, they were doing all the work. It was easy money for Mr Griffin. She resolved to have a word with him when she next set eyes on him.

* * *

The opportunity presented itself the following morning, when he entered the kitchen.

'Coffee?' she offered. She'd just brewed a pot.

He smiled and nodded at her. 'Please.'

The dark rings beneath his eyes and his unusual dishevelled appearance told her how tired he was, and she wondered why he wasn't still in bed. 'How come you've risen so early?' she asked.

'I haven't. I've only just arrived home. I'll have that coffee and then it's off to bed for me.'

'What a life you lead!' she said good-naturedly as she poured the steaming coffee into the awaiting cup. 'Milk and sugar?'

'Both, please.'

She added them, and then handed the cup and saucer to him. 'I haven't stirred it,' she said, 'but there's a spoon in the saucer.'

He nodded at her.

This was as good a time as any to approach him, so she cleared her throat and took a seat opposite, setting down her cup and saucer. 'Mr Griffin, I've been meaning to speak to you…' she said hesitantly.

'That sounds ominous. Don't tell me you've changed your mind about taking on the girls?'

'Oh no, nothing like that.' She shook her head.

'What then?'

'I think that to do well here, you need to up your game, as it were.'

'Go on, I'm all ears,' he said, then took a sip of his coffee. 'You brew a nice cup,' he complimented, 'but do go on.'

'I think if we decorated one of the back rooms in a more lavish style, charged a little more for the girls' services and concentrated on the food side of things, we'd attract a better clientele.'

'Carry on, I'm listening...' he said, straightening his pose.

'The girls would need good grooming as well, some much nicer gowns. Also, I think they need to be paid more for their services.'

'P... paid more!' Griffin spluttered on his coffee as it went down the wrong way. When he'd composed himself, he said, 'I think I'm very fair to those girls.'

'Maybe you are in some respects, but they're the ones putting all the work in. Without them you wouldn't have the extra income. And after all, they're the ones putting themselves at risk. Poor Gwenda could have ended up dead the other night, if no one had heard her screams.'

'True,' said Griffin, wiping his moustache with the back of his hand. 'So how much do you think they ought to be paid, then?'

'Eighty per cent of their earnings instead of twenty!'

'I'd go out of business then!'

'No, you wouldn't. If we attracted a higher-class clientele they'd pay more and you'd make money from them dining here too and from the bar takings. Though the upper-class sorts would need to be served their drinks in the back room and not at the bar.'

'I suppose it might work...' said Griffin, mulling things over.

'I guarantee it would. But that back room would require

some new furnishings: velvet drapes, flock wall paper, a few large green leafy plants, a couple of fancy gasoliers, crystal chandeliers... that sort of thing.'

'Hey, I'm not made of money, you know!' Griffin's eyes widened with the shock of all Elin was suggesting.

'Aren't you? You're not Morgan Griffin the moneylender then? Or Morgan Griffin who owns this pub and goodness knows what else?'

He loosened his collar as though somehow it was too tight for him now. 'I am, yes. You know that, of course I am, but it's a big risk for me to take.'

'Just think about it though; there's no other place near here that might attract such gentlemen. All are a bit below par, seedy sorts of places from what I've heard, like that washhouse across the way.'

'I'll think about it,' he said, shaking his head, and then a small smile began to dance upon his lips. Maybe he liked the idea more than she realised.

* * *

When Elin returned to the house, Lawrence was already there waiting for her, pacing up and down the hallway as though expecting her at any given moment. He looked up when she entered.

'Elin...' he said, walking towards her. He took one of her hands in his. 'I must speak with you.'

She gently removed her hand from his grasp. 'Not here,' she whispered. 'I need to get your mother ready for breakfast. I'll be missed. I don't want any attention drawn towards us.'

He nodded. 'That's understandable. I wasn't thinking,' he said, lowering his voice. 'Where and when, then?'

'Out in the garden at the back of the shed in one hour,' she said, 'but I can only spare a few minutes.' Her heart was thumping so hard and fast, she feared he'd hear its heavy thrum.

'I'll take anything I can get.' He nodded, causing her to smile nervously at him.

Lawrence's thoughts were obviously echoing her own. Just to be in his company for a few minutes, with the rest of the world blocked out, would have to do for now. What that might lead to, she had no idea but was prepared to find out.

It was no use – whenever she was in his company, she just melted like a snowflake on a hot surface; that was the kind of effect he had on her.

She needed to clear her thoughts before speaking to him later, realising she couldn't afford to slip up. She had a new path to lead now; a new chapter in her life was due to unfold. *In with the new and out with the old.*

'Right, I'll see you in one hour,' she said, glancing around to ensure they weren't being watched. She couldn't afford for Molly to hear their clandestine conversation; that just wouldn't do. The girl could cause trouble for her as her feelings for Lawrence were strong. But then again, she wanted to leave the house anyhow, so should it really concern her? She paused for a moment while they searched one another's eyes. They were able to speak without words, and she knew without a shadow of a doubt that he was in love with her. And she with him.

'Now, I have to go to see to your mother,' she said sharply, breaking the spell.

'Later,' he whispered, and when she reached the first step of the staircase, turning to glance over her shoulder, she found he had disappeared.

* * *

That hour of waiting seemed to drag and just when the hands of the mantel clock in the drawing room had reached the hour and it began to chime, she was summoned by Mrs Brightman.

'Oh, Elin, dear, can you watch those apple pies for me in the kitchen? I wouldn't ask but I have to nip out, as my sister is unwell. That's why I've been quite testy of late; she's continually on my mind. I just need to check on her. I won't be a tick as she's only living in Pond Row, so not too far away.'

Oh dear! What was she to do now? She couldn't very well refuse the woman. 'Are Floss and Molly not around?'

'No, they're busy stripping the beds upstairs.'

'Not again!'

'You know how fussy Mrs Langton is when Mr Lawrence is home.'

Elin nodded. She knew full well and thought the woman would have a fit if she knew he had a yearning for her. 'Beatrice, is she about?'

'She's busy in the laundry room washing those sheets. I wouldn't ask you normally but I trust you.'

Elin smiled. 'Very well. Seeing as everyone else is up to their necks in it, I'll keep an eye on those apple pies for you. How much longer do you think they'll take to bake?'

'Only a few minutes. But I need to leave right now. My niece sent word to me about her mother – sounds like she's getting sicker by the minute and she's ever so worried.'

'You go, now, Mrs Brightman. I'll manage here.'

'Did you have anything important you needed to do yourself?' Cook's eyes were full of concern as she tied the ribbons of her bonnet, which she'd placed on her head at a jaunty angle.

'Nothing that can't wait.' Elin smiled.

Then the woman turned her back and was gone, the back door slamming behind her.

Elin entered the kitchen and, approaching the oven, lowered her head to gaze inside, feeling a hot blast as she did so. The smell of the cinnamon from the apple pies was heavenly. Oh yes, they'd need a few minutes longer. She should have time to run to the garden and explain things to Lawrence.

Anxious from rushing, she arrived at the wooden shed, disappointed to see Lawrence wasn't there, but then she heard a rustling noise and he jumped out at her from behind a bush, which made her giggle.

'Come here,' he said, taking her hand, and he led her behind the shed, which backed onto a high brick wall. 'No one can see us here,' he said breathlessly as he held her in his arms. She wanted to resist, she really did, but she melted as he held her in his strong embrace and planted a kiss on her lips that robbed her of all breath. The kiss seemed to go on and on as her heart beat faster and faster. She was having feelings she shouldn't be having as a married woman. No one had ever kissed her in such a fashion before.

'What are we going to do about this?' he said finally as he drew away, holding her at arm's length to gaze into her eyes.

'I... don't know,' she said.

'I do know I want us to be together,' said Lawrence.

'B... but that's impossible.'

'Nothing's impossible. You could divorce your husband.'

'Not a woman like me. I could never afford such a thing; only rich women can afford to divorce.'

'That is true, but I have the right contacts and I would be prepared to pay whatever it takes to make you my wife.'

She had no doubts that maybe he might find some legal loophole for her to divorce her husband and fork out for it too, but that didn't make things right in her book. Could this really be happening to her? She loved him; she always had from that very first time he'd knocked on the door, coming to visit her in her time of sorrow. She'd been impressed with how compassionate he'd been. Lawrence Langton was a real gentleman and if she were to marry him, her life would change forever.

'I'll have to think about it,' she said. 'I've got a lot going on work wise at the moment.'

'Work?' He frowned. 'I know you enjoy making pies and working at this house but I could make things easy for you, Elin. You'd need never work again. And if you did want to carry on running your pie business, you could employ people to work for you. Just think, you could be a lady of leisure for the rest of your days!'

Oh no, this wasn't what she wanted at all. Her chin jutted out as she said, 'Lawrence, I value my independence. You might be used to women who are compliant, who love the finer things in life and who do not wish to dirty their fingernails, but I'm not one of those!'

'*Those*, referring to Arabella, I suppose?'

'Yes!' she snapped and hated herself for doing so. 'Oh, my goodness!' Her hands flew to her face in horror.

'What's the matter, Elin? I do understand what you meant about wishing to remain independent but—'

'It's not that; I've totally forgotten that I was supposed to be watching some apple pies in the oven for Cook!' She began to run towards the kitchen, where the back door was ajar. Even before she arrived there, the smell of burnt pastry came wafting towards her. Yanking open the oven door, she was devastated to see the blackened tops of the pies. Cook was going to pulverise her. All that woman's hard work was for nothing and all she'd done was ask a favour of her. *Think! Think!*

Elin took some deep breaths to compose herself. Then she removed the two trays from the oven with a thick towel, setting them down on a griddle to cool down. Could she possibly salvage those apple pies? She'd just have to remove the burnt tops to see if they were ruined inside too. To her relief, once she'd carefully removed the tops with a serrated knife, she discovered the insides were fine, just well baked. If she quickly prepared some pastry and cooked new tops in the oven, hopefully Cook would be none the wiser.

In amongst all the palaver, Lawrence had followed her into the kitchen.

'Now that's what you call a pair of burnt offerings!' He chuckled.

'It's no laughing matter – it's all your fault!' she scolded good-naturedly.

Soon, new lids were prepared and baked for both pies. She sealed the tops of them using a little egg wash around the rims and popped the complete pies back in the oven for a couple of minutes. She carefully hid the evidence from Cook though, leaving the back door wide open to allow the smell of burnt pastry to drift away.

'There we are,' said Lawrence, taking her into his arms. 'There's no harm done, is there?'

The click clack of footsteps alerted them to the fact someone was walking down the corridor, so they broke apart – just as the door burst open. Molly was stood there with a few fresh tray cloths over her arm.

'I thought you might like some of these,' she said, looking the pair up and down.

'Thank you, Molly.' Elin tried to keep a straight face.

'I just smelled apple pie and came to see if I might try a slice,' Lawrence said, teasing the girl.

'Don't do that!' yelled Molly, moving to stand in front of the oven, as if in the pies' defence. 'Cook will have your guts for garters!'

That had been a close shave. The girl seemed to swallow Lawrence's quick repartee, appearing none the wiser as to why he was in Elin's company, but if they'd not heard those footsteps approaching, Elin dreaded to think of what the outcome might be. She'd had it on good authority from Cook that Molly now had designs on the young butcher's lad who delivered meat to the property, which was a blessing in more ways than one.

* * *

Before heading off to the pub that evening, Elin decided to call on Frank to see how he was doing. She'd felt enormously guilty about leaving him to his own devices but had told herself that to stay would be folly. Hopefully, Wyn wouldn't be there. But even if he was, he'd not hurt her in front of his father; she was sure of that. She hoped he wasn't at home, as she'd have no idea what to say to him after what had occurred. Maybe he'd be remorseful in front of his father and that surely, going by his previous behaviour, would be an act on his part. Yes, he'd been an excellent actor up until now, fooling all the audience; only the leading lady had known the truth. His father, though, had only recently had his eyes opened to his son's violent behaviour towards her, so she appreciated his feelings would be particularly raw right now.

Tentatively, she knocked on the door, feeling that she couldn't walk straight in there, as it was no longer her home.

The door swung open and she was surprised to see Dilys standing there. Upon seeing her, the woman smiled broadly. 'Oh, *cariad*, we've been so worried about you. Come in.'

We? It was obvious to Elin that the woman had been back and forth at the house several times since she had left it. Frank and Dilys would be great company for one another, having both lost their spouses.

'Thank you, Dilys,' Elin said as she stepped over the threshold. The woman stood to one side to allow her to pass and then she closed the door behind them. Elin's eyes darted around the room.

'Have no fear,' said Dilys. 'Your husband's not here and hasn't been since that dreadful incident. Frank filled me in.' She touched Elin's forearm lightly. 'Oh, not that we've been gossiping about you, dear.'

'I didn't think for a moment you had.' Elin smiled at her, less nervous now she'd been reassured Wyn wasn't at home. 'So, have you seen him at all?'

The woman shook her head. 'According to his father, he's not shown up at work either. He has no idea where he is right now.' She paused for a moment and then let out a small sigh. 'Frank and I have been dreadfully concerned about you. I knew a little of what you've been going through when you explained to me, but Frank had absolutely no idea at all. He was right shocked about it all.'

'I hid it well,' Elin admitted. 'Where is he, by the way?'

'He's out in the backyard, chopping up some logs for firewood.'

Elin glanced at the hearth where the flames of the coal fire were dancing merrily. A delicious smell of stew emanated from the scullery. Yes, Mrs Evans had made it really cosy for Frank when he'd returned home from work. All her concerns for the man began to ebb away. Dilys would look out for him, for sure.

There was the sound of the back door opening and closing, and then Frank was in the living room with a big smile on his face, tears filling his eyes. 'Elin…' he said, walking towards her. 'It's so lovely to see you. Have you come to stay for good?'

She shook her head and then hugged him warmly. 'No. It's best I don't return here,' she said, drawing away.

'I expect you're staying at the big house then?'

'No. Actually I'm staying at…' She was about to tell him she was lodging at Griffin's pub but thought better of it. She didn't want Wyn to know where she was. 'I'm staying with a friend for the time being.'

He let out a little smile. 'That's good to know. You'll always be welcome here, any time. You've been like a daughter to me.'

She wondered how the man would feel if he discovered she'd been in someone else's arms only that morning and of her plans to look after a group of prostitutes at the pub – he'd be shocked for sure.

'Now then,' said Dilys. 'I hope you'll stop for a bite to eat?'

Elin nodded. 'Yes, I'd like that.'

She glanced at the pair of them. Why hadn't she seen it before? Frank and Dilys were good companions for one another and even if it didn't turn into marriage, she realised they'd be solid friends. When her mother-in-law was alive, of course, she and Dilys were best friends and she supposed, back then, Frank was a little out on a limb in their presence, but since his wife's death, they'd grown close to one another. Maybe as they both missed Olwen, their friendship brought them together in her memory, bringing comfort to them.

16

There were obviously things that needed discussing between Elin and Lawrence, but he had to return to London for work. There was an important court case upcoming that was expected to drag on for several weeks. Maybe it was just as well, as it would give time for things to cool down between them. He'd be mortified if he knew what her new role at the pub involved – she was sure of it – but her idea behind it all was to keep those girls safe. If they were intent on working in such a field then the best thing to do was to watch out for them. Otherwise, they might end up injured – or even worse. It was a dangerous profession for any woman to undertake, but one that put food on the table.

Arrangements were made over the following couple of weeks to decorate the back room of the pub for 'clients'. Elin had insisted on referring to them in that manner as she said it sounded more sophisticated and upmarket. They were no longer to refer to the men as 'customers' or 'punters'. She realised, of course, that it would take some time for the girls to become accustomed to this as old habits died hard. Another habit she intended putting a stop to was any of the girls taking advantage of the men by stealing from them. She explained it was a practice that needed to stop from here on in, and any girl found stealing from a client would be given her marching orders. The girls assured her they'd be on their best behaviour, and she guessed it was too much of a risk for any of them to take now they were all going 'upmarket' as it were.

Finally, the room was wallpapered with heavy duty flock paper, and the doors, skirting boards and ceiling given a fresh coat of paint. A fancy crystal chandelier was suspended from the ceiling and gasoliers installed either end of the alcoves flanking the large mantelpiece. An oriental rug in a multitude of rich colours was placed in the middle of the room, along with two chaise longue leather sofas facing one another, as well as several armchairs and low tables. And the pièce de résistance in the corner of the room was an upright piano that Mr Griffin had bought privately, or so he said. Elin reckoned maybe someone had given it to him as payment for a debt owed. Dotted around the room were several leafy tall green plants: ferns, palms and aspidistra, settled in large colourful pottery vases, creating an exotic effect. The gasoliers came in handy given the circumstances, as they could be turned up or down to increase or decrease the level of lighting in the room. Elin suggested that early evening when the men were dining, they be turned up full, and then dimmed later, when the evening's seduction began.

One rule she maintained was that no girl was allowed to have any relations with any of the men within the confines of that room. They were allowed to eat or drink with the clientele and even flirt a little, but any kissing, cuddling or intimate relations were strictly for the bedrooms upstairs. Mr Griffin had said they'd have to be careful as some of those men had reputations to uphold – they held high offices at the ironworks and at local businesses within the town and couldn't afford to be caught in flagrante in front of the local constabulary. There were some sneaky journalists around too. So, for those reasons, discretion was advised.

The girls seemed fine with this and Gwenda, although she said she felt ready to return to work, was given orders by Elin that instead, she carry on helping in the kitchen – more hands were needed now to provide high-class meals for the men. A cook had been employed to prepare simple but nourishing meals, but Elin thought it might only remind them of what they'd been getting at home – wholesome, plain fare. The object was to take the men away from their everyday lives where they might be under a lot of strain from being a boss or running a business. Instead, she decided it might be an idea to employ a proper hotel chef who might offer some French cuisine – onion soup, steaks cooked in various sauces, mussels in a white wine sauce and scrumptious desserts like crêpes Suzette and tarte tatin – knowing a little about such things from Mrs Brightman, who had schooled her well. Mrs Brightman had once told her she'd been to Paris in her younger days when she worked for another well-to-do family, so she knew all about French cuisine, even incorporating it into her menus at the Langton house on occasion.

It would be important too, she realised, that the menu be written in French to give it an exotic flavour. All the while, she reassured Mr Griffin this would set them apart from many other establishments in the area who offered little more than a pie and a pint. It would be a whole new experience for them.

Mr Griffin became quite excited about it all. 'I realised there was something special about you the first time I ever met you, Mrs Edwards,' he enthused. She realised he was deeply fond of her, but felt in her heart that he was a ladies' man in more ways than one. It was rumoured by the staff at the pub that he had several women on the go, but to be fair to him, he did not take advantage of his position as landlord – that seemed an unwritten rule.

* * *

The day finally arrived when Elin decided to hand her notice in at the house. She'd given Mrs Langton enough time to recover from the recent disturbance between her sons. Before telling the woman, though, Elin explained all to Cook when the other maids were busy elsewhere.

Cook let out a little sigh. 'I can't say I'm happy with the path you've chosen to take, Elin, but I do understand *why* you've chosen to take it. You need to earn good money now that your husband will no longer be supporting you.'

Elin shrugged. 'Did he ever financially support me, though?'

'I suppose he didn't really, acquiring all those debts. In a way, he was leeching off you and his parents too. I bet he had no intention of ever buying or renting a house for the pair of you. It's just as well you got out when you did, my girl.'

'I suppose so.'

'There's no suppose about it!' Cook pursed her lips. 'Imagine if you'd had little ones too! He'd have stolen sweets from your babies' mouths by the sound of it!'

She honestly hadn't considered that. 'I still wouldn't wish any harm to come to him,' she said with a sigh.

'Maybe not,' said Cook, thoughtfully, 'but he harmed you often enough. I would save your sympathy for someone who deserves it, if I were you.'

Elin realised Cook was right: Wyn hadn't done her any favours whatsoever. 'I'm going to inform Mrs Langton this morning about my intention to leave.'

'Yes, best do that. She'll miss you though, Elin, and I expect she'll find you hard to replace.'

'I'll miss her too but I think it will be for the best.'

Cook arched her eyebrows. 'And what about Mr Lawrence? Will you miss him, too?'

Elin's mouth dried up. Did the woman know anything? 'Er, yes, I suppose so,' she said a little too quickly.

Cook looked at her for the longest time. 'I have eyes and ears, you know,' she said in a sage fashion. 'I know how fond you are of one another. I've seen how he looks at you. Even when you served him in the dining room the evening of his birthday party, he only had eyes for you.'

There was no fooling the woman, that much was for certain. 'It wouldn't work out between us anyhow,' Elin said, with a note of regret to her voice.

'In most cases, no, it wouldn't,' said Cook, huffing out a breath, 'but love is a powerful thing. It can make fools out of us all...'

'Is there something you're trying to tell me, Mrs Brightman?'

'Oh, I'm just reminiscing, that's all – about that family I worked for when I was young. The one that took me to Paris with them. I fell in love with their son. He was astonishingly handsome...' There was a twinkle in the woman's eyes as she spoke. 'We really had something special going on. He wished to marry me but his parents had him lined up for marriage with a family friend's daughter; it would have made good business sense.'

'And what happened?'

'We were going to run away together one evening and get married without his parents' approval. I packed my bags and waited for him outside the railway station, but a fifteen-minute wait turned into a half hour and, as the moments ticked away, I realised in my heart he wasn't coming.'

'He got cold feet?'

'No, it wasn't that at all. Gilbert had every intention of meeting me...' A tear trickled down her face as she sniffed loudly, and she dabbed at her watery eyes with the back of her hand. 'No, his father found out about it and kept him under lock and key in his bedroom for days. He finally managed to escape and found me, but by then, I'd decided I didn't want to mess up his life any more.'

'Oh, that's so sad...' Elin said, shaking her head with disbelief. 'But why didn't you follow your heart?'

'It was because I loved him so much. You see, sometimes it's better to let someone go for their own sake, no matter how much they love you or you love them.'

Elin nodded, now with tears in her own eyes. She understood that Cook was saying this to her for her own benefit.

* * *

Mrs Langton had taken Elin's resignation very well and said, given the circumstances regarding her husband, she quite understood why she should want to leave the village. Elin didn't, of course, explain what she was doing instead, just that she was staying with a friend who owned a pub. Mrs Langton had even written a character reference for her should she need it someday. She'd suggested working out her notice but the woman wouldn't hear of it, saying that Molly could help her now until she found a suitable replacement.

It was just a shame Lawrence wasn't around. She wanted to make sure they parted on good terms.

In light of Cook's sad story, and not wanting to get her own heart broken, Elin left the house, turning back to look at it as she approached the main gates with tears in her eyes.

* * *

Over the following couple of weeks, Elin threw herself into work at the pub. Gwenda was still helping with the pie-making business and Elin had plans for the young woman to share the work so, if necessary, she could concentrate on the working girls' welfare. She'd trained her well, teaching her how to make both shortcrust and puff pastry and how best to cook the meat so it was tender and juicy to use for the various fillings. It was her hope that the young woman wouldn't return to prostitution now there was a perfectly good role for her in the kitchen of the pub.

Everything was going quite well with the vetting of the men. Most of them managed to pass muster, except for a couple of undesirable sorts whom Elin had bad instincts about, and who were given short shrift and sent on their way.

She always kept a chatelaine of various keys on a chain around her waist. These were to allow her access to the girls' bedrooms at any given moment should something go wrong. Elin had taken to occasionally patrolling the landing area outside their rooms and listening for anything that sounded a bit untoward. So far, she hadn't had to go barging into any but she would if necessary. It was probably what she'd endured with her own husband that was putting her on such high alert. And even now she wasn't resting on her own laurels, because she feared Wyn might one day seek her out here at the pub, should he ever learn of her whereabouts.

One afternoon, a smartly dressed gentleman who was probably in his twenties turned up at the pub asking to speak to her.

She led him through the back of the premises and into a

small room that she'd acquired as an office for herself, instructing him to take a seat.

'I understand you need to speak to me before I request the company of one of the girls?' he asked, raising his brows.

'That is correct – you heard right,' she said. 'I need your details, which will be kept in that bureau behind me, and locked away in a drawer so everything will be kept confidential – have no fear about that.'

He nodded at her.

'Does that meet with your approval?' she asked.

'Yes, thank you. I have nothing to hide.' He smiled at her, displaying his open palms in a gesture of transparency.

The man reminded her of someone, or was it that she'd encountered him someplace before?

She stood and made her way to the bureau, then, taking a little silver key from her belt, unlocked it and proceeded to remove a small black ledger from the drawer. Settling herself in a chair at the desk, she looked at him.

Then she lifted a fountain pen. 'Name, please?'

He stood to make his way over to the desk. 'Benjamin.'

'I'll need a surname too,' she said curtly, quirking an eyebrow.

'Langton.'

Elin opened her mouth as she gazed at the man before her in astonishment. No wonder this man looked so familiar to her! This was Lawrence's brother. She quickly closed her gaping mouth and composed herself. She knew him to be twenty-two years of age and eligible for marriage, so why would he need the services of a place like this? Though from what she could gather from some of the girls, not all the men who attended the place were after that sort of thing. There was one who just wanted to be held and cuddled, and he liked to talk to the woman he was with, as apparently his wife was a cold fish who gave him no love at home.

But judging just how handsome the man sat before her was, she couldn't imagine he was here to speak to one of the girls and pay good money for it; he'd have no problems whatsoever attracting eligible young ladies.

He gave his address as a place in Aberdare, which was in a neighbouring valley. Strange that, as hadn't someone told her he'd been banished to the wilds of Scotland? His copper-coloured hair made her wonder if he had a bit of a temper and that's what had led to the fracas that night following the party.

After taking his details, she told him the rules for the establishment. If he was surprised by them, then he didn't say so. He seemed quite a nice person to her but despite all the finery of his blue silk cravat, crisp white shirt and black astrakhan coat, she was aware that sometimes a person might be a wolf in sheep's clothing. But for now, she'd give him the benefit of the doubt.

She had toyed with telling him who she was and the role she'd played at his mother's house but then thought better of it, as it might make him too familiar with her and put him on his guard. Better he didn't know as this way was more professional. She hoped though it was a fallacy that his red hair indicated he had a fiery temper as she couldn't afford to have someone on their books who might take it out on one of the girls. Tempers put the girls in danger, but so far, he'd been a proper gentleman who seemed placid in nature.

* * *

All was running smoothly for a few days, but one evening, when Elin came downstairs to the bar room to start her work, she noticed a familiar figure slumped over a table, his head lowered and a tankard of ale in front of him. It was Wyn! Although he seemed worse for wear, she felt that familiar dread take hold of her. What on earth was he doing here? Had he managed to discover her whereabouts? What could she do now? She needed to take care of the girls and couldn't do so from a distance.

Approaching the bar, she summoned Jim. 'See that fella at the back of the pub...' she whispered.

'Aye, I see him, the one with his head almost falling into his pint, looks as though he's had over the odds?'

'That's the one,' she said, realising that if he was drunk, he probably had no idea she was here.

'What about him?'

She released a breath. 'That man is my husband. I recently left him, as he's been quite violent, so I don't want him causing trouble for me...'

'I see,' said Jim in a knowing fashion.

'If he spots me, he's liable to get angry. He has no idea I'm staying here.'

'Don't worry, I'll have your back for you, Mrs Edwards.' Jim smiled in a reassuring fashion. 'I'll warn Freddie, the other barman working here this evening, too.'

Jim had the most beautiful Irish accent and she guessed he'd be one for giving the ladies all the blarney.

'I'd appreciate it, if you would. I'll be in my office for a while. Hopefully, he might leave here soon.'

'Let's hope so,' said Jim as he tossed a bar towel on his shoulder and began to collect the empty tankards. Elin guessed he was doing so to check Wyn out.

She made her way to the back room to keep an eye on the girls. Everything appeared to be ticking along nicely there. No one misbehaving themselves. The gentlemen were chatting back and forth with the girls and amongst themselves too, while Bridget was sat at the piano playing a song, which she'd said she'd heard as a little girl in the old country. It was called 'Ramblin' Rosie' and as she sang along, it seemed to bring a tear to some of the girls' eyes. Bridget's melodic voice had a haunting quality to it. As Elin listened to the lyrics, she could see the girls related to the young girl who had fallen on hard times in Dublin city. These gentlemen here, though, seemed bemused by it all. For all their finery, they would hardly have experienced anything like that.

She had to admit how nicely the girls were turned out this evening. She had taken them to a costumier to get them fitted out with some lovely gowns – gowns that wouldn't look out of place in one of those posh balls the Crawshay family held at their castle on the hill.

She checked all was going well in the kitchen and was pleased to discover the cook there had everything under control with Gwenda's assistance. He informed her he was baking stuffed trout that evening with a selection of winter vegetables, followed by fruit pudding with fresh cream. Bart Bevan was a local young man, who in fairness could throw a decent meal together. Maybe there'd be no need to hire a fancy chef to cook those French meals she aimed to provide after all. If she got hold of some French cookbooks for him, the man could learn all about them and then he'd have free rein to experiment with the recipes.

It was an hour or so later before she checked out the bar room and, by then, there was no sign of her husband.

'What happened to him?' she asked Jim.

'I didn't notice him leave,' he said with a shrug, 'but now I know what he looks like, I shall be on my guard in the future. I won't be taking any messing from the likes of him.'

Elin nodded in an approving fashion.

When Gwenda finished tidying up in the kitchen and Bart had headed off for home, she had a quiet word with the girl. 'Did you issue a description of the man who attacked you to the police?' she asked. She hated having to remind her about the incident, dredging it all up again, but it was necessary in case any of the girls encountered the man.

Gwenda's bottom lip trembled and her eyes filled with tears. 'I… I couldn't give them much to go on…' she said. 'I can't remember much about it. All I remember is he started out so nice at the beginning of my time with him, but then he seemed to turn on me by the end of it.'

'I'm sorry to make you think about such a horrid experience, Gwenda,' Elin said, 'but it is important.'

'I know it is, Mrs Edwards.' Gwenda sniffed loudly. 'It's like my mind can't make any sense of it. I can see him doing what he did to me, but for some reason his face is like it's blacked out.'

'You mean like he's in shadow?'

'Yes, that's it.'

'Is there anything else you can remember about him, like his accent, maybe? Or if there was any particular odour about him?'

Gwenda nodded. 'I do remember he had a local accent; he wasn't a stranger to the town like some are.'

'That's something to go on, anyhow. What about how he was dressed?'

'How'd you mean?' Gwenda angled her head to one side.

'Was he well dressed like the new clientele we have here, or was he dressed more like a workman? One of the lower classes?'

Gwenda pondered a moment. 'Something just came back to me. He was wearing a jacket and a white muffler and a flat cap – they were quite dusty, so I guess he worked somewhere that got him dirty in some way.'

'That's interesting,' said Elin as a fleeting thought passed through her mind. Gwenda might well be describing Wyn there – it was how he dressed for work, but on the other hand, so did many men in this town. In any case, Wyn might be capable of violence towards women, but to go as far as trying to murder one? Surely not! Dismissing the thought as quickly as it arrived, she added, 'Now then, I won't push you for any more details at present, but if you remember anything about him, no matter how small, you will tell me, won't you?'

'I promise,' Gwenda vowed.

She left the girl to tidy up the kitchen and then went in search of Mr Griffin, who was scanning the evening paper in the bar room, in the same corner she'd first encountered him. Elin was no fool – she knew he must be pretending to read so he could keep a check on the customers, particularly after what had happened to Gwenda. Every once in a while, he looked up and glanced around the room. From his viewpoint with his back to the bar, he could see every customer. He turned to her as she approached and folded his newspaper.

'Anything of interest in that?' she enquired.

'If you can call the press making out the infamous Jack the Ripper might be incognito in Merthyr Tydfil, then yes!' He shot her a smile.

She took a seat opposite him, unsurprised really, as she recalled that headline she'd read a few weeks back: *Has Jack the Ripper Left London?* Maybe the man had left one heaving metropolis for another.

'You know what those reporters are like,' he continued, making mountains out of molehills. 'They hardly deal in facts, preferring to embellish stories to suit themselves.'

'I hope we haven't got a murderer on our hands, though,' said Elin thoughtfully. 'I had a word with Gwenda just now and she barely remembers anything about her attacker. She sees his face as blacked out, though she could tell me he has a local accent.'

'That definitely narrows things down,' said Griffin in a sardonic fashion as he lifted a sceptical eyebrow.

'Oh, and the other thing she just recalled is that he wore work clothes. She said they were very dusty.'

'That could describe most of the men in this establishment.' He gave a rueful laugh. 'It's my guess the man will never be caught – there's not enough for the police to go on.'

'Do you really think so?'

'I saw it happen many years ago when I first bought this pub, at another place on the high street where the landlord was running some girls. One girl was dreadfully beaten up there; they never found the culprit. And don't get me started on those girls who walk the streets and don't even have a place to work from – they run the biggest risk of all, but it does seem to go with the territory.'

'At least we're making things as safe as they can possibly be for the girls who work here,' Elin said.

Mr Griffin nodded before studying her face for a moment. 'I bet you can't believe that you've gone from working in a fancy house to a place like this?'

'No.' She chuckled. 'If anyone had told me that about a year ago, I'd never have believed them.' She paused. 'By the way, my husband was in here earlier.'

His eyes grew large. 'Did he approach you or hurt you in any way, Elin?'

She shook her head. 'Fortunately not. He didn't even see me, he was in that much of a drunken state. I tipped Jim off about him. He said he'll keep an eye out.'

'How that man has the nerve to take a drink in my pub!' said Griffin, clenching his teeth.

'Yes, as far as Wyn's concerned, he hasn't paid off his debt to you and thinks he's had one up on you. He has no idea I've been working off his debt for him.'

Griffin's eyes looked sad. 'Is that how you really view me now, Elin? That you're still working off your husband's debt, and so in some ways are indebted to me? Because if so, you paid that off the first time you baked those pies for me. You don't owe me a thing now; it is I who is in debt to you.' He lifted her hand from across the table and planted a kiss on it, totally taking her by surprise.

'I suppose I did think that way, yes,' she admitted.

'Then please, do not any longer. You are free to leave here any time you wish but I do admit to needing you and wanting you around.'

His words caused a tear to trickle down her face so she wiped it away with the back of her hand. 'Thank you,' was all she managed to say before having to leave the table. He was just so kind to her and at that moment, she didn't quite know how to handle it.

* * *

Later that evening when Griffin left the pub, explaining he was off to discuss business with some associates, Elin wandered around the bar surveying the room. There was nothing out of the ordinary to tell but then, two men who were fairly smartly dressed in tweed jackets and bowler hats entered the premises. Her senses told her to watch them closely. She did not for a moment think either of those were the attacker but there was something instinctive inside her, informing her they weren't merely here for a quiet drink.

She approached the bar, catching Jim's attention. 'Any idea who those pair are?' she asked, casting a glance in their direction. They had settled themselves down in a quiet corner and were now supping out of tankards. The one with bushy sideburns had lit his pipe.

'Oh those – they work for one of the local rags,' he said, nodding in their direction as he pulled one of the beer pumps, filling a tankard with a frothy top of ale. 'Just a second, Mrs Edwards...' He handed the customer his tankard and took his money. And as no one else availed themselves of his services, he now gave her his full attention, lowering his voice. 'I overheard their conversation when they ordered those drinks. They reckon the police have caught the attacker! I'm going to tell Mr Griffin as soon as he returns.'

'Pardon?' Elin's eyes widened as a chill ran down her spine.

'Yes, by all accounts an arrest has been made!' Jim said with some excitement.

Elin gasped. 'Jim, I have to find out more about this.'

'B... but Mrs Edwards, please don't interfere. Mr Griffin wouldn't like that.'

Elin did not heed the barman's words; instead she walked directly over to where both men were seated and began to strike up a conversation with them. If they were surprised, neither showed it and they invited her to take a seat. She explained she worked at the pub for Mr Griffin but did not extol the virtues of her role there.

When she raised the topic of the attacker, both men exchanged knowing glances with one another and said they had a major scoop, which would go to press that very evening. 'We even have the suspect's name!' the man with the pipe boasted.

Elin swallowed. 'Wh... what is it?'

The man shook his head. 'Now that would be telling, wouldn't it? You'll have to wait and read the *Merthyr Herald* like everyone else!'

'How did you find out about him, though?' Elin wanted to know.

'A reliable source informed me he violently attacked another young woman last night, but thankfully was disturbed by a group of men while in the act, which probably saved the poor unfortunate's life. He made his escape before he could be captured by the police.' The man with the pipe nodded sombrely at her, then he took a puff from his pipe as though it were some sort of solace for him, sending up a cloud of acrid smoke.

Taking charge of the situation, Elin said, 'This sounds like a celebration. What will you have to drink, gentlemen? A double whisky each, perhaps?'

Both men grinned, nodding appreciatively at her. By hook or by crook she was going to get that name out of them before the newspaper went to press.

It took less than an hour of buying the pair drinks and some gentle cajoling but when she did, a feeling of shock and revulsion, washed over her.

Surely not Benjamin Langton?

Thankfully, so far, he'd not returned to visit any of the girls, but hadn't there been an element of violence between him and his brother? Maybe he was capable of losing his temper? She still found it hard to believe that the polite docile man she'd spoken to was a vicious attacker who had harmed Gwenda.

'So, you're confident the police have the right man?' she asked the one with the bushy moustache. She was dubious about it all because Gwenda had described her attacker as a working man in dusty clothing, not a handsome young gentleman in all his finery.

'Yes.' He nodded at her. 'The police told us he's been in trouble before for fraud. And to add to the scoop, he's one of the well-known Langtons associated with that confectionery business of the same name. He's a right one anyhow; he tried to embezzle funds from his own family!' He raised his whisky glass and gave a cheer, causing Elin to feel sick to her stomach. She was going to have to find Lawrence and tell him about this. She made her excuses to leave the men, who would no doubt be there for a time yet celebrating his capture and the success of their precious article. It turned out the one with the sideburns was a reporter for the newspaper and the other, quieter man, an artist who had sketched Benjamin's arrest to grace the front page.

* * *

Elin quickly located Mr Griffin's coachman and asked him to take her to Abercanaid. Thankfully, her employer had set out on foot that night, so she guessed any business he was doing wasn't all that far away. The coach driver parked up the coach just outside the Langton house, and she asked him to wait for her as she wouldn't be too long.

When she arrived at the back door, she was surprised to see Cook still working in the kitchen. She appeared flustered and gave a slight shriek when she saw Elin stood there.

'Oh, you gave me a right fright then, Elin!' she said, placing the heel of her hand to her chest.

Elin blinked. 'What's going on then, Mrs Brightman? How come you're still here?'

'It's Mr Lawrence; he has a guest tonight and they're dining together!'

'Oh?' she said, wondering if it was a family friend or an associate he was entertaining, but she didn't ask who it was.

'I need to see him urgently,' she said breathlessly.

'Anything I can help with?'

Elin shook her head. 'No, not really. I've just discovered that Mr Langton's brother has been taken into custody by the police.'

'Never!' said Cook. 'What's he done?'

'There were two men who work for the *Merthyr Herald* at the pub talking about the arrest – they were quite gleeful, saying the police have the man who attacked Gwenda. I got Benjamin's name out of them. Apparently, he attacked another young woman too last night and might have killed her, only he was disturbed by some men and ran away.'

'Oh, my goodness!' Cook began to tremble. 'I know there's been a lot of argy-bargy with him over the years, but nothing to suggest he's capable of something like that!'

Elin bit on her lower lip, deliberating on telling Cook what she knew, but ultimately she felt it best to be truthful. 'To be honest with you, he's registered as a client at the pub! I interviewed him myself.'

Cook pursed her lips. 'I'm not surprised, but did he realise who you are?'

Elin shook her head. 'No, up until then we'd never met. He must have heard his mother referring to me, of course, but wouldn't have put two and two together.'

'You might have had a lucky escape there then, Elin. And more importantly, so did those young women at the pub.'

Elin nodded, still feeling incredulous about the situation. 'I better go and have a quiet word with Mr Lawrence then,' she said, making her way to the dining room.

'No, don't do that right now...' said Cook guardedly as she grabbed Elin by the arm. 'The person he's dining with, and I don't want to upset you, is Miss Arabella...'

Elin felt her heart plummet. 'M... Miss Arabella?' She almost choked on the words.

'Yes. And from what Floss and Molly told me earlier, they think he's about to pop the question.'

'Ask her to marry him?'

Cook nodded. 'It appears so. They both said he was speaking very nicely to her and she had his full attention.'

Elin's eyes glazed with tears and, suddenly, she felt quite unsteady on her feet, prompting Cook to guide her over to the table so she could take a seat. 'I know it's hard for you to hear, Elin dear, but it's probably for the best.'

All the while as she let the woman fuss over her, she thought how fickle Lawrence must be – it was only the other day he'd told her he wanted her to be his wife, but she hadn't exactly been all that receptive, had she? Maybe he'd decided to simply move on, especially as she'd left the house without saying goodbye to him. Perhaps he considered her departure the answer to his proposal.

'I'll fetch you a glass of water, Elin,' she soothed. 'I tell you what, I'll look for some paper and a pen and you can write a letter to Mr Lawrence explaining what's happened. You need not see him and I can get one of the maids to pass it to him later.'

Of course, Cook was correct. Given the circumstances, it was probably the best thing to do. After penning the letter and placing it into an envelope, she handed it to the woman.

Elin could barely take it all in. All she could think of was that Lawrence was going to marry someone else, and there wasn't a thing she could do about it.

17

By the time Elin returned to the pub, both newspaper men had left and Morgan Griffin had returned. He approached her as soon as she entered, his eyes full of concern. 'Jim told me you want to have a word with me,' he said, leading her into the kitchen, which had now been cleared, the cook having departed. Elin explained what had occurred since he'd gone.

Morgan's eyes widened. 'I know it's shocking who they have arrested,' he said, 'but that's got to be good news, hasn't it?'

'Not for Lawrence Langton it isn't!' Elin said, with an edge to her voice.

'But good news for the girls here,' said Morgan, smiling. 'Especially Gwenda. She can sleep soundly now, knowing the police have their man.'

Something suddenly occurred to Elin. 'But she won't be able to identify him, will she? She remembers something about him, his clothing and his accent, but her mind is blanking out his face.'

'I suppose so, but that won't matter. Maybe the police can get a confession out of him anyhow. Blinking heck, I can't believe it's

Lawrence Langton's brother they have in custody, but he does have a chequered past by all accounts.'

'So have you!' Elin barked at him.

'Elin! This is so unlike you to be like this. Why are you so angry with me? I'm on your side. You realise I'd do anything for you, don't you?' He laid his hands on her shoulders and looked directly into her eyes, and she could see the love he had for her there.

'It's not you.' She sniffed. 'It's me. I'm in love with Lawrence Langton and I thought he loved me too, but when I went to tell him about his brother tonight, he was dining with this woman he knows and the staff at the house think he was going to propose to her!' She began to weep like a fool as he held her in his arms, softly comforting her, patting her back.

'Elin, you mean the world to me,' he said, and then he planted a kiss on her forehead in a fatherly fashion, making her realise his love was almost as one would care for a child, their own flesh and blood. He was significantly older than her, after all. 'I don't want to see you getting hurt.'

'I already am,' she bawled as she buried her head in his chest.

* * *

Elin was strolling along Merthyr High Street with Gwenda, the bustling crowds in evidence due to the open-air market. Elin had decided to focus on the girl instead of her own woes. There was nothing she could do about it – Lawrence Langton was out of her life, though she realised he'd never be truly out of her heart. She'd asked Mr Griffin if she might take the girl out to treat her to something nice to wear to cheer her up, and when he'd agreed and she told her, Gwenda had smiled, nodding enthusiastically. The swelling and bruising to her face had now subsided so she was free to face the world once again, instead of hiding away in the kitchen. Though Elin realised it would be a long time until her inner scars faded.

Elin had the idea of visiting a little shop she knew where the girl could try on maybe a new bonnet or a blouse; it wasn't too expensive there and the proprietor was so friendly and welcoming – nothing was too much trouble for Mrs Parry. And if she didn't have what you wanted, she'd try to get it for you somehow.

It was a bright morning, nearing midday, and the sun was high overhead, unseasonally warm for the time of the year. They had both perused a stall at the market that sold costume jewellery and were about to head towards the clothing shop when Gwenda froze in her tracks.

'What's wrong?' Elin laid down the glass and paste brooch she'd been admiring to look at her. Something was up, that much was evident.

But Gwenda was unable to speak. She opened her mouth and closed it again, reminding Elin of the way the young woman had behaved following the attack.

Elin wrapped a comforting arm around her shoulders. 'Nothing will happen to you while you're with me,' she said with some confidence.

Gwenda turned her head to look at her and then pointed in the distance. 'He...' was all she managed to say.

'He what?' Elin frowned.

'H... he's the man!' Gwenda said, in a trembling voice.

Elin's eyes widened. 'The man who attacked you?'

'Yes.'

Elin strained to see in the distance, holding her hand to her eyes as the sun dazzled her. 'Did you see in which direction he went?'

'Towards the chapel, that one on the high street,' the young woman said with some conviction.

A thought occurred to her. Maybe her suspicion that Benjamin Langton was innocent was correct then as, after all, he was now in police custody. Unless Gwenda was mistaken, then it couldn't possibly be him. 'Come with me. I'm going to see exactly who he is...'

Gwenda nodded, following in her wake as Elin pushed forward through the throng with some urgency.

As they neared the chapel, where the marketplace thinned out to just one or two stalls, Gwenda whispered, 'Look, there he is – he's buying hot chestnuts from that stall.'

Elin could see a man beside a metal burner being served by an elderly woman. As he paid for his purchase and turned to the side, Elin could finally see his face. Her heart hammered. It was him – Wyn! There was no mistaking those broad shoulders and that strong jaw in profile.

'A... are you sure now you have the right man, Gwenda? You said you couldn't remember his face?' Her mouth had dried up and her palms perspired.

'Yes, I am now. I glimpsed him pass us as you were admiring that jewellery. It all came flooding back to me.'

'Do you ever remember him mentioning anything of a personal nature to you, just to be sure it's him?'

'I'm remembering things now,' she said excitedly. 'He did tell me he was married but not what his wife's name was. He told me he waited until Mr Griffin had left the pub that night as he owed him money and he didn't want to be spotted by him. Reckoned he'd once sent some thugs to his house, and they'd smashed the window and door. But said he had the last laugh as he still hadn't paid Mr Griffin what he owed him!'

'You have the right man,' said Elin firmly. For now, she wasn't going to tell Gwenda who the man was to her; she'd inform the police first, to get Benjamin Langton off the hook. 'I'd better not approach him to be safe. We'll call in to the police station as I have a name for him.'

'You do?' asked Gwenda, sounding surprised.

'Yes, I know him very well. I'll explain all later. But we need to get a move on,' she said, lifting her skirts as she began to run in the direction of Graham Street where the police station was located. 'Come on! We haven't got a moment to lose!'

* * *

It had happened so quickly that Elin felt her feet hadn't touched the ground. She explained to the sergeant that Gwenda had recognised her attacker on the street as the memories of what had happened that night came back to her and she'd begun to piece things together. The hardest part for Elin had been explaining that it was her own husband who had done that and that he used to attack her too, the very person who should have loved her the most in this world. The police sergeant said she'd done the right thing as he might have eventually gone on to murder someone and they'd do everything in their power to track him down and put him under lock and key.

She deliberated for a moment before asking, 'What about Benjamin Langton? Now you know he's not the attacker, is he free to go?'

'I'm guessing you've read the newspaper headline, then? He will be shortly,' said the sergeant. 'His brother called here earlier and brought someone with him to represent him should it go to court, but, in light of this new evidence, there's a good chance he'll be released.'

Elin let out a little sigh. 'I never really thought it was him,' she said with some conviction.

Gwenda was beginning to look a little weary, so Elin decided to take her back to the pub and explain to Morgan Griffin what had happened.

'Don't worry, Gwenda,' she said softly, 'I'll take you out to buy that new bonnet some other time.'

Gwenda nodded gratefully at her. There'd be time enough to explain who the perpetrator was when she'd recovered from today's shocking ordeal.

Morgan Griffin was mortified to discover that it was Wyn who'd been the attacker. 'You never know,' he said to Elin later when they were taking a tot of brandy together in the bar room, 'maybe it was the man's bitter and twisted way of getting back at me?'

'Possibly,' said Elin, though she sincerely doubted it. The truth was, in her heart she knew there had been other women. She remembered her father-in-law accusing him of smelling strongly of perfume that one night, and the occasions too when he reckoned he'd been helping out that farmer – it had all been a pack of lies. Wyndham Edwards despised women for some reason. The only one he'd shown any respect towards was his own mother, whom he'd listened to. But it was when she passed away that a monster was unleashed.

'Look at this!' said Jim as he came crashing into the bar room ready to begin work. 'The headline here!' He held up the front page of the *Merthyr Herald*. 'That journalist has written another piece and all within twenty-four hours of the Glamorgan Constabulary having the wrong man banged up to a man hunt now being underway!' He slapped the newspaper onto the bar.

Griffin was on his feet to read it, scouring the front page, with Elin stood beside him. The headline read: *Fallen Woman's Attacker Disturbed by Vigilante Group!*

Elin sucked in a surprised breath. So, the men that had almost stumbled over Wyn the other night had been a group actually looking for him, probably in the mistaken belief that he was Jack the Ripper. That newspaper had set the bait by egging people on to sell more copies.

'Will you read it to me, Elin?' Griffin asked. He paused for a moment before adding, 'I can read, but sometimes I have difficulty with long words.'

'Of course, I will.' She smiled and, lifting up the newspaper from the counter, read from the front page.

'"In the early hours of this morning a very shocking event occurred. A woman of dubious morals was attacked in an alleyway in the notorious area of China, Merthyr Tydfil. The man was cold and callous and the victim said she feared for her life following the recent Jack the Ripper murders in Whitechapel, London."'

'They're linking the two events to sensationalise things!' Griffin scoffed.

Elin realised all too well what the press could be like at times. She raised her brows. 'Hmm, I was just thinking the same thing myself.'

'Carry on,' he urged.

'"The woman was savaged and bled profusely at the hands of the beast who overpowered her petite frame. This unfortunate feared she was about to meet her maker when she heard a flurry of footsteps headed towards her. They were enough to scare off her attacker who took flight, and the men immediately escorted her to a place of safety.

'"Unfortunately, what now appears to be an innocent man in the wrong place at the wrong time was walking close by after leaving a house of ill repute. The man, who appeared intoxicated, was immediately arrested by two constables and carted off to the police station where he was detained overnight. The police eventually told the prisoner he was free to go the following day, due to a previous victim identifying the real perpetrator of the crime at Merthyr Marketplace while the innocent man was still in custody."'

'That must have been Benjamin Langton,' said Griffin thoughtfully.

Elin nodded at him. 'It must have been,' she agreed. 'You can see now why the police might have thought it was him, if he was near the scene of the crime.'

'Carry on,' Griffin said once more.

'"A man hunt is now underway to find the perpetrator who has been named locally as Wyndham Edwards of Abercanaid. Edwards is a coal hewer at the Gethin Pit, but he has failed to show up for his shift at the pit for several days. Whether Edwards has any links with Whitechapel has yet to be discovered. The hunt continues."'

Elin folded up the newspaper and threw it down on the bar. 'How daft is that!' she scoffed. 'Wyn has never been to London in his life! The farthest he's travelled is to Barry Island!'

Griffin shot her a smile. 'No doubt they'll milk that Ripper connection for all it's worth!'

The artist's impression of several men holding lanterns aloft as they discover a woman bleeding on the ground was inserted above the article. Of course, Elin realised that sketch artist would have been nowhere near the actual scene at the time, so it was all simple supposition on his part and he'd probably doctored it to resemble similar sketches of a Ripper murder scene that had been printed of late.

'Oh no.' Elin folded the paper and slapped it down on the bar.

'What's wrong?' Griffin looked intently at her. 'It's a good thing, ain't it, if he's been named?'

Elin felt her blood run cold. 'What about Wyn's father though? It'll be a shock for him. Someone is bound to tell him, or the police will find him to speak to soon enough. I should have thought before going directly to the police.'

'Now Elin,' Griffin soothed. 'You're not thinking straight, darlin'. The only way he's going to get caught is if the word is out about him. Someone might dob him in. In any case, he might buy a copy of the newspaper and read it for himself!'

'I suppose you're right,' she admitted. 'I just wish I'd had a chance to tell his father first.'

'Well, you didn't. What's the most important thing? Capturing your husband and putting him under lock and key or being too nice about everything by saving your father-in-law's feelings?'

'You're right of course,' Elin admitted.

'I know I am. Now I'll get us both another drink. You look like you could do with one.' He summoned Jim over who was polishing a tankard with a cloth.

* * *

By midday the following day, Wyn had been arrested and Elin was to learn it was his own father who had turned him in to the police. When they visited the house, he informed them they'd probably find him at the White Hart Inn where he was prone to gambling. Poor Frank, what a thing to have to do; she did feel for the man. First, he lost his wife and now he was about to lose his son too.

Out of the blue that evening, Cook turned up at the pub asking to see Elin to check she was all right. Elin realised what it would have taken the woman to turn up to such an area, at her age too.

'How are you doing, dear?' she asked as Elin ushered her into her office. The woman was well dressed with two shawls around her shoulders and she carried a wicker basket in her hand.

Elin offered Cook a seat, which she took, placing the basket down on the floor beside her. 'That's why I've come; I've heard all about what's been going on. Oh, Elin, that could have been you, almost beaten to death like that, *cariad*. It doesn't bear thinking about. Thank your lucky stars you managed to escape his clutches.'

'I do.' She forced a smile.

Mrs Brightman leaned over towards the basket and she whipped away the cloth covering the contents. 'There's not much I could do for you, so I thought to bake some cakes.'

Elin moved closer to peer into the basket. There on a plate inside was a pile of sugared Welsh cakes. 'That's so kind of you – and going out of your way too, making a special journey to see me.'

'I can't stop long as it's a fair walk back to Abercanaid.'

'Yes, you can stop,' Elin insisted. 'I'll ask Gwenda to brew us a pot of coffee to go with these, or would you like something a little stronger?'

'A little stronger.' Cook laughed. 'A gin and lemonade would be grand.'

Elin nodded and she went off to fetch a glass for Cook and a lemonade for herself.

'Now then,' Mrs Brightman said as they both sat nibbling on the Welsh cakes that smelled of cinnamon and nutmeg, the plump currants inside tasting lovely. 'We all miss you at the house. And we heard how you spoke up for Mr Benjamin when he was arrested.'

Elin quirked a surprised brow. 'How did you find out about that?'

'The police told Mr Lawrence. He spoke very highly of you and said he had a lot to thank you for.'

Elin smiled. 'What's he doing these days?'

'He's returned to London for a while and Mr Benjamin has now set up residence in the house, at least for the time being. Mrs Langton is thrilled. She's missed him over the years – you can tell.'

'I'm pleased to hear that.' Elin longed to ask Cook about Lawrence and Arabella's wedding plans, but thought better of it. Instead, she said, 'You won't be walking back to Abercanaid this evening, Mrs Brightman. When I nipped to the bar earlier, I asked Mr Griffin if it was all right if his coach driver gave you a lift home, so you shall be travelling in style. Of course, I had to bribe him with your Welsh cakes. I promised I'd keep him a couple.'

Mrs Brightman threw back her head and laughed. 'There's plenty to go around,' she said.

* * *

'Get out of here!' Elin heard Morgan Griffin shouting as she entered the bar. Mrs Brightman had not long left the pub to head off home in his coach.

Who could he be shouting at? She scanned the room to see the two newspaper men she'd spoken to recently leaving the place with their heads lowered. The one who smoked a pipe nodded at her as they left but the other one gave her a peculiar stare.

'What on earth's the matter?' Elin headed towards Griffin, her skirts rustling as she walked the length of the room. The bar room was fairly quiet of an evening and everyone must have heard what he'd said as a deathly hush had descended over the establishment.

'Come through to the back, Elin,' Griffin advised as he glanced at the astonished faces of the men. And putting his arm around her waist, he escorted her through to her office.

'What's wrong?' She blinked.

He closed the door behind her. 'Take a seat.' He gestured towards the armchair and she did as instructed.

'Please, you're scaring me now. Just what did those two gentlemen do that was so wrong?'

He rubbed his chin, before dragging the chair from her desk to sit opposite her. 'They came in here to gloat, I reckon.'

She frowned. 'Gloat about what?'

He swallowed hard. 'Something has happened and it's going to upset you, Elin. That's why I asked you to sit down. It's your husband.'

For some reason she didn't know what to do with her hands, so she clasped them together, almost as though she were praying. 'Has he escaped from the police station or something of that nature?'

Griffin shook his head. 'No, it's not that. There's no easy way to tell you this, but he's dead.'

She heard a loud scream and then realised it was herself who had made that noise. Suddenly it felt as though she were outside her body and was watching the scene unfold before her, but it was someone else's story and not her own. 'Dead? But how could that possibly be so?'

'He hanged himself in the police cell. Apparently, according to that pair, he somehow used his leather belt to string himself up from the bars on the cell window. The police station was busy at the time so the sergeant hadn't checked his cell for a couple of hours, and when they found him like that, it was already too late – all signs of life were gone.'

A sudden peal of laughter rippled through her entire being, which became uncontrollable. She couldn't seem to stop herself, and yet she didn't know why she was laughing at all because she didn't find any of this amusing. Not at all. On the contrary, it was horrific.

'Elin! Elin!' Griffin was shouting at her. Everything became a blur until she felt him apply a couple of light slaps to both cheeks. 'I'm sorry, darlin',' he said, and then he took her into his arms while she wept. 'You had started to go hysterical there. I think it was the shock of it all. I needed to slap your face to bring you back to reality.'

She didn't know how long he cradled her in his arms for, but then he said, 'I'll fetch you a stiff drink.'

Elin took a composing breath to steady herself. 'B... but I still don't understand why you threw that pair out of here just for delivering bad news like that.'

'I heard them talking by the bar,' Griffin explained. 'They were going to drop that piece of information on you out of the blue. Somehow, they'd discovered you were his wife – don't ask me how as I didn't tell them. But no doubt they wanted to see your reaction as it would make a good news story for them. That sketch artist would probably want to sketch you when you were at your most vulnerable. They're like a pair of scavengers, picking over the bones! I couldn't bear having any of that. I wanted to protect you.'

A tear trickled down her cheek. 'Thank you for that, Morgan,' she said softly. 'I expect they'll print what they want to print anyhow...'

He nodded. 'I like it when you call me Morgan like that. You always refer to me as Mr Griffin,' he said, before leaving the room to fetch her a drink.

While he was gone, Elin made a decision: she was going to have to leave the pub soon, find somewhere else to live and work from. No way did she want any of the press sniffing around her – it was all too much to bear. Hadn't she suffered enough at the hands of her own husband? It was like he was taunting her before he'd even reached his grave. And if that bloodhound press pack from London came to Merthyr with a view to making out there'd been another Jack the Ripper – or even that it was the same person – then she didn't want her name associated with any of it.

* * *

Over the following months, Elin realised she still had to grieve for her husband. Not because she'd now become a widow but for the memory of the man she had initially thought he was. Eventually, she'd managed to find digs with a lady named Mrs Peterson at Pontmorlais, which wasn't too far from the pub. Mr Griffin had allowed her to carry on baking her pies on his premises until she found another suitable place to work from. He quite understood her reasons for leaving but said he'd always be around should she need anything.

She had done what she'd set out to do and that was to help the girls at the pub to keep safe. Well, they'd all sleep better in their beds now that Wyn Edwards was no longer roaming around. She had informed them just who he was to her, and if any of the girls were surprised, they didn't show it. But Elin guessed that Mr Griffin had already put them in the picture anyhow, before she'd even uttered a word.

She'd been to visit Dilys to check on how Frank was doing but didn't feel up to speaking to the man just yet, as she didn't want to hurt him any more than he was already hurting.

* * *

Several months later, on the approach to Christmas, she was on the way back home to her digs from the pub when she noticed a female shop assistant place a small notice in the holly-decorated window of the bookshop on the high street. It read:

> *Seeking a suitable person to take over recently vacated tea room at lower end of high street, Merthyr Tydfil. Reasonable rent, small apartment included. For further information, please contact Mr John Mason.*

The address given was in Georgetown. That wasn't too far away for her to call there. If she went straight away, she'd be in a good position as by the look of it, she was the first to view that notice.

As she set off in that direction, she wondered if she was mad, acting on impulse like this, but she had wanted her own place for a while. She'd managed to accrue some savings since her pie business had taken off, and from the extra wages that Mr Griffin had paid her to take care of the girls. No, she decided, this was as good an opportunity as any! She'd grieve no longer for a man who had little or no care for her.

Locating the house, she discovered it was one of the larger houses just off Iron Lane. When she knocked the door, a little old lady answered, identifying herself as Mr Mason's wife, and the woman welcomed her inside.

Looking around the house, Elin was reminded of her grandparents' home from when she was a child – totally charming with many relics of the past.

She was asked to wait in the parlour and as she sat listening to the tick of the mantel clock, she tried to keep herself composed, until presently, an elderly, well-dressed man appeared, who didn't look short of a bob or two.

'Oh, my dear,' he said as he headed towards her, 'I'm afraid there's been some mistake. I'm sorry you've wasted your time coming here.'

'Mistake? But how is that, Mr Mason?' She just couldn't understand it. 'Has the property already been rented out to someone else, then? Am I too late getting here?'

'No,' he said. 'But I was looking for a gentleman to take it over, someone who would make a success of the business. You see, I owned the tea room myself. My wife and I did actually – she served in the tea room and I ran the business side of things. It was ours for over twenty years but we're both getting on in years now, so we thought we'd just rent out the property instead.'

'But if that's the case, then I don't see what the problem is?' She frowned.

'We've had problems with people trying to break in there since vacating the building, so I don't want it kept empty for too long. I feel a man's presence might stop all of that.'

Elin stood, feeling she was being judged now. 'And you don't think that I can look out for myself? Is that it, Mr Mason?'

Appearing nervous now, his lower lip trembled. 'That's the sum of it, yes.'

'Well, let me tell you something, I had a bully of a husband to contend with who has since passed away, but no man shall ever tell me what to do, ever again! And more recently, I've had to help some young ladies out, watching out for their welfare in case any men hurt them. I'm more than capable of taking care of myself and your property, too! I'm a hard worker and I've built a successful pie-making business up from scratch, so don't tell me what I'm capable of doing!'

Realising that she'd possibly gone too far now, she took a deep composing breath. 'I'm sorry, I shouldn't have raised my voice like that but it's most unfair. It's a man's world!'

Suddenly, he smiled at her. 'No, you're right. It is I who have been most unfair. I can see now that you're a force to be reckoned with, Mrs...?'

'Edwards, Mrs Edwards,' she said, politely.

'Please sit back down and I'll ask my Dorothy to make us some refreshment. How will that do?'

She smiled at him. 'Thank you. That'll do nicely, Mr Mason.'

* * *

Elin was glad she'd spoken up for herself as Mr Mason said he was prepared to rent the property to her for a peppercorn price, providing she reside on the premises, as he didn't want it remaining empty a moment longer. She had promised him a small share of the profits, which he agreed to. They'd shaken on it, and that evening, she'd told her landlady of her plans to move out within a fortnight or so.

She'd asked Gwenda to carry on working for her, with Mr Griffin's approval, of course. The attack had been too much for the girl and Elin was pleased she'd accepted her offer, as she didn't want her to return to prostitution.

For a couple of weeks, the pair had been busy setting everything up. The painters had been in to give it a fresh lick of paint and everywhere was now cleaned up and as shiny as a new pin. There was already an oven and a stove, which had been used when it was a tea room, so the place was ideal for them to work from. Elin, though, wanted to give it a more homely feel, so she had red and white checked tablecloths placed on every table, and in one corner of the room was an area with a comfortable sofa, leafy plants and an oil lamp.

Customers could order pies to take away or they could eat on the premises at an extra cost. There was also a more elaborate menu than at the pub, with a variety of pies with mushy peas and baked potatoes on offer too, along with seasonal vegetables.

The place became an overnight sensation as news of 'Elin's Pie Shop' spread far and wide. Work kept her so busy that there was hardly a moment to think. A big hit with folk that festive period was her turkey and ham pie, along with a selection of mince pies, dusted with icing sugar.

It was the week before Christmas, and Elin was feeling excited. Dilys had called to the shop to invite her to her home on Christmas Day, where Frank would be joining them. Elin was understandably a little apprehensive about accepting the woman's invitation, as she hadn't seen her father-in-law since his son had passed away. She realised she'd have to face up to meeting him at some point, so she was pleased to accept.

The sky had turned pewter grey and customers were complaining how cold it was outside, but it was warm and cosy inside the shop with its log fire. Elin had just closed the door on her final customer of the day after sending Gwenda home when the bell over the door tinkled. Oh no, this was all she needed. Couldn't whoever it was read the sign?

Sighing as she made her way from the back of the place to the counter, she saw a familiar face smiling at her. Dressed in a black woollen coat with an astrakhan collar and top hat, which he'd now removed, was Lawrence Langton.

'Hello.' She smiled at him as her heart skipped a beat. He was the last person she thought she'd encounter, as she figured he'd be spending time with Arabella, but she was so happy to see him. 'I wasn't expecting to see you.'

'Weren't you?' he said, returning the smile as her breath hitched in her throat. 'I thought I'd pop in to wish you every success with your new business. I read about it in the local newspaper.'

'Not the *Merthyr Herald*!' she scoffed, as she thought back to the memory of those two newspaper hacks.

'No.' He shook his head. 'It was one of the others.'

'You're back from London then for Christmas?'

'I am indeed. Not just for Christmas though. I'm starting my own business here in my home town.'

'As a lawyer?'

'Yes. I've bought a property at the top end of the high street.'

Her heart began to thud, but then she thought of him and Arabella. Deciding it was better to be direct with him and say exactly what was on her mind, she said: 'I suppose you've moved your business to Merthyr because you're getting married soon?'

Lawrence's eyebrows lifted with surprise. 'Married? And just who am I supposed to be marrying?'

'Arabella, of course!'

'That's news to me. I didn't know that!'

Puzzled now, she looked into his eyes. Was he jesting with

her? 'But I was told some time ago that you pair were getting engaged.'

'When exactly was this supposed to have happened?' He laid his hat on the counter; then, removing his gloves, he paired them up and placed them inside.

'The night I sent word to you that your brother was being held at the police station. You and Arabella were dining together.'

'Oh yes, that did happen. But it's not what you think. I asked her to visit because I wanted to tell her as gently as I could that I *wouldn't* be marrying her, not then, not ever. I didn't want to keep her dangling on the hook, so it would give her time to find someone else. And do you know what?' Elin's heart began to thud once again. 'She has. I did her a big favour in the long run as I could never love her the way that I love you. Oh, Elin, you are all I think about day and night. I've kept away as I know you were a little annoyed when I suggested we wed and you give up your business for me for others to run while you lived a leisurely life, but I was wrong. You've proved me wrong. I also thought you needed to grieve, but the real reason I've brought my business to Merthyr is to be with you, if you'll have me, my darling?'

To her astonishment, he dropped down to the floor on one knee and said, 'Elin, please do me the honour of being my wife. You are free to marry now. I promise I'll let you do as you wish with your business but just be a part of my life, won't you?'

'B... but we're not of the same class, you and I, Lawrence. What on earth would your mother say?'

'Mother loves you, as you well realise, almost as much as I do. She knows what you did for Benjamin. There is nothing to fear, for you could hold your own with a pauper or a prince and you know it. What do you say?'

He was looking up at her with such imploring eyes. And as she gazed out of the window, his question lingering in the air, awaiting her answer, she noticed it had begun to snow. It would be a new beginning for the pair of them.

'What I say is "yes!"' she said, with no hesitation whatsoever. She had loved Lawrence Langton from the first time she'd ever laid eyes on him, and he had loved her too.

As people scurried past the pie shop, keen to get on with their own Christmas celebrations, they had no idea there was a celebration going on inside. Lawrence stood and took Elin into his arms for a lingering kiss that seemed to go on forever.

'Come on, Elin, let's get out of here and tell everyone at the house the good news,' he said, taking her by the arm.

As she closed the shop door behind them, she realised she was finally closing a chapter of her life but had a new one to look forward to with a man who loved her and one who would take care of her for the rest of his life.

EPILOGUE

'Now then,' said Elin as they left the pie shop late Christmas morning, loaded with festive packages, 'do we have everything?' She glanced at Lawrence who was smiling by the side of the coach as he awaited to help her inside.

'I think you've more than enough Christmas cheer there for the whole of Abercanaid!' He threw back his head and laughed.

'I suppose so,' she said, 'I just didn't want to leave anyone out.'

They were newly engaged and planning a spring wedding for next year. Lawrence had already been looking for a suitable property for them to live in and thought he'd found the perfect choice: a large house on the mountainside, overlooking the village. He had plans to take her to view it in the New Year. But for the time being, Elin was still residing above the shop. Gwenda had agreed to live in the apartment above the premises when Elin finally married and moved out. Indeed, the girl had been delighted with the news as it was cramped in the digs she'd taken since leaving the pub.

Elin glanced back at the name, *Elin's Pie Shop*, situated just over the door, in gold lettering, before leaving, realising that although she was to marry, she was still going to carry on with the business with Gwenda by her side.

They were on their way to Christmas dinner with Dilys and Frank. Following her engagement to Lawrence, she'd politely asked the woman if she might bring him along. Dilys Evans had been delighted with the news but Elin told her to hold out telling Frank as yet. She wanted to do that herself as she didn't know how he'd react to the news. A little knot of tension in her stomach was increasing at the thought of seeing the man again and telling him she was to marry someone else, but Lawrence's reassuring smile told her the future with him would be bright.

* * *

As the coach drew up outside Dilys Evans's house, several heads turned in the street – they didn't often see a fancy coach here. Several children ran towards them, clutching various toys they'd obviously been given for Christmas. One little girl of around five years old held a colourful rag doll to her chest, while an older boy, who Elin assumed was her brother, sported a red wooden train in his hand. Their eyes were shining with hope and expectation.

When Lawrence had assisted Elin down from the coach with some of the packages, leaving the remainder inside, he said to the coachman, 'If you could return for us in two hours?'

The man nodded at him and smiled as Lawrence handed him a gold sovereign, a Christmas tip no doubt.

Before Elin even had a chance to knock on the door, Dilys Evans was on the doorstep welcoming them inside. 'Come in out of the cold, the pair of you,' the woman fussed as the smell of roast goose wafted towards them, making Elin's mouth water at the thought of it.

Elin hugged the woman warmly, planting a kiss on her soft cheek.

'Where's Frank?' she asked as there appeared to be no sign of him. 'I do hope he's well after everything that's happened lately?'

'He is, yes, and he'll be along shortly,' said Dilys with a twinkle in her eyes. 'Now take off your over garments and hand them to me. I dare say you'd both like a glass of sherry?'

Dilys was obviously pushing the boat out for them today.

A thought occurred to Elin: someone else was missing too. 'Where's Joshua?'

'Aw he's too busy at the moment, got himself a pretty young girlfriend living in Troedyrhiw. He was invited to her house for Christmas dinner this year!' she said, smiling. 'He's bringing her back here for tea, for me to meet her later.'

'That's nice,' said Elin, feeling that love was in the air for a few folk she knew lately as well as for herself.

Lawrence, who had been quiet up until now, turned to Dilys and said, 'Mrs Evans, I've heard you've been a good friend to Elin during a difficult time for her and I'd like to thank you for that.'

Dilys nodded and smiled at him and then she handed the pair a glass of sherry each. 'And you've been a good friend to Elin too, but I'm sorry both… I do have a confession to make…'

Elin and Lawrence exchanged dubious glances with one another. 'I was so excited about you pair getting engaged to one another that I found it hard to contain my excitement. Frank knows me so well that he managed to wheedle it out of me in the end. Please both forgive me, but he now knows all about it.'

'Oh, my goodness!' said Elin, and then her hand flew to her

face and she lowered her head. 'I hope I haven't upset him. I wouldn't want to hurt him for all the world, Frank's been like a father to me.'

With tears in her eyes, she looked up to see Frank stood before her with something wrapped in tissue paper in his hand.

'You'd never hurt me. I know that, Elin. And I'm pleased for you both – honestly, I am. You deserve a man who treats you well. I heard everything you said as I nipped back home to get something for you and returned through the back door. It's an engagement present from Dilys and myself to you.'

'He made it for you himself,' said Dilys proudly. 'He's worked on it for ages; every spare moment he had he was carving outside in the shed. Go on give it to them, then!'

Frank handed Elin the tissue-wrapped gift, and when she unfolded it, she could see it was a wooden love spoon with carvings of hearts and horse shoes.

For once, Elin fell speechless, then she opened her mouth. 'Aw Frank, it's so beautiful!' She admired the intricately carved spoon, made with fatherly love. 'Thank you!' she said, giving him a big hug and pecking a kiss on his rugged cheek.

'That's not all,' said Frank with a tear in his eye. 'On the back of the two hearts are your names. Once you decide on a wedding date, let me know and I'll carve it on the spoon for you.'

'I don't know what to say, Mr Edwards,' said Lawrence, stepping forward and offering the man his hand.

Frank took Lawrence's hand for a firm shake. 'No need to say anything – Elin's happiness means the world to me,' said Frank, looking at Dilys, 'to us both actually.'

After Christmas dinner they exchanged presents. Dilys was thrilled with a new brightly coloured shawl threaded with fine ribbon that Elin had bought from Mrs Parry's shop on the high street. She'd finally purchased a pretty bonnet there for Gwenda too, remembering her promise to the girl. For Frank she brought a bottle of whisky to keep him warm on the cold nights ahead. Dilys's present to the pair was a homemade Christmas cake, laced with brandy and neatly packaged up in a muslin cloth that was tied with red and green ribbons.

'Thank you for such an enjoyable feast,' said Elin as they were leaving, her mouth still watering at the taste of the roast goose with pan-fried leeks, roast potatoes and other seasonal vegetables, and all covered in a rich brown, tasty gravy. And what a Christmas pudding too! Made by Dilys herself and brought to the table with a sprig of holly on top and lit up until the flames died down – Mrs Brightman herself could not have done any better.

It was wonderful spending Christmas Day with Dilys and Frank, creating a special memory that would last for time to come.

Lawrence nodded his thanks at the pair as they stood to wave them off as the coach left the street, headed in the direction of Lawrence's home. Elin felt another knot return to her stomach. What would Mrs Langton have to say about their engagement? she wondered, realising she would soon find out. The woman had been given the news last evening by Lawrence, when they'd both called to the house, but his mother had been resting in her bedroom at the time, so despite Lawrence's reassurance that all was well, Elin wouldn't quite believe it until she heard from the woman herself. It was of extreme importance to her that Muriel Langton gave their union her full blessing.

* * *

The coach pulled up outside the Langton house and Lawrence alighted first to help Elin down the steps. 'Johnson, can you fetch those packages into the house for us?' Lawrence enquired of the coachman, who was more than happy to oblige after being awarded a gold sovereign earlier in gratitude for his service.

Molly smiled as she opened the front door for the pair. What a difference in the girl there was! She'd gone from being a sullen, sulky young girl to a more mature young lady who looked pleased to see them.

'Good afternoon, sir... er... Mrs Edwards...' she said, lowering her head as they crossed over the threshold.

'Good afternoon and a Merry Christmas to you, Molly!' said Lawrence in a courteous fashion, and then, as if to remind the girl he was to be married to Elin, he added, 'But don't forget in a few short months I am to marry this good lady here after which time you shall refer to her as Mrs Langton or ma'am. Understood?'

'Quite, sir.' Molly dipped her knee, then waited while Lawrence removed his hat and coat to hand to her, and Elin removed her cape and bonnet. Then with arms full, Molly steered herself over to the hat and coat stand in the middle of the hallway to hang the items up.

When she'd done so, she turned to them and said, 'Mrs Langton told me to inform you that she's expecting to speak with you both in the drawing room.'

Lawrence quirked an eyebrow and huffed out a breath. 'Both of us or just myself?'

'I assumed it was the both of you, sir.'

'Thank you, Molly. That will be all for now.' Lawrence turned towards Elin and, laying a hand of reassurance on her shoulder, whispered, 'Please don't fret; there is nothing to fear.'

Elin nodded at him.

'Shall we?' he said, taking her hand as they headed towards the drawing room. He knocked lightly three times on the door until they heard his mother telling them to enter.

As she saw them approach, Mrs Langton sprang out of her armchair to greet them and all of the earlier tension Elin had felt slipped away.

'My dear,' she greeted as she took both of Elin's hands in her own. 'You don't know how pleased I am that you'll be marrying my son.'

'Really?' Elin blinked several times; she hadn't expected to hear the woman say those words.

'Yes, really.' Mrs Langton smiled. 'I think you and he are perfectly matched. You're a young woman who has a mind of her own and he likes that.'

Elin hazarded a glance in Lawrence's direction to catch him smiling broadly. 'That's so true, Mother,' he said, stepping forward and kissing her on the cheek.

'I understand from Lawrence that you'd like to get married in the spring?'

Elin nodded. 'Yes, that's right, Mrs Langton. If that's all right with you?' she asked tentatively.

'Yes, of course it is. I can't wait. Benjamin will be here in a moment; he has something to say to you.'

'To me?' Elin couldn't for the life of her think what that might be. It might prove an embarrassment for the pair of them considering they'd both been frequenting an area of Merthyr known for its loose morals and now she was to marry into the Langton family. What if Mrs Langton were to discover the truth? Her heart began to pound profusely at the thought of him letting the cat out of the bag.

They all chatted amicably with one another, until Mrs Langton, rising from her armchair, said, 'Oh, he's finally arrived!'

Elin's gaze was drawn in the direction of the latticed window where she glimpsed Benjamin striding up the pathway, dressed far more informally than the last time they'd encountered one another. This time he wore a short, dark, casual jacket and a flat cap like the one she'd seen Lawrence wear when they'd first visited China. A sprinkling of snow had settled on his head and shoulders. They heard the front door open and close and voices, as Elin realised Molly must be taking his jacket and cap from him.

Then the drawing room door opened as Benjamin stepped into the room, his face flushed from the cold but his eyes sparkling warmly as he said, 'Compliments of the season to you all!'

'Come and sit by the fire,' his mother beckoned.

Benjamin nodded at her and smiled at his brother, then as he made his way towards the hearth, his gaze fell upon Elin. She held her breath. What was he likely to say now? '*Welcome to the whore mistress from China!*'?

But instead, he took her hand and laid a kiss on the back of it. 'So, this is my lovely sister-in-law to be! Very pleased to meet you.'

She wasn't sure if he had recognised her or not from that time she'd registered his name in the book at the pub but then realised he must have as he continued, 'I'd like to thank you very much,' he said, in a serious tone now. 'If you hadn't spoken up for me when you did, I would have spent much longer in that police cell.'

'That's all right.' She smiled. 'I just knew it couldn't be you and I had the proof when you were in custody as the young lady who was attacked picked out someone else walking the streets at that time.'

'Well, I'm grateful to you anyhow,' he said, releasing her hand.

'So, exactly where have you been?' Lawrence wanted to know.

'I've been working for a well-known man from China!' he exclaimed.

'Yes,' Mrs Langton interrupted. 'For years there was a man in this town who wished to remain an anonymous benefactor to the poor people in the area. He would come to the factory and order various boxes of confectionery during the festive season – it was one of our largest orders each year. Pink and white sugar mice, sherbet bonbons, chocolate drops, peppermint creams, block toffee, packets of fudge and even boxes of chocolates from our finest range! Then he'd distribute them amongst those in need, like the children, the elderly and the vulnerable in the area. Over the years, he has always disguised himself to distribute them, so people won't recognise him. That man is no other than the notorious Morgan Griffin! And he's still doing it to this very day! But we mustn't tell anyone, we'll keep it between ourselves.' Mrs Langton tapped the side of her nose with her index finger in a surreptitious manner. Elin began to splutter on her coffee as it went down the wrong way. Muriel Langton passed her a clean handkerchief.

'That's how I came to help,' said Benjamin, as his mother looked on proudly. 'I wanted to give something back after all my wrongdoing, so when he called this Christmas to pick up the stuff from the factory, I offered to assist him. I spent most of yesterday and this morning helping him to deliver the Christmas confectionery to the needy.'

'Well, I'll be blowed!' said Lawrence in astonishment. 'It's as if Griffin has transformed into Father Christmas himself for the season!'

'Yes, apparently he dresses up as a different character every year, so no one recognises him,' added Mrs Langton. 'I always knew there was goodness in that man, somewhere.'

Of course, Elin had always known this to be true, but now Lawrence was faced with the truth himself. He sat there stunned for a moment, then he turned towards his brother. 'So, what exactly did you do, Ben?'

'I helped him on his cart, he drove and I took the confectionery to folks. He particularly wanted the children and the elderly to have something. It wasn't just sweets and chocolate from our factory though; he gave out gifts too. Toys for the children, food for families as well.'

Elin sat there taking it all in, at just how generous the man was. 'B... but how come you got involved in all of this?' she asked in astonishment.

Benjamin's face flushed for a moment. 'It's my way of making some sort of recompense for all I've done over the years, Elin,' he said sombrely. 'I put this family through a lot by taking funds from the factory in the first place and my, er... my more recent behaviour.' He glanced at his mother, who just smiled and nodded at him.

'We'd both like to thank you very much, Elin,' she said, 'for believing in Benjamin's innocence and going to the police about it when you and the young lady who was attacked recognised the man, who I understand was actually your own husband.'

'Yes,' said Benjamin. 'I hated being banged up in that police cell. It made me reflect a lot on my behaviour, but it wasn't too long a spell, thanks to you.'

Elin blushed. 'It was nothing.'

'Mr Griffin speaks highly of you, in any case...' Benjamin said.

Elin glanced in Mrs Langton's direction. 'I suppose I should tell you I helped him take care of his working girls when I left here. I wanted to ensure they were protected after that savage attack on one of them.'

'I quite understand, dear.' Muriel Langton smiled. 'Think no more of it. You did more than help to save my son...'

'You saved me too,' whispered Lawrence by her side.

'Come on, let's finish this coffee and these mince pies!' said Mrs Langton as she poured a cup for Benjamin and handed it to him as he finally took a seat by the fireside.

* * *

Afterwards, Elin went in search of Cook in the kitchen. Mrs Brightman had her head over the stove, busily stirring something bubbling away. She turned to see Elin stood beside her. 'Oh, Elin, it's so lovely to see you, *cariad*!' she said, resting her wooden spoon in the saucepan to give her a warm hug. 'Let me just take this off the hob and we can have a nice chat by the table,' she added. Elin smiled at her, loving all the familiarity of being back in the kitchen with Cook, albeit in a different manner of speaking. Now she wasn't far off being one of the Langton family, instead of the hired help at the house.

'Well, tell me all about it, then...' urged Cook as they both seated themselves at the table. 'You look quite the lady now!'

Elin ended up telling the woman about the afternoon Lawrence had sought her out at the pie shop just as she was about to lock up for the evening and how he'd asked her to marry him.

Cook beamed. 'We heard about your engagement from Mr

Lawrence himself! He summoned all the staff together to inform us. Oh, he was bursting with excitement, he was!'

Elin nodded. 'I stayed put in the drawing room when he told you all. I couldn't quite face everyone...'

Cook nodded her understanding. 'You were probably overwhelmed that he'd proposed to you like that.'

'I suppose I was when it came so out of the blue, particularly as in my mind, he was about to marry Arabella, which couldn't have been further from the truth.' Elin's forehead broke out into a soft frown. 'And how did Molly take it?'

'Oh, you don't want to be worrying about her any more; she's absolutely fine with it. She only has eyes for that butcher's boy I told you about. He's been calling here at the back door to see her on a regular basis. He's even taken her out on more than one occasion.'

Elin breathed out a sigh of relief. She didn't want to start out married life with the girl despising her, particularly as she'd be a regular visitor to the house from now on. 'I've brought you a little something to thank you for your kindness,' she said, handing the woman a gift-wrapped package.

'That's ever so nice of you, Elin, but I didn't think to buy you anything. To be honest, I didn't imagine I'd even see you today as Lawrence said you were both dining at your former neighbour's house.'

'We were, we did, but he wanted to spend time with his family too. Go on, open it then,' she urged, glancing at the package on the table. Mrs Brightman undid the red ribbon and unfolded the wrapping paper to see a little box inside, which she opened.

'It's beautiful,' she gasped as she fingered the blue jewelled brooch inside.

'It's not much, I know, but I picked it up from that stall on the outdoor market. I was going to buy it for you a while back but it was the day I spotted it in the marketplace with Gwenda, when she caught sight of the man who attacked her, who of course turned out to be Wyn…' She bit on her lower lip.

'I completely understand,' said Cook, patting her on the hand. 'Even after all Wyn did, I was sorry to hear of his death. Not sorry for him but for his father, and you too, as it must have affected you tremendously.'

Elin nodded and then, sniffing, said, 'I couldn't purchase the brooch for you that particular day as I went to the police station but I remembered it when I was in the market earlier this week. It was still there, so I bought it for you.'

'And I shall treasure it always,' said Cook. 'I hope you'll stay in touch once you marry, Elin.'

'Of course I will,' she said, rising from the table. 'I'll see you later as Lawrence wants us to exchange gifts with his family next.'

Cook nodded. 'I better get on, I suppose. Things to do. Now where are Floss and Molly when I need them?' She chuckled. It was reassuring to know some things never changed at the house.

* * *

Lawrence had bought a fur stole for his mother from himself and Elin with a matching muff. 'We thought they would keep you warm when you're in the coach.' He smiled at her. 'Your neck and hands will be as warm as toast while wearing those!'

'They're absolutely beautiful!' Muriel said, running her hand over the dark brown fur of both items.

'Elin chose them. She has such great taste!' He winked at his wife-to-be.

Then he handed a present to his brother. 'Also from the both of us,' he said.

Benjamin quickly unwrapped the boxed package to see there was a silver silk cravat inside with matching handkerchief. 'Thank you so much, both of you!' He beamed.

'I understand now that you're involved in the family business once again, you'd want to look your best!' Lawrence enthused.

Benjamin nodded eagerly.

When the gift giving was over after Elin had received a pair of ladies' white gloves and a box of handkerchiefs from Mrs Langton and Benjamin, and Lawrence a smart walking cane, Elin noticed there was still one small package beneath the Christmas tree. Puzzled, she said nothing of it, thinking maybe it was an extra gift that Benjamin wanted to give to his mother in privacy once they'd departed.

As Lawrence and Elin stood to leave, Lawrence said, 'Oh, I've forgotten about this gift here...' She thought he was going to take it to his mother, but then he dropped to his knee in front of Elin as he had when he'd proposed. 'Elin, I know I've already asked you to be my wife and you've accepted, but there's something you need to be my fiancée.' He handed her the little package, which she unwrapped to see a velvet box inside.

She gasped as she opened it to spot a gold ring with a ruby stone surrounded by miniature diamonds. 'Oh!' She held her hand to her chest in astonishment.

'It's your engagement ring,' he said, pulling himself to his feet to slip it on her finger.

She discovered it fitted her finger very nicely indeed. Just like she and her future husband were a perfect fit for one another.

In the background, she heard Mrs Langton's shrieks of

delight and Benjamin slapping his brother on the back saying, 'Congratulations, both! Aren't you going to give the lady a kiss, dear brother?'

Lawrence's lips curved into a smile as he took Elin into his arms. 'Oh yes, you just watch me,' he said, taking her breath away.

* * *

MORE FROM LYNETTE REES

ABOUT THE AUTHOR

Lynette Rees lives in Wales and has been writing since she was a child. She enjoys the freedom of writing in a variety of genres including: crime fiction and contemporary romance, though her first love is historical fiction. When she's not writing, or even when she is writing, Lynette enjoys a glass of wine and the odd piece of chocolate as she creates stories where the characters guide her hand. She honestly has no idea how a story will turn out until the characters tell their own tales in their own unique ways.

Download your exclusive bonus content from Lynette Rees here:

Visit Lynette's website: www.lynetterees.wordpress.com

Follow Lynette on social media:

- facebook.com/authorlynetterees
- x.com/LynetteRees0
- instagram.com/booksbylynetterees7
- bookbub.com/authors/lynette-rees

ALSO BY LYNETTE REES

The Winter Waif

The Workhouse Girl

The Cobbler's Apprentice

The Pit Girl

The Coal Miner's Wife

Printed in Dunstable, United Kingdom

83574247R00170